A BEE IN HER BONNET

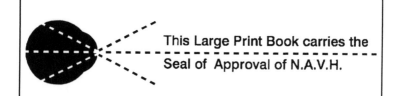

This Large Print Book carries the
Seal of Approval of N.A.V.H.

THE HONEYBEE SISTERS

A BEE IN HER BONNET

JENNIFER BECKSTRAND

KENNEBEC LARGE PRINT
A part of Gale, Cengage Learning

GALE
CENGAGE Learning·

Farmington Hills, Mich • San Francisco • New York • Waterville, Maine
Meriden, Conn • Mason, Ohio • Chicago

GALE
CENGAGE Learning·

LIBRARY OF CONGRESS CATALOGING-IN-PUBLICATION DATA

Names: Beckstrand, Jennifer, author.
Title: A bee in her bonnet / by Jennifer Beckstrand.
Description: Waterville, Maine : Kennebec Large Print, 2016. | Series: The
    Honeybee sisters | Series: Kennebec Large Print superior collection
Identifiers: LCCN 2016037291| ISBN 9781410495020 (softcover) | ISBN 1410495027
    (softcover)
Subjects: LCSH: Amish—Fiction. | Sisters—Fiction. | Bee culture—Fiction. | Large
    type books. | GSAFD: Love stories. | Christian fiction.
Classification: LCC PS3602.E3323 B44 2016 | DDC 813/.6—dc23
LC record available at https://lccn.loc.gov/2016037291

Published in 2017 by arrangement with Zebra Books, an imprint of
Kensington Publishing Corp.

Printed in Mexico
2 3 4 5 6 7 21 20 19 18 17

A BEE IN HER BONNET

CHAPTER ONE

Poppy Christner was screaming her lungs out.

Well, she wasn't exactly screaming — more like yelling, as if she were mad as a wet hen and everybody within a mile was going to hear about it. Even though Luke couldn't see her around the bend in the road, that shrill voice certainly belonged to Poppy. She'd spent too many recesses in primary school yelling at Luke for him not to recognize it. Poppy always seemed to be irritated about something.

He furrowed his brow and snapped the reins to get the team moving a little faster. Not that a team pulling a wagon laden with wood would ever win a race, but he wanted to see why Poppy was making all the racket, and he hoped to get there before Christmastime. Even though she sounded more angry than distressed, Poppy might be in trouble. Maybe he could help.

A smirk tugged at his lips. Maybe he would need to rescue the person being yelled at.

When his wagon lumbered around the bend, it took him a second to make sense of what he saw. Poppy, unapologetic tomboy and Luke's nearest neighbor, jogged alongside an old rusted-out car, yelling at the driver as the car inched slowly down the dirt road in front of Poppy's farm. She clutched the top of the driver's side window as if the mere touch of her fingers could keep the car from speeding off.

Hold on there.

Only when Luke brought the horses to a stop did he realize that the window was almost completely closed, with Poppy's hand stuck between the top of the window and the car door. The driver had rolled up his window on Poppy's hand, and she had no choice but to jog alongside the car or be dragged down the road.

Luke's heart all but leapt out of his chest. If that car sped up, Poppy could lose her arm.

No wonder she was shouting at the top of her lungs.

"Roll down this window right now," she yelled. "Let me go!"

Whoever was behind that windshield

didn't seem to care that he might rip Poppy's fingers off with a careless foot to the gas pedal.

Without a moment's hesitation, Luke vaulted into the back of his wagon and pulled out the long crowbar from his toolbox. He jumped from the wagon bed and raced toward the car. "Don't be afraid, Poppy," he called.

She turned her eyes in his direction. "I'm not afraid," she snapped, as if he'd insulted her. Not acting the least bit surprised that Luke had appeared to rescue her, she glared at her own reflection in the tinted car window. "Show your face, you coward."

Luke planted his feet three yards in front of the car, looked daggers at the figure behind the windshield, and didn't even flinch as the car inched closer. If they ran him over, they ran him over. He wouldn't stand aside and let a girl get hurt.

Holding the crowbar aloft, as if he was about to take a swing, he yelled loud enough for the driver to hear. "Roll down your window, and let her go."

"And be prepared to answer for your sins," Poppy added.

Luke wasn't sure what sins Poppy wanted the driver to answer for, but now was not the time for her to make such a demand.

Righteous indignation would only make it more likely that she would be parted from her fingers.

The windshield was so dirty Luke couldn't make out the face of the driver, but the person in the passenger seat ducked his head and pulled his wide-brimmed straw hat over his face.

The car kept right on coming, slowly, but still on course to smash Luke like a bug. He held his breath and raised the crowbar higher. "Stop the car, or I'll take out your headlights."

He didn't know if a threat broke his vow of nonviolence, but he could consider that question when he wasn't about to get plowed over. The bigger question was whether the driver cared if his headlights were taken out. The car looked to be in pretty bad shape. What was one more dent?

The car kept coming, still dragging Poppy by the hand, still on course to imprint a tire mark on Luke's chest. His heart pounded against his rib cage so hard he could feel it in his throat. Would whoever was driving really mow down a defenseless Amish boy? Well, he wasn't completely defenseless, but he felt pretty certain a crowbar didn't stand much of a chance against the hunk of metal rolling toward him.

He saw movement behind the windshield and heard the two people in the car yelling at each other. Loudly. He hoped that whoever wanted to set Poppy free would win the argument. Luke would rather not die with a weapon in his hand. What would the bishop say?

The car jerked to a stop, and Luke heard a squeaky groan, much like the hum of one of Poppy Christner's beehives in springtime. The driver's side window stuttered open about three inches. In a flash, Luke raced to the side of the car, grabbed Poppy around the waist, and pulled her back just as the driver gunned the engine and drove away, spitting gravel and dust twenty feet into the air.

Poppy pried herself from his grasp faster than he could put hammer to nail. With her gaze glued to the disappearing car, she took several quick steps down the road before stopping. Was she considering chasing after the car on foot?

With her back to him, she stood motionless and stared in the direction the car had gone, almost as if she were longing for it to return. Her labored breathing matched his own. They were both shaken up. He'd nearly been run over, and she'd nearly lost her hand. Or worse.

He'd probably saved her life.

Luke Bontrager comes to the rescue. You're welcome, Poppy Christner.

"Poppy, are you okay?" he said, because she was waiting a wonderful long time to express her undying gratitude. "Poppy," he said again. "Is your hand okay?"

With posture as rigid as a flagpole, she spun on her heels and glared at Luke as if she were about to smack him in the face, which was not altogether unheard of. She had once given him a bloody nose. No one was as unpredictable or as aggravating as Poppy Christner.

It was why Luke usually steered clear of her.

But wasn't she grateful that he hadn't avoided her today? Wouldn't she at least thank him for saving her life with his crowbar?

A fire raged behind her eyes. "Why did you do that?"

"Maybe because that man was about to rip your hand off," he said, returning her scowl.

His sarcasm only made her madder. "I was trying to get a good look at his face."

"Believe me. You were never going to get a good look. The only thing you were sure to get was a new nickname."

She narrowed her eyes. "Oh, really?"

"Poppy Five Fingers."

A hint of disdain played at her lips. "I had everything under control."

"Unless he decided to drive off and take your fingers with him."

"I needed to see his face, Luke Bontrager, and you ruined everything."

He clenched his jaw. "Next time I'll let you get run over."

"I hope you do," she replied. She cradled her hand close to her body, and Luke could see a nasty bruise already beginning to form along the back of her hand. Poppy was tough, but while she tried not to show it, Luke had a pretty good idea just how badly that hand hurt.

He expelled an annoyed puff of air from his lungs and held out his hand. "Here. Let me have a look."

"I'm fine," she said, folding her arms to hide her hands from view. That small movement sent pain traveling across her face.

He set his crowbar on the ground. "Look. I have put down my weapon. You have nothing to fear."

"I'm not afraid."

"You seem to be afraid of a little first aid."

She lifted her chin higher. "My hand is fine, and you don't know anything about

13

first aid."

Shoving aside the urge to get about his business and let Poppy fend for herself, he reached out his hand until he was practically touching her. "I've hammered my thumb and staple-gunned my own leg. I splinted my brother's arm when he broke it last year, and I super-glued my own lip back together when I was sixteen."

In spite of her obvious pain, she relaxed enough to cock an eyebrow. "You glued your lip?"

He fingered the half-inch scar running through his upper lip. "My mouth met the claw of my brother's hammer. I glued it back together with super glue. No harm done."

She seemed to eye him with greater appreciation. "I can barely see the scar." Maybe she would decide he deserved a little appreciation for saving her fingers. And her life.

"So let me see your hand."

"I don't want you to look at my hand. I'm mad at you."

He didn't know why he let that surprise him. "Mad at me? For saving your life?"

With her arms still securely folded, she started toward the lane that led to her house. "You let those boys get away."

14

Stifling an aggravated growl, he ignored his better judgment and followed her. He had almost run out of patience, but he wouldn't abandon a girl who needed help, even a girl as bullheaded and disagreeable as Poppy Christner. He could be stubborn too. "Poppy, I'm not going to go away until I make sure your hand is all right."

She stopped in her tracks, puckered her lips in frustration, and blew a wisp of hair out of her face, eyeing him as if he were a pesky fly. "It doesn't hurt that bad."

"Can I see?"

His persistence finally paid off. She slipped her hand from under her arm and held it out to him. If he'd asked for permission to touch her, she probably would have started arguing with him again, so he simply took her hand as if it were the most normal thing in the world. She didn't even flinch.

Her skin was soft and smooth against his rough carpenter's hands. His calluses probably felt like sandpaper. No matter how abrasive Poppy was, he would try to be gentle.

An ugly red welt ran across the length of her palm where more than a few layers of skin had peeled off. Blood oozed from the wound, but it was barely enough for a Band-Aid. He grimaced. "It must sting something wonderful."

"I'm okay." She stared straight ahead, her face a mask of cool detachment, as if she couldn't care less about her hand. Luke knew better. He could hear her unsteady breathing and sense the trembling just below the surface of her calm exterior. She was hurting, but being Poppy, she had to be proud about it, especially in front of a boy.

He slipped his fingers around her wrist and turned her hand so her palm rested on top of his. She tensed, but Luke didn't know if it was from the pain or embarrassment that they were practically holding hands — not that *he* was embarrassed by her warm palm against his or the smell of honey and vanilla that seemed to float about her — but she might be.

A long, purple bruise ran along the back of her hand just below her knuckles. The swelling had already begun. He looked up. She stared intently at him with those leaf-green eyes that always unnerved him a bit. "The most important thing is to get some ice on it and then make sure it's not broken. By the grace of *Gotte,* you still have your fingers. Where would one of the Honeybee Schwesters be if she couldn't tend bees?"

Poppy might have curled her lips slightly at that.

The Amish neighbors in Bienenstock, the settlement in northern Wisconsin where they lived, had nicknamed Poppy and her two *schwesters* the Honeybee Sisters because they kept beehives, sold their honey at a local market, and made all sorts of wonderful-*gute* honey desserts.

He should have stopped at that, but he never could resist needling Poppy just a bit. "Think of all the boys who would never get the thrashing they deserved if you only had one good hand."

She yanked her hand from his and winced at the sudden movement. "You know perfectly well that I don't hit boys anymore. That was when I was a girl, and I've grown out of it. Though for you, I might be willing to make an exception."

"I'd rather not be the exception." He casually twined his fingers around her wrist again, pulled her hand close, then pressed gently in search of broken bones. "After I see you safely home, I think we can agree to stay away from each other unless your hand gets stuck in another car window. I prefer girls like Dinah Eicher who are pretty and demure and who don't hit people. You don't like boys at all."

He saw something deep and aching flash in her eyes before she snatched her hand away from him again. With a speed he had not thought possible for a girl, let alone a girl with a bad hand, she took off down the road. "You don't need to see me home," she called over her shoulder.

"*Jah,* I do. What if you faint?" Dinah Eicher would have fainted.

"I don't faint," she said, without breaking her stride.

He frowned. Had he hurt her feelings?

He hadn't said anything that they both didn't already know.

With long strides, he followed her over the small bridge that marked the beginning of the Honeybee Sisters' property, down the lane past the red barn with the orange door, and practically raced her to the house. He had definitely hurt her feelings. No one would be that diligent without reason.

Had it been his comment about liking pretty girls? Surely Poppy wouldn't be bent out of shape over that. A girl like her didn't much care if she was pretty. Luke liked girls who were delicate and graceful, like flowers. Poppy was pretty in her own way — a fact Luke usually ignored because of all her other bad qualities. A boy would have to be blind not to notice the shocking green eyes and hair the color of golden honey, the smattering of freckles across her nose or the

18

hint of a dimple that appeared every time she moved her mouth. But he'd also be *deerich*, foolish, to forget the stubborn independence and hot temper that were as much a part of Poppy as her green eyes.

He wasn't about to apologize for the "pretty" comment. *Pretty is as pretty does*, Mamm always said, and if Poppy wanted boys to think she was pretty, she would stop yelling at people and show some gratitude when someone risked his life to save hers.

Poppy didn't get her feelings hurt. She punched people.

CHAPTER TWO

Poppy walked so fast she surely sent up a cloud of dust behind her. Her hand throbbed, her throat felt raw from screaming, and there was an ache in her chest that she tried valiantly to ignore.

She scolded herself for letting Luke Bontrager get under her skin. What did she care if he thought she was *hesslich*, ugly? He was arrogant and selfish and in sixth grade hadn't let her join in schoolyard games of tackle football because "girls shouldn't play rough like the boys."

Ach, she wanted to punch him all over again.

Why did the lane have to be so long? She could hear his steady footsteps immediately behind her as she passed some of their beehives, the honey house, and finally the barn. If her hand hadn't been throbbing, she could have easily outrun him, escaped into the house, and slammed the door on that smug, superior scowl of his.

She'd made it perfectly clear that she didn't need his "help." Why was he still following her? Did he honestly think she would faint?

He dogged her steps up to the porch, but surely he'd go away once he saw her to the house. Unfortunately, he was arrogant enough to think that he was the only one who could tend to her hand, even though her sisters were just inside.

She reached for the door handle and looked down. A dead mouse lay on the welcome mat. Poppy caught her breath and tried not to shudder. She hated mice, but she refused to show any weakness in front of Luke.

Luke's gaze followed the path of hers. The mouse's mangled body rested on top of one of the bright yellow flowers on the mat. He bent over and picked it up by the tail. "Do you use this to ward off unwelcome guests?"

"If we do, it's not working."

Much as she hated to touch the thing, it was her job to dispose of the cat's little gifts. She took the mouse out of Luke's fingers and flung it off the porch into the rosebushes at the side of the house.

Surprise flitted across his face. "You're not afraid of anything, are you, Poppy

Christner?"

"No, but I'm annoyed by boys who don't know when to go away."

"I only want to make sure your hand is okay yet. Then I'll leave."

She could only hope.

"We got a new cat last week. He leaves something dead on our porch almost every day. I think it's his way of trying to be accepted into the family." She opened the front door and barreled into the house with Luke in tow. The sooner in the house, the sooner she could get rid of him.

Poppy's older sister, Lily, stood at the butcher-block island stirring something in a bowl while her younger sister, Rose, kneaded bread dough. Aendi Bitsy, whom Poppy affectionately called "B," sat at the table reading a cookbook. Aunt B's salt-and-pepper gray hair was mostly tucked under her *kapp,* but enough peeked out that Luke would notice it was tinted purple. Aunt B wore a pair of dangly pink earrings that matched the hair quite nicely.

Lily froze with her spoon clutched tightly in her hand. Rose's eyes grew as wide as extra-large eggs. She picked up her bread dough and pressed it to her like a security blanket. It would make a mess of her apron.

Aunt Bitsy rose to her feet and glowered

22

at Luke as if she was trying to make him cry. "Have you brought home a stray, Poppy?" Her glare could have curdled water. She did not like boy visitors.

What did Luke think of the fluorescent pink earrings dangling from Aunt B's ears just below her prayer *kapp*? Aunt B had lived as an *Englischer* before coming back to the Amish when Poppy's parents had passed away, and she didn't quite fit the mold of an Amish *fraa.* She often dyed her gray hair pastel colors, wore very un-Amish earrings, and sang loud *Englisch* songs with strange lyrics.

Aunt B's appearance didn't seem to ruffle Luke's feathers one bit. He marched right up to her as if he found nothing shocking about her earrings or her bone-chilling glare. Poppy couldn't help but be impressed. And perhaps a little disarmed. "Poppy's hurt her hand, and I want to make sure it gets taken care of."

Lily, Rose, and B pulled their curious gazes from Luke's face and converged on Poppy. Rose didn't even put her bread dough down as she and Lily came around the island.

"What happened?" Aunt B said, brushing past Luke as if he were invisible.

"I'm okay," Poppy said. "It's just a little bruise."

"It's broken," Luke said.

Ach, he thought he was so smart. "It's not broken," Poppy insisted. Lily took Poppy's hand to look at it. Poppy hissed in pain before clamping her lips together. She wouldn't in a million years give Luke a reason to gloat over her.

Lily frowned, her features lined with worry. "Poppy, what happened? This looks terrible."

Aunt B turned her wrath on undeserving Luke. "What did you do, young man? Are you aware I have a shotgun in my possession?"

Luke didn't back down, not one little bit. He remained unexpectedly calm at the threat of getting shot. "If it weren't for me, she wouldn't have any fingers left."

Poppy lifted her chin. "You can't take credit for all ten. No matter what might have happened out there, I would still have at least five fingers."

He folded his arms across his chest. "*Ach,* at least five? Forgive my arrogance."

Deciding to ignore him, she flexed her fingers just to prove they weren't broken. Pain tore up her arm. She stifled a gasp and swallowed her tears. "I was walking home when I saw a car parked in front of our farm. It was just sitting there, and I wondered if it could be the person who's been making all the trouble."

The mischief had started over a month ago. First someone had tipped over one of their beehives. A few nights later, the troublemaker had torn all the laundry off the line and stomped it in the mud. He had even taken one of their buggy wheels off one night while they slept.

"You think they were the ones who . . ." Luke glanced at Rose, shut his mouth, and practically choked swallowing his next words. The vandal or vandals had painted a horrible message on their barn four weeks ago, and Luke, Dan Kanagy, and Josiah Yoder had been good enough to paint over it in the middle of the night before Rose had a chance to see it. The thought of someone trespassing on their farm and making mischief troubled all of them, but it terrified Rose. The less she knew, the better.

Poppy felt a spark of warmth on her cheeks. Luke had sacrificed a good night's sleep for Rose's sake. He had at least one redeeming quality.

But probably only that one.

Rose squeezed the bread dough in her hands until it oozed between her fingers.

"Poppy, you saw the man who hurt our bees?"

"He had his window rolled down, and I got close enough to see what looked like bee stings on his face. That's when I knew it was him."

Lily looked at Luke. "Last night they tipped over another beehive. We figured whoever did it would have been stung."

"I yelled at him as I came up beside his car," Poppy said. "He started to roll up his window, so I reached my hand in to stop him. I didn't think he'd roll me right up with it."

"*Ach, du lieva,* oh my goodness," Lily said, probing Poppy's bruise with her thumb.

"The car started going, and I had to jog alongside or get dragged down the road."

"That must have hurt something wonderful," Rose said.

"I never got a good look at his face. Luke pulled me away from the car before I had a chance to see."

A frown looked to be chiseled into Luke's face. "I'm not going to apologize for saving your fingers."

Lily had recently become engaged to Luke's best friend, Dan, so she didn't find Luke completely disagreeable. "*Denki,* Luke. Poppy could have been run over."

Don't be nice to him, Lily. We don't want him to think he's our friend.

Luke grunted dismissively. "The car was rolling down the road with Poppy's hand half in and half out. I got in front of the car and threatened them with my crowbar."

Lily's mouth fell open. "You put yourself in the path of a moving car?"

"I wasn't about to let them drive off and hurt Poppy. They didn't want their headlights smashed in, so they rolled the window down far enough for Poppy to pull her hand out."

Aunt B's expression softened around the edges. "You've done a very *gute* thing, Luke Bontrager."

Poppy's family fell into awed silence, gazing at Luke as if he were an angel, or at the very least, a bishop. Poppy couldn't share their admiration, but she should have been humble enough to admit that Luke had saved her from something that could have turned out very badly. But it galled her that it gave him one more reason to feel superior.

Ach, his head was puffed up enough already.

She cleared her throat. "I . . . I didn't say it before, but I'm grateful that you made them stop."

It had to be said, even if it felt like swallowing a mouthful of sawdust.

Luke nodded, a smug curve to his lips. "With the four of you living here alone, I always try to keep an eye out for your protection."

Aunt Bitsy very nearly snorted. "You think we need protection? I suppose it's better than thinking we need therapy."

"I'm always happy to do what I can," Luke said.

B folded her arms and smirked. "It must be such a burden for you."

"I don't mind. It's a man's duty to watch out for the women."

Should Poppy warn him that he was walking headlong into a hornet's nest? He was so cheerfully oblivious. She almost felt sorry for him — but not sorry enough to stop him.

"My *dat* says women can't be expected to withstand the things a man can."

"Young man," Aunt Bitsy said, looking at Luke as if he were a little slow. "I have my yellow belt in karate, one very fierce cat, and a shotgun for emergencies. Completely without your help, we've managed to support ourselves from what we produce on this farm. We lift honey supers, drive horses, bake bread, and use chain saws."

Luke didn't seem the least bit impressed. "You shouldn't. A chain saw will chew your fingers into hamburger."

Aunt Bitsy gazed at the ceiling. "Dear Lord, thank you for sending Luke Bontrager into our home. We don't know how we have managed without him for so long."

B liked talking to *Gotte* out loud, but her sarcasm was lost on Luke.

"I don't know how you've managed without a man for so long either," he said, digging himself deeper and deeper. "Women are delicate and sweet. You need a man here to shield you from a hard world."

Aunt B raised an eyebrow. "The only thing sweet about me is the butterfly tattoo on my ankle."

Poppy resisted the urge to laugh out loud at the look of befuddlement on Luke's face. No argument existed to counter an ankle tattoo.

Sometimes there were no words.

He must have found it wise to change the subject. "I'll run home and unhitch my team, then bring the buggy over and take Poppy to the hospital for X-rays. Or I could call a driver."

"*Nae,* you won't," Poppy said.

The muscles of his jaw twitched slightly. "Since I'm the one who saved you from that car, I feel responsible. I'm taking you to a doctor."

Poppy wouldn't let Luke boss her around, no matter how bad her hand hurt. "You needn't bother. If I need to go to the hospital — which I don't — I can take myself."

The lines in his forehead piled up on themselves, as if no one had ever refused his help before. "Why should you, when I've already offered?"

"I don't want your help."

His eyebrows traveled upward, matching his obviously heightened irritation. "You'll never get a husband by digging in your heels, Poppy Christner. I'm just trying to help."

If he thought to change her mind with that piece of advice, he was sorely mistaken. Poppy's grandfather, Dawdi Sol, had been very clear that she would never get a husband. The threat didn't even hurt her anymore. Mostly. "If all the boys are as thick and conceited as you, I'd rather be an old maid."

"Well, don't come crying to me when you are."

"I don't cry."

He threw up his hands. "Of course not. You're tough as a whole bucketful of nails."

"And I don't need a man."

"And a man doesn't need the frustration."

They stared at each other for five awkward seconds. Aunt B and Lily had managed to slide out of their way, so nothing stood between Poppy and Luke to divert her attention from those brooding eyes and the strong, angular chin. There was no denying Luke Bontrager had a good face. Too bad he didn't have a personality to go along with it.

He tapped his fist on the table as a signal of finality. "I've done all I can do, Bitsy. You're on your own. I hope she doesn't come to regret her stubbornness."

Aunt B grunted. "Never accuse someone of weakness to cover up your own, Luke Bontrager."

He stomped to the door and yanked it open.

"Luke, wait," Rose said, in the timid voice she used with strangers.

Poppy eyed her sister. Luke's imposing presence should have rendered Rose completely mute.

Rose bustled to the counter by the oven, put down her bread dough, and rinsed her hands in the sink. Then she took three honey cookies from the cooling rack, wrapped them in a napkin, and gave them to Luke. "*Denki* for saving my sister."

The surprise was evident in his expression

31

before he flashed Rose a tentative smile. "You're welcome," he said. Taking the cookies as if Rose were handing over her most prized possessions, he made his voice low and sweet. "Your cookies are the most delicious thing I've ever tasted."

Men, in general, made Rose extremely nervous. She only seemed completely at ease with Lily's fiancé, Dan. Any boy who was sensitive to Rose's feelings melted Poppy's heart into a puddle of mush.

She bit down hard on her tongue. She wouldn't let Luke make up for past sins with one soft word to Rose. He'd painted their barn and said something nice. That didn't compensate for his many faults, like his inclination to call girls ugly, his arrogant confidence, or his belief that girls were helpless.

He glanced at Poppy, and his expression hardened like mud on a hot day. "I hope your hand feels better, Poppy. If I were you, I'd stay away from strange cars and suspicious-looking people. I'm next door. Fetch me, and I'll investigate for you."

Probably knowing exactly what she'd think of that, he didn't stick around long enough for her to reply. He stomped out of the kitchen, shut the front door, and left them in blessed peace. Was it too much to hope that he'd never cross their threshold again?

Aunt B propped her hands on her hips. "Rose, you have a kind heart, but I wish you hadn't given him those cookies. Boys are like stray cats. You feed them once, and they'll keep coming around."

Lily laughed. "I don't think Luke will ever want to set foot on the farm again. Poppy put him down right *gute.*"

Aunt B shook her head. "Mark my words. He'll be back. We made the mistake of feeding Dan Kanagy, and look how that turned out."

"It turned out wonderful-*gute,*" Lily said, her eyes dancing with a thousand lovely possibilities. "I got a fiancé out of it."

Aunt B growled. "See what I mean? A complete disaster."

All three sisters giggled. Aunt Bitsy's sour disposition often scared fainthearted boys away, but she only wanted the best for her girls. On the day Lily and Dan got engaged, she had cracked a smile and put on her long, green earrings in celebration. She had been ecstatic.

Aunt B went to the window and peeked out between the curtains. "Luke Bontrager is too big for his britches. I'm tempted to toilet-paper his house."

"He only wanted to make sure Poppy was okay," Rose said.

"He wonders how we've managed without him for so long," Poppy said.

Aunt B shrugged. "Let him think what he wants to think. He's young. He'll learn — and probably the hard way."

Rose went back to her bread dough. "He saved Poppy, and I'll always like him just for that. What if that car had driven away? Poppy might have been run over."

Aunt B examined Poppy's hand. "Rose is right. And it won't be said of me that I don't give credit where credit is due. You might not have been able to get a good look at those boys in the car, but you still have your fingers. Luke is no coward. We should probably give him some token of our gratitude."

"Rose already gave him some cookies," Poppy said. She sounded sullen and pouty, even to herself. Wouldn't Luke Bontrager just *love* to gloat over her.

"You could write him a thank-you note," Rose said.

Gute idea. She could shove it in his mailbox and never even have to talk to him.

Lily's smile grew gradually, like a flower opening to the sun. "Make him a honey apple pie. It's one of your best recipes."

"Nae," Aunt B said. "We mustn't feed him."

"But, Aunt Bitsy," Rose said, glancing at Lily, "he saved her life. It's got to be big."

Aunt B tapped her finger against her cheek. "What about a bouquet of flowers? He can't eat flowers."

"The way to a man's heart is through his stomach," Rose said.

Lily nodded while B shook her head. "We don't want to get anywhere near his heart, so you can just forget about that idea."

Lily looked sideways at Rose. "Let Poppy decide."

Poppy stifled a frustrated groan. Conceited Luke Bontrager had saved her hand with his frightening crowbar. Rose was right. The thank-you would have to be big. She'd have to make him a honey apple pie, but she wouldn't have to be happy about it.

Aunt B took out one of her earrings and set it on the table. "Now," she said, starting on the other earring, "we're going to the hospital. I think your hand is broken."

Ach! She'd never hear the end of this from Luke.

She wanted to smack herself upside the head.

With her good hand, of course.

CHAPTER THREE

The sun hadn't yet peeked over the horizon as Poppy and Rose went outside to gather eggs in the dim morning light. During the day the chickens wandered about the yard, pecking at feed or scratching for juicy worms and snails. At night they roosted in the small coop behind the barn. There were only eight chickens, but they supplied enough eggs that the Honeybee Sisters never needed to buy extra, even when they made cookies and a cake on the same day.

Poppy linked arms with Rose, and they skipped down the porch steps together. "I think Tilly has stopped laying," Rose said. "But don't tell Aunt Bitsy. She'll want to cook her for dinner."

"That's where she'll end up eventually," Poppy said.

Rose sighed. "I know, but I hate thinking about it."

"It's too bad it's not Big Bertha who's quit

laying. She pecks my hands something wonderful every time I reach for her eggs."

Rose used to collect the eggs by herself every morning, but ever since the first time their beehive had been upended, over a month ago, no one had felt completely comfortable letting Rose go by herself. They were all a little spooked by the mischief making.

Rose carried the egg basket because Poppy's hand still felt sore. At least it wasn't broken. Poppy smiled to herself through the pain. She loved that Luke Bontrager had been wrong about her hand. On her way home from the hospital two days ago, Poppy had been tempted to stop by Luke's house, flex her fingers in his face, and gloat. But then he probably would have taken great pleasure in the fact that she had followed his advice and gone to the doctor in the first place, so she couldn't see much of a victory in an unbroken hand. She hadn't made Luke a thank-you pie. It hurt too much to even think of rolling out a crust yet.

When they strolled around to the south side of the barn, Rose caught her breath and pulled up short, almost yanking Poppy's arm out of its socket. "Look, Poppy."

Instead of being nestled safely in the coop, their eight chickens were on the ground huddled against the side of the barn, fast asleep. At the sound of Rose's voice, Big Bertha stirred and squawked and flapped her wings as if the cat were chasing her. She made such a fuss that the other chickens awoke and disintegrated into a skirmish of feathers.

"What is this all about?" Poppy said. "Did Billy Idol scare you out of your coop?"

Billy Idol was their new cat. He was fierce enough to rid the farm of mice, but he also made the chickens quake in their boots — if chickens had boots. Lily's fiancé, Dan, had brought Billy Idol last week as a gift to Aunt B, but Aunt B had never appreciated a gift less. She wasn't all that fond of the cat they already had.

"Aendi Bitsy is going to get rid of Billy Idol for sure this time," Rose said, furrowing her brow at the possibility of losing their new cat.

Poppy couldn't share Rose's concern. Billy Idol might have been a good mouser, but he was the orneriest cat alive, and he left his victims on the porch almost every day. Poppy could just as well do without the sight of a dead mouse greeting her first thing in the morning.

"Let's go see," Poppy said.

Tiptoeing around the agitated chickens,

they went behind the barn. If Billy Idol had cleared out the chicken coop for a place to sleep, he'd be in big trouble.

"Oh no," Rose whispered as they came around the corner.

Poppy took in a sharp breath.

The chicken coop was gone.

Well, not exactly gone. Nothing remained of it but a tangled heap of straw, wire, and splintered lumber. It looked as if a tiny tornado had blown by and reduced it to a pile of kindling in the middle of the night.

The troublemaker had returned.

Fear and anger tightened in Poppy's chest. Could someone truly hate them this much? What had any of the Honeybee Schwesters ever done to warrant chopping down their chicken coop or painting threatening messages on their barn? Aunt Bitsy wore earrings occasionally and hid money between the pages of their Bible, but surely no one could be this angered by her eccentric behavior. Lily read books to the schoolchildren once a week, and Rose was so timid and sweet that people were afraid of offending *her*, not the other way around.

Poppy nibbled on her bottom lip. She had socked more than her fair share of boys in primary school. Could one of them still be angry after all these years? At the moment, it was the only explanation that made sense. This whole mess could very well be her fault.

Tears slowly trickled down Rose's cheeks. "Why would he chop up our chicken coop? What did the chickens ever do to him?"

Poppy put her arm around her sister. After this, they'd be fortunate if they could convince Rose to leave the house. "The important thing is that he didn't hurt our chickens. That means he has a little kindness inside him."

To Poppy's surprise, Rose's expression brightened considerably. She wiped her eyes and sniffed back new tears. "That's true. He cared about the chickens. He must not be all bad. Jesus can still touch his heart."

Well, maybe. The best Poppy dared hope was that he'd get arrested for sneaking around people's houses and quit bothering them.

"Let's go break the bad news to B and Lily," Poppy said. "We'll have to buy some eggs at the market today."

"*Nae,* look," Rose said, gazing at the side of the barn where the chickens had been roosting.

Six eggs lay on the ground in a nice little row against the barn wall. Rose quickly snatched them up and put them in her basket. "It's a chicken coop miracle," she said, with an unexpected smile.

Maybe she wouldn't shut herself in her room today.

Billy Idol strolled around the corner of the barn and mewed loudly. His voice was gravelly and deep, as if he'd been a smoker all his life. At the sight of the chickens milling near what used to be their coop, he crouched and crept closer, no doubt preparing for an attack.

Poppy folded her arms and gave him the stink eye. "Don't even think about it, Billy Idol."

Rose handed Poppy her basket of eggs and scooped Billy Idol into her arms. "Oh, you sweet little kitty. Did that man scare you too?"

Poppy's lips curled into a reluctant grin. Only someone as pure-hearted as Rose could love a cat like Billy Idol. He had unruly black-and-white fur, lopsided whiskers, and one ear split right down the middle. One eye only opened halfway, and part of his tail was missing. But it wasn't his looks that made him so unlovable. Billy Idol regularly hissed and spit at the members of his new family, as if he would have rather taken a bath than be picked up and snuggled.

41

Even in Rose's loving embrace, he struggled and swiped at her as if she was choking him. Rose patiently ran her hand along his back and scratched what was left of his ears, until he gave up the struggle and sat quietly in her arms. He looked like a five-year-old enduring a haircut, but at least he kept still.

Rose nuzzled her cheek against Billy Idol's fur. "There, there, kitty. It's all right. You're safe now." Billy Idol frowned at the indignity of being babied, but Rose didn't notice. "Maybe he saw our intruder last night."

"I hope Billy Idol gave him a good scratching."

Rose held the cat up so she could look him in the eye. "Did you scratch that mean man?" she said, in her most precious baby voice. "That's naughty. No scratching or Aunt Bitsy will banish you from the house."

It was a *gute* sign that Rose could talk about the incident, even with the cat.

Poppy couldn't even think about it without the bile rising in her throat. She bit her lip. How dare someone leave their chickens homeless and scare everyone half to death? Who was the young man behind that rolled-up car window, with his shifty gaze and his face swollen with bee stings? If only she'd gotten a good look.

If Luke Bontrager hadn't interfered, their

chickens would still have a coop.

She pressed her lips together. Then again, maybe she wouldn't still be in possession of her fingers. She gingerly flexed her hand. If the vandalism incidents were retaliation for something she'd done, she'd face twenty car windows to find out the truth, no matter what Luke Bontrager said.

He would surely scold her if he ever found out.

Well, he could try.

She'd give him as good as she got.

Luke, Dan Kanagy, and their friend Josiah Yoder stood behind the Christners' barn regarding the woodpile that used to be the chicken coop. Dan had come by the Honeybee Farm earlier to see Lily. Lily had told him about the coop, and Dan had fetched Josiah and Luke after supper to survey the damage.

Luke was doing a valiant job of keeping his blood from boiling over. *Whosoever was angry with his brother without a cause shall be in danger of the judgment.* Well, a destroyed chicken coop seemed to be a pretty *gute* cause for anger. Why would someone spend several good sleeping hours reducing a chicken coop to rubble?

"Lily's pretty upset about it," Dan said,

43

picking up a jagged piece of wood and turning it over in his hand.

"What about Rose?" Josiah said. "Is Rose okay?"

"They're all shaken up," Dan said. "Even Poppy, and her confidence isn't easily rattled."

"You're telling me," Luke muttered. She didn't even bat an eye at a broken hand.

Josiah poked his foot around the splintered wood. "They didn't hear anything in the middle of the night?"

Dan shook his head. "There was some wind last night. Those big trees blowing in the breeze would have covered up the sound. I wish I knew a way to stop him from destroying their entire farm piece by piece."

"Maybe we should call the sheriff," Josiah said. "I don't like the idea of the four of them being here alone."

Josiah must have been really worried. It wasn't the Amish way to involve the police in anything.

Luke tended to agree with him. Four women living alone on a country farm needed more protection than a shotgun could provide — even if the community frowned on calling the police. Bitsy used to be *Englisch.* She colored her hair and wore tattoos. Surely she wouldn't mind calling

44

the police.

Dan nodded as his brows inched closer and closer together. "Bitsy's already talked to the sheriff, but there's not much he can do except keep a closer eye on the place. I'm here almost every day, but that doesn't keep things from happening in the middle of the night. All we can do is keep fixing what's broken." He poked a piece of wood with his foot and glanced at Luke. "Could you help me rebuild it?"

"I'll help," Josiah said, "but I'm no carpenter."

"I'm a dairy farmer," Dan said. "I can hammer nails, but it won't be done right unless you're the one in charge, Luke. I know it's a lot to ask."

Luke folded his arms across his chest and grunted his displeasure. "I'm insulted you even think you have to ask. Of course I'll rebuild it."

"And we'll do whatever we can to help," Josiah said.

Luke raised an eyebrow. Josiah couldn't hammer a nail straight even if someone drew a line for him. "You can hold my lunch box."

Josiah's lips twitched sheepishly. "*Ach,* I'm better than I used to be."

Luke glanced sideways at him but didn't

argue. "Monday is the Fourth of July. The Johnsons don't want me working on their floor anyway. And I can't lay their floor until I get those planks. I can take Monday and Tuesday to build a new coop."

It was certain Dan hadn't expected anything less, but relief flooded his expression. "I'll come as soon as I finish milking on Monday."

Josiah cupped his hand around the back of his neck. "I can come after nine o'clock."

Luke raised an eyebrow. "At night?"

"*Jah.* I feel really bad about not being more help, but I've got to make hay while the sun shines."

"Literally," Luke said. He thumped a hand on Joe's shoulder. "I know how laden you are right now with the farm. Don't worry about coming. Dan and I can manage without you."

Josiah narrowed his eyes in mock indignation. Luke had never seen him truly angry in his life. "You just don't want me touching your tools."

"That too," Luke said.

"I want to come, just in case I catch a glimpse of . . ." Josiah turned bright red and lowered his eyes. "Well . . . you know."

Luke smirked. "You're pathetic, Joe. Just go knock on the door and talk to her. She won't bite you."

Josiah gave Luke a friendly shove. "I've got a plan," he said. "And it can't be rushed. Unlike you, I don't knock girls over like a freight train."

Luke shrugged and flashed a smile. "It's not my fault I knock girls over with my good looks."

"Don't fool yourself," Dan said. "You haven't knocked Poppy Christner over yet."

"And thank the *gute* Lord for that. I like my nose just the way it is."

Dan stuffed his hands in his pockets and leaned against the barn. "Poppy isn't prone to hit people anymore."

Luke rolled his eyes. "So she told me."

"She's wonderful pretty," Josiah said. "Don't you think she's pretty?"

"Who cares if she's pretty? If you haven't noticed, she's a little hard to get along with." A lot hard to get along with. "And stubborn. And contrary."

Dan rubbed the whiskers on his chin. "Sounds like someone we know, doesn't it, Joe?"

Josiah's lips curled upward. "Except for the part about being pretty."

Luke squinted at his two friends. "Are you talking about me?"

"You're as hardheaded as they come,"

Dan said.

Joe nodded. "But we like you anyway."

Dan held up his hands as if to stop traffic. "Well, we put up with you. Besides, Poppy isn't contrary. She's feisty. I would think you'd like someone with some guts yet."

"I want someone sweet who understands what a good catch I am and adores me for being a wonderful-*gute* man," Luke said.

Dan twisted his mouth into a funny grin. "I don't think that girl exists."

Hearing movement behind him, Luke turned to see Poppy, Rose, and Lily Christner walk around the side of the barn. They looked like a trio of angels by the light of the setting sun. Rose wore a light pink dress, and Lily wore yellow. Poppy's dress was a royal blue that Luke liked very much. The blue highlighted the color of her eyes and made them stand out from her face like stars on a summer's evening.

She also had a bandage wrapped around her hand. It had been only two days since the car incident, and it probably still hurt something wonderful. He hoped she didn't wait too long to go to the doctor. The sooner she got it in a cast, the sooner it would heal.

"It was sort of rickety anyway," Lily said, motioning to the pile of splinters that used to be the chicken coop. "Maybe he did us a favor."

Rose and Poppy stood next to Lily with their elbows linked. Would it look too obvious if Luke suddenly switched places with Joe so Joe could stand closer to Rose? Probably. Joe said he had a plan. Joe tended to be too deliberate for Luke's liking, but Luke wouldn't court Rose for him. Joe could set his own pace, no matter how slow.

Joe took one step forward. "Hello," he said, not even daring to look Rose in the eye.

A snail could have beaten Joe in a footrace.

"*Wie gehts,* Josiah," Poppy said. "It's nice to see you."

Rose didn't lift her eyes from the ground, so Luke had no idea if she even knew who Joe was.

Dan had focused all his attention on Lily the minute she walked around the side of the barn. Everybody else might as well have disappeared, because he acted as if he couldn't take his eyes from her. Luke hoped a girl would look at him like that someday.

Come to think of it, Mary Schrock and Dinah Eicher both looked at him that way. The biggest challenge was choosing which of them would be the lucky girl to get his undying love.

"Luke is going to build you a new chicken coop," Dan said, squeezing Lily's arm with his free hand.

"That is so very kind of you," Lily said. She nudged Poppy with her elbow. "Isn't it, Poppy?"

Poppy nearly coughed out her answer. *"Jah. Jah,* very nice. *Denki."*

Luke didn't acknowledge Poppy's existence. She didn't like him, he didn't like her. Theirs was a mutual understanding. Why rock the boat? "I have a couple of extra days without work next week. I'll be here Monday morning. It shouldn't take too long to put up."

"All by yourself?" Lily said.

"Dan will be by after milking yet," Luke said.

Josiah tried to glance at Rose without looking like he was glancing at Rose. "I'll come by every night as soon as my chores are done."

"Then our chickens will have a proper place to sleep," Rose said. *"Denki."*

Luke wasn't sure if she was talking to Josiah or him, but since Josiah moved as fast as a turtle taking the long way around, Luke decided to answer for both of them. "We'll do our best to make it comfortable for the chickens."

"I can help in the mornings," Poppy chimed in.

"No need," Luke said, hoping with the lighthearted and pleasant lilt of his voice to kill that idea before it ever took flight.

Poppy pinned Luke with a no-nonsense gaze. "I want to help."

Poppy was a gathering storm, and Luke did not want to get struck by lightning. He clenched his teeth and measured his words very carefully. Lightning or no lightning, under no circumstances would he let a girl wield a hammer. If Joe wasn't allowed to touch his tools, Poppy certainly wouldn't be. "I won't need any help but Dan's and Joe's." He remembered just in time to add that cheerfulness to his voice so Poppy wouldn't suspect he didn't want her near his tools.

The storm on her face got cloudier. "I want to learn how to build a chicken coop in case I ever need to build one of my own."

"You'll never need to build your own. I'm happy to do it." He didn't feel all that happy at the moment. Mostly he felt annoyance at Poppy's hardheaded independence. Why couldn't she accept that it was his duty to do what he could?

She pressed her lips together in a hard line. "Both you and my *dawdi* say I'll never

51

get a husband. An old *maedle* needs to know how to build her own chicken coop."

Josiah raised both eyebrows. "You told her that?"

"It wasn't like that," Luke said, sputtering like an old gas generator. Why did he always stick his foot in his mouth? "I was only trying to talk her into seeing a doctor. I didn't want her hand to fall off."

"It didn't," Poppy said, as if Luke hadn't already noticed.

He glanced at Poppy's hand. It gave him a perfect excuse to refuse her help. "You're injured, so you can't help anyway."

"The doctor took X-rays. It's not broken."

He couldn't keep the smugness from his voice. "You took my advice and went in."

She matched his expression with plenty of scorn of her own. "I went in to prove you wrong. You're not so smart, Luke Bontrager."

He shrugged. "I'm not usually wrong. Maybe the doctor missed something on the X-ray." He didn't really mean what he said. He was wrong and stupid and thoughtless on a daily basis, and he was glad that her hand wasn't broken, but a show of arrogance always made Poppy furious. He shouldn't take such perverse pleasure in getting a rise out of her, but she looked fierce

52

and oh, so pretty when she got angry.

The storm flashed in her green eyes. She could have taken on a whole den of badgers. Luke stifled a grin. Nope. He shouldn't enjoy seeing Poppy so irritated.

She unwrapped the bandage from her hand and made a fist. Luke took one step back.

Lily grabbed Poppy's elbow. "Don't hit him."

Dan grinned. "Hit him, Poppy. He could use a pop in the mouth."

Lily's mouth fell open. "Dan Kanagy!"

Poppy rolled her eyes. "I wasn't going to hit him. I just want to show him."

Luke frowned until it felt like his eyebrows met in the middle. A sickly bluish-black bruise ran across the back of Poppy's hand. He had to take a deep breath to keep from growling.

No one should hurt a girl like that.

"It looks sore," he said, keeping his expression blank so she wouldn't know how much it upset him. "You should be crying like a baby."

"I can hold a hammer just fine."

The only thing to do was to be perfectly honest with her, but honesty would make her pretty angry. "This is a man's job, Poppy. I won't let you help me."

Her green eyes were flashing before. Now they burst into flame. "That is the stupidest, stubbornest thing I've ever heard."

She might have started hissing at him, but Lily grabbed her wrist and tugged her toward the house. "*Cum,* Poppy," Lily said. "We've got bread to make, and I know we'd all like to see Luke reach his twenty-third birthday, even if he deserves a dozen scoldings."

Rose slipped her hand around Poppy's waist and managed a weak smile. "Let's go see if Billy Idol left something on our porch."

With her glare firmly focused on Luke, Poppy let her sisters lead her away without protest. Maybe she realized she would have said something to regret. Maybe she wanted time to plot revenge.

As long as she stayed out of his way, he didn't care how mad she was.

The three sisters disappeared around the corner of the barn, and Dan gave a low whistle. "You sure know how to impress the girls, Luke. It's a wonder they don't fall at your feet the minute you walk into a room."

Josiah seemed genuinely concerned. "You told her she's going to be an old maid?"

"I was annoyed. It just popped out."

"You're never going to persuade her to

54

marry you if you talk to her that way," Dan said.

Luke didn't even pretend to be amused. "Very funny."

Dan propped a hand on Luke's shoulder. "You're going to be sick in love with her before the year's out."

Luke thought his jaw might scrape the ground. "Even you can't be that thick, Dan. Poppy hates me, and I can't stand her."

The laughter behind Dan's eyes made Luke a little irritated. "You've always liked a challenge."

"What I like is a nice, sweet girl like Dinah Eicher or Mary Schrock."

"Where's the fun in that?" Dan said, still with that annoying grin on his face, as if he were smarter than Luke and Josiah put together.

Josiah chuckled. "It's more likely Poppy and Luke will kill each other than fall in love."

Luke shook his head in mock disgust. "And it's more likely you'll turn fifty before you dare have a conversation with Rose Christner."

Josiah was unimpressed with Luke's teasing. "I told her I would come to help with the coop, and she said *denki*. Did you hear her say *denki*? That's a conversation if I've ever heard one."

Luke's laughter came out as a single grunt. "Only if you were a clerk at the market. *Hello, Rose,*" Luke said, making his voice extra high. "*Could I interest you in a nice heavy bag of flour?* Then you could carry it out to her buggy to show her your muscles."

Josiah looked as if he were actually considering the possibility. "Do you think that would help?"

Dan draped his arm around Josiah's shoulders. "Don't let Luke talk you out of your plan. I like the plan. Rose is a wonderful-*gute* girl." He glanced at Luke. "So is Poppy."

"Just as long as she's wonderful-*gute* from a distance," Luke said.

Joe frowned. "You're not going to let her help with the chicken coop?"

Luke shook his head. "She'll hurt herself."

Dan seemed to be barely containing his laughter. "Maybe you should wait to start on the coop until I'm done with the milking on Monday. I wouldn't want Poppy to intimidate you."

Luke smirked at Dan's lack of faith. "I can handle Poppy Christner."

"I hope so," Dan said. "I wouldn't want to see her get the better of you."

56

CHAPTER FOUR

Poppy stood outside Luke's workshop and listened to the high-pitched sound of his saw as it met a piece of wood. For as loud as it was outside, the noise must have been deafening inside the workshop. Poppy waited until she heard him finish cutting a piece of wood, and then she knocked on his door, her heart pounding rebelliously at the thought of having to face Luke Bontrager and thank him for saving her hand, even though it probably hadn't needed saving.

Ach. It had to be done, but after the day she'd already had, she wasn't looking forward to it.

Every Saturday afternoon, Poppy and her sisters paid a visit to Mammi and Dawdi Kiem, and every Saturday evening, Poppy came home in a sour mood. Dawdi Sol admonished Poppy constantly about her "stubborn heart." He nearly fell over when he caught a glimpse of Poppy's hand today.

Don't you want to find a husband, Priscilla?
Don't you want to be a godly Amish fraa?

It didn't take too much imagination to figure out why Aunt B had decided to leave home when she was a teenager.

Poppy had come home from Mammi and Dawdi's house and made Luke his pie, and she had decided to deliver it as soon as it came out of the oven. Her day was ruined anyway. It couldn't get much worse.

On the other hand, she was paying Luke Bontrager a visit. There was a real possibility of a lot worse.

No indication on the other side that he had heard her knock. The saw hummed and screeched as it chewed through another piece of wood. Poppy knocked again, louder this time, but there was too much noise on the other side of the door. She lifted the latch, and the door, twice as wide as a normal door, swung open. Luke stood with his back to her and guided a piece of wood with his long, deft fingers as if he had been born with a sturdy piece of oak in his hand.

She waited until he'd cut the wood and taken a step back from the saw. "Luke," she said, loudly enough to be heard over the machinery.

He snapped his head around as if she had startled him. No doubt she was the last

58

person he expected to see in his shop. He pulled some bright orange earplugs from his ears and flipped a switch on his saw. It sputtered before coming to rest and leaving the workshop in blissful silence. A layer of fine sawdust covered his face and clothes, and it looked as if he was in desperate need of a washing machine. A carpenter's laundry was no doubt plentiful. He tilted his head to one side, folded his arms, and eyed her suspiciously.

With him looking at her like that, she suddenly had trouble finding her voice. "I went to your house first, and they told me you were out here."

"I have some table legs to finish." He sounded only mildly hostile. At least he wasn't growling.

Oy, anyhow, she hated to be beholden to Luke Bontrager. "I . . . I wanted to tell you thank you for stopping that car from driving away with my hand."

He didn't take his eyes off her as he shrugged and shook his head. "Lots of boys would have done the same."

She took the dish towel off the pie. Steam rose from the crust, and the smell of cinnamon and apples permeated Luke's wood shop. "I made you a pie to say thank you."

Luke softened like ice cream on the counter as his dark eyes lit up with a look of pure joy. He took three long strides toward her and very nearly buried his face in the pie. "It's still warm," he whispered.

"I just took it out of the oven."

"Ach, du lieva," he said. "It smells like cinnamon." He held out his hands as if to take it from her.

"It's hot," she said.

He cleared a space off his worktable, and Poppy set it down, slipping her oven mitt off her hand and underneath the pie in one motion. Luke looked like he was very nearly dying of starvation. "Can I eat it?"

"Now?"

"Jah."

His eagerness coaxed a smile from her. "Do you keep a plate and silverware in your workshop?"

Beaming like a flashlight, he reached into his pocket and pulled out what looked like a pocketknife. "I don't need one," he said. He slid a shiny spoon out of the handle where Poppy would have expected a blade to be. With not even the least hesitation, he thrust the spoon into the middle of the pie and scooped out a steaming, hot spoonful of apple filling. He blew on it twice and stuffed it into his mouth.

Poppy pursed her lips to keep her chin

from scraping the ground. Had he not eaten dinner?

He sighed as if she had baked all the bliss in the world into one pie. "This is the most *wunderbarr* thing I have ever tasted." He shoveled another bite into his mouth and then another. Was he planning on eating the whole thing here and now?

Apparently so.

A ribbon of warmth threaded its way down Poppy's spine, and she felt a blush travel up her neck. She wasn't quite sure why she was so pleased that Luke liked her pie. He was just Luke, and it was just a pie. She had to get out of here before she turned bright red. Luke would mock her mercilessly.

She probably could have slipped out without Luke's even noticing. He was completely engrossed in her pie. "Well," she said, "I'm glad you're enjoying it. I'll be going now."

Luke stopped inhaling Poppy's gift long enough to acknowledge he'd heard her. "*Denki,* Poppy." He pulled a tissue from his pocket and swiped it across his face. "Why do you want to do boy stuff when all you'd have to do is feed your husband a pie every day, and he'd do anything in the world for you?"

Her chest tightened at his veiled criticism. "I'm going to be an old *maedle* like Aunt Bitsy, remember?"

He shook his head. "Not when you make pies better than any boy ever could."

She twitched her lips upward. "You're a better eater than I am."

"Wouldn't you rather bake pies all day than build a chicken coop?"

"I would rather do both."

He took another bite and savored it slowly. "If this pie was meant to butter me up, it worked."

Poppy's heart fluttered. "It did?"

"I give you permission to watch me build the chicken coop."

She stifled a growl and made her voice and her smile sickly sweet. "Why would I want to watch you build it when I despise you?"

He paused with his spoon halfway to his mouth. He was probably wondering if she'd spit in his pie. "Girls like watching me build things."

"I'm going to help build instead of watch."

He took the drastic measure of putting down his spoon. "You're not going to help, Poppy."

She clamped her mouth shut before she said something else she would regret. What

62

was the use of digging in her heels tonight? She was supposed to be expressing her undying gratitude, not arguing with Luke for the sake of arguing. Monday would come soon enough. She relaxed her expression and tried to look calm and at peace with herself. "I hope you enjoy the rest of your pie, Luke," she said. "And I will see you tomorrow at *gmay.*"

He narrowed his eyes. "And what about Monday?"

"Monday will be a *gute* day to build a chicken coop."

"Don't get your hopes up," he said, nearly growling as he picked up his spoon.

He was mad, all right. But not mad enough to give her back the pie. By the time she stormed out of his workshop, it was more than halfway gone.

CHAPTER FIVE

Poppy ignored the throbbing in her hand as she pushed the full wheelbarrow to the woodpile. Wouldn't Luke be surprised that a girl could clear all the old wood away before he even got there?

Nae. He'd be angry that Poppy did his job just as well as he could, and he'd be mad that she hadn't obeyed his every command. Girls who didn't swoon at his presence made him very irritated.

She dumped the last of the splintered wood onto the woodpile and with one hand pushed the wheelbarrow back behind the barn. She could maneuver it easily enough, but her right hand ached so badly, she would have thought it was broken if she hadn't seen the X-rays.

She looked up and caught her breath.

Luke stood right in the spot where the coop used to be, with his hands propped on his hips and a scowl on his face. He didn't act surprised to see her, but it was as plain as an old man's wrinkles that he was angry. His coffee-brown eyes smoldered with heat, and someone might as well have plowed a deep furrow right between his eyebrows.

He had wide shoulders and muscular arms, a carpenter's arms, as if he were accustomed to ripping trees from the ground by their roots. Girls like Dinah Eicher or Mary Schrock or Treva King might have found his gaze terrifying. Poppy only found it aggravating. Lots of girls thought Luke Bontrager was handsome, even as formidable as he was. He did have a certain appeal. Along with his *gute* face and dark walnut hair, his eyes shone with intensity and passion, and the lines of his mouth were set and determined.

But Poppy didn't care how good-looking he was. What kind of girl could be attracted to a boy who looked like he wanted to growl at her instead of have a normal conversation?

Speaking of growling . . . "Poppy, I told you I don't want your help."

She returned his glare with one of her own. "Well, you're getting it. It's our chicken coop."

In three long strides he was at her side, nudging her away and commandeering the wheelbarrow. "You shouldn't be pushing this. Your hand's gotta hurt something wonderful." He propped the wheelbarrow on its edge against the side of the barn. "It wonders me why you would want to be out here when you despise me."

Poppy clamped her lips together before a smile escaped. She was mad at him. He shouldn't be able to make her laugh. "You've described my feelings perfectly."

"Then why? Especially with a bad hand."

"Because I want to learn how to build a chicken coop."

He leaned closer and studied her face. For some stupid reason, her heart did a little flip-flop. It must have been those eyes. They could have bored a hole clear through her skull. "You can go to the library and check out a book on chicken coop construction," he said.

"Just like you can go to the library and learn how to bake honey apple pie?"

A soft, longing moan came from deep in his throat. "I could never make a pie like that. Don't try to soften me up."

"But if I stay away . . ." she said, her voice trailing off into nothingness. She hated letting him think he had a chance of talking her out of helping. She squared her shoulders and looked him in the eye. "If I stay away, you win."

His eyes softened at the corners. "I always win."

Ach, no one got her as worked up as Luke Bontrager could. Every blood vessel in her neck was going to pop. "You do not," she said. "Not this time."

His laugh was deep and rolling, and she would have loved the sound had it not been at her expense. "Your eyes are so green," he said.

Your eyes are green? What kind of a response was that? He was laughing at her because she had green eyes? There was no end to this boy's arrogance.

He lost his smile and expelled a breath. "Poppy, I am stronger than you."

"I moved all the wood before you got here."

"*Jah,* with a sore hand. Any man who lets a woman do the heavy lifting should be ashamed of himself. I am stronger and more able to do the work. Let me do it."

Poppy blew an imaginary wisp of hair from her face. "You're not stronger."

He huffed out another breath. "You'd lose in an arm wrestle."

"All those muscles you have is one kind of strength. What about smarts? Do you think you're smarter than me?"

His lips drooped downward. "I . . . I don't know." They kept drooping. "Even when I was in eighth grade and you were in sixth, you understood fractions better."

Poppy tried not to show her complete and utter surprise that Luke would remember or admit that. She should be at least as gracious. "It's because of all the cooking I do. There are fractions in every recipe."

"The way you cook, it's easy to tell you are a master at fractions."

"You were better at geometry."

He grinned reluctantly, as if wary she was still trying to soften him up. "Carpentry. I'm always fitting corners and cutting shapes."

She turned her gaze to the field and studied him out of the corner of her eye. He was tall, probably six feet, and solid, like the maple tree that stood in the center of town. His arms were thick. She wouldn't dare suggest an arm-wrestling contest.

She stood about five inches shorter, so his legs were longer, but she was wiry and fast. There were many different kinds of strength, after all.

"What about faster?"

"Faster than what?" he said.

"I'll bet you can't beat me in a footrace," she said, feeling quite pleased with herself.

"I'll race you to the bridge just to see who's faster."

He shook his head. "I've got work to do."

"If I win, you teach me how to build a chicken coop."

"And if you lose?"

She swallowed hard. Would she be willing to surrender? "Then you don't."

He rubbed the stubble on his chin. "And you quit bothering me?"

"*Jah,*" she said, frustrated at the little prick of pain that he thought she was a bother. Her *dawdi* had often told her the same thing.

He eyed her as if sizing up the competition. "Hmm. You think you're faster than me?"

"*Jah.* I do."

He lowered his gaze and shook his head. The movement almost looked like resignation. Or determination. "You're going to get beat."

"I'm giving you a clear advantage because I have to run in a dress."

He cracked a smile. "I'm not the one who needs an advantage. I should give you a head start, just to make it close."

"I don't want any favors."

Another great sigh, as if he were carrying the weight of the world. "Okay. Even though

I'll regret this, I agree to a race."

Poppy grinned. Even his agreement was a huge victory. "You'll regret it because I'm going to win."

He gave her a smug, sideways glance. "Not in a hundred years, Poppy Christner." He took off his hat and hung it on one of the wheelbarrow handles. "Let's get this over with."

She ambled toward the lane that ran in front of the barn with the orange door. "And you'll let me help if you lose?"

"Against my better judgment, I'll teach you all you need to know about chicken coop building. But it's not going to come to that." They got to the lane, and Luke scratched a line in the dirt with his boot. "The first person to step on the bridge wins, and the loser goes back in the house and leaves me in peace."

Poppy merely nodded. She could be irritated later. Right now, she needed to save her energy for the race.

Luke stood at the starting line as if he were standing in line at the market. He truly thought he was going to win. *Gute.* Overconfidence would be his downfall. Her dress was a disadvantage, but his work boots couldn't have been light.

"Should I say go or you?" he said.

70

"Ready . . ." Poppy said, putting her toe on Luke's line and leaning forward. Luke didn't even crouch. "Set . . . Go."

Since Luke was bigger and slower, Poppy came off the starting line ahead of him, but it didn't take much for him with his long stride to catch up. She glanced to her right, but didn't let him distract her. She had to run with all her might. She lengthened her stride, grateful she was wearing her black rubber-soled shoes and that she could run well enough in her dress.

The long lane, lined on one side with flowering bushes, curved to the left. Her hand throbbed with every jarring step she took, and it didn't take long for her lungs and legs to feel like they were on fire. Lord willing, her legs wouldn't give out before her determination did.

All those recesses spent trying to prove herself to the boys paid off. She pulled ahead of him, but only by a little, and she could hear his heavy steps close behind her. Oh, *sis yuscht*! Luke Bontrager was a lot faster than he looked.

The bridge waited twenty feet ahead. In a surge of speed, Luke came even with her. She made the mistake of glancing at him. He grinned, as if he were enjoying himself or confident he was going to win. "You're pretty fast for a girl, Poppy Christner," he said, panting and chuckling as he pulled ahead of her.

Luke Bontrager would *not* win this race. His laughter slowed him down enough to give Poppy a chance to catch up. She didn't think she was even breathing as she ran for all she was worth, stretched out her foot, and stomped on the bridge half a second before Luke did.

She felt so happy, she could have taken flight. Unfortunately, she didn't have wings. Her last desperate stretch to reach the bridge catapulted her through the air with no place to land gracefully. Though she was too busy falling to see it, for sure and certain it was a truly spectacular landing.

And truly painful. By the grace of the good Lord, she caught herself with her left hand — instead of her already injured right one — and her knees. Her left knee hit the bridge hard. She'd probably have a very large bruise by the end of the day. Her right knee landed on something sharp, like a pebble or the edge of one of the boards on the bridge. The searing pain took her breath away.

Oy, anyhow.

Since her face was getting to know the bridge up close, she didn't see him, but she could feel Luke looming near her like a black storm cloud. "Are you okay?" he said, with more anxiety in his voice than Poppy would have expected.

Before she could right herself, he slipped a firm arm around her waist, pulled her to a sitting position, and squatted next to her. Taking her left hand in his, he brushed the tiny pieces of gravel from her palm and examined the scrape she'd gotten from falling. His big hands were amazingly gentle, and she could almost have believed he cared that she'd gotten hurt. "Does it sting?"

She nodded, not about to let Luke hear her shaky voice. He had enough to gloat over. Her embarrassment was almost as acute as the pain, but she met his eye, ready to show him contempt if he wanted to laugh at her.

He didn't laugh. Gone was the arrogance and self-assurance of a few minutes ago. His eyes glowed like dark, liquid chocolate. She saw nothing but concern. She hadn't expected that. His look made her iron will feel sort of mushy.

"Where else does it hurt? Did you get your knees?"

Her knees throbbed with every breath she took, and she could feel warm, sticky moisture oozing down her right leg, but if Luke knew there was blood, he'd probably insist that she go into the house and take a nap. Or he'd run to the phone shack and call for an ambulance to take her to the hospital. She didn't want a nap or the emergency room. She wanted to build a chicken coop.

"I'm okay," she said, trying to sound perfectly healthy. "No harm done." Almost no harm done — if she managed to stand up.

A lock of hair had come loose from the scarf around her head. He nudged it behind her ear with his thumb.

A butterfly fluttered its wings in her stomach.

Okay.

Luke Bontrager wasn't the kind of boy who tenderly smoothed girls' hair. He was the kind of boy who wouldn't let her join in a game of tackle football.

She held perfectly still and watched him carefully, just in case he did something else unexpected.

"Can you stand up? Do I need to carry you?"

If she needed any motivation to stand, that was it. Luke Bontrager wasn't going to carry her anywhere. "*Nae*. I can do it." She wanted to jump to her feet and take off running, just to show him he didn't have any reason to feel smug. Instead she decided to try for simply standing. He didn't need to know she wouldn't be running again.

Probably ever.

She pushed herself from the ground, and he took her arm and tugged her to her feet. If he hadn't helped her up, she might have been crawling home. She stifled a groan as she took a few tentative steps.

"Are you sure you're okay?"

"I will live," she said, flashing what she hoped passed for a smile. It hurt too much to manage much more than a grimace.

"I should never have agreed to a race," he said. "I didn't want you to get hurt."

Suddenly a smile came easily. Amidst the pain she had almost forgotten. "There is a happy thought in all of this."

"What's that?" he said.

She arched an eyebrow. "I won."

CHAPTER SIX

Poppy Christner was a pain in the neck.

And an unexpectedly fast runner.

And, *ach, du lieva,* very good with a hammer.

And a pain in the neck.

Luke would never say out loud that she was good with a hammer. He didn't want her to get her hopes up that he would ever let her build something with him again. It was too nerve wracking trying to do his own job while watching her closely to make sure she didn't injure herself yet again.

He pried the last of the planks from the pallet and stacked them in a pile next to Poppy. He had insisted on using the crowbar because it took two good hands and a lot of arm strength. Poppy didn't even have one good hand, but he had given up trying to get her to go into the house, even if she winced every time she put hammer to nail. He wasn't going to get her to agree with him on anything, and he wasn't going to argue. He'd argued enough already.

He'd lost the race.

But only because he had on his heavy work boots — that and because Poppy had looked so cute running with all her might, and he had let himself get distracted by her green eyes. The distraction had only lasted for a second, but it turned out to be enough for Poppy to take advantage and beat him.

Still, Poppy had won fair and square, and he was a man of his word. He would teach her how to build a chicken coop, and he wouldn't complain about it. No use stewing over it now anyway. Besides the fact that he had given his word, he felt guilty for agreeing to race in the first place. He'd given in to a childish notion, and Poppy had gotten hurt.

Poppy picked up another plank and hammered it into the cross planks of another pallet. Luke had gotten the pallets for free. The coop wouldn't cost nearly so much if they used old wood.

Poppy finished hammering and ran her finger along the planks. "Nice and sturdy," she said, pressing down with her hand to test the panel's strength.

Pain flitted across her face. She didn't fool him for one minute. Hammering was not a job for someone with a bad hand.

"Okay," he said. "That was very good."

Her smile might have bowled over a weaker man. "Surprised?"

"*Jah.*"

Laughter tripped from her lips, as if his reluctant compliment had made her very happy. "I used to follow my *dat* all over the farm. He bought me a small hammer and a box of nails and let me play with scraps of wood from his shop, even though my *dawdi* Sol told him it was useless to teach a girl anything. I got to be very *gute.*"

"I should probably be glad you didn't spend your time playing with dolls. At least I don't have to worry you'll smash your finger with a bad swing."

Still kneeling in the dirt, she brushed off her hands and picked up the hammer. "I cuddled my share of dolls. Rose would have been heartbroken if I hadn't played house with her at least once a day. And we cooked with Mamm." A shadow of something deep and longing darkened her features but passed as quickly as it had come. "I think of her every time I bake a loaf of bread. I think of her all the time, but especially when I bake."

"How old were you when she died?"

"Seven. My favorite thing was to watch

her long fingers shape dough into pretzels. At night when she read to me, I would listen to her soft voice and trace the veins in her hands with my finger. I'll never forget her hands."

"I'm sorry," he said.

She tilted her head and studied his face. "I'm sorry too."

"Bitsy took you in after your parents died."

"We stayed with our grandparents until the courts sorted out custody." Poppy stiffened, as if every muscle in her body had pulled tight. "Aunt B moved us to Wellsby for a short time, but then she bought this farm and we came back up here." She sighed and tried for a resigned smile. "Our grandparents are strict, but Aunt B thought it best to live close to our *mamm*'s only relatives. At least we didn't have to live with them."

Sol Kiem, Poppy's *dawdi,* was a stern and rigid man, with a long, gray beard and a perpetual frown. He and Poppy's *mammi* lived in town in a little house on a couple of acres with a *gute*-sized garden and a small stable for their horse. Luke could only imagine how having a granddaughter like Poppy would rankle Sol's sense of what was right and proper.

Sol wouldn't look too kindly on a tomboy

for a granddaughter.

"I'm sorry," Luke said again. Maybe there was a reason for Poppy's stubborn insistence that she help with the chicken coop.

"Aunt B says that one day all tears will be wiped from all faces. I hope that's true, but if I ever get to heaven, I'm going to sit down with *Gotte* and give Him a piece of my mind." She frowned. "You probably think that's wicked of me — to want to scold *Gotte* for taking my parents."

"There's nothing you can tell *Gotte* that He doesn't already know. He doesn't want you to hide yourself from Him. He wants you to give yourself over to Him with your whole heart, not just the nice pieces."

"I don't know if there are any nice pieces."

He looked to the sky and pretended to think about it. "There must be something."

With a tentative curl of her lips, she waved her left hand as if swatting flies. There was a nasty scrape on the palm from her fall this morning. Luke flinched for her. Did pain ever stop this girl? "Don't worry, Luke Bontrager. I know exactly what you think of me."

It was the closest to teasing each other they'd ever gotten. He felt like a little kid with his hand in the forbidden cookie jar. Would she smack him down if he let down his guard? Better to not find out.

"We've got six more pallets to do," he said. "Are you up for it?"

She smirked. "You're having a hard time keeping up with me."

He hadn't hoped for a quick surrender, but it didn't hurt to ask.

She shifted on the ground slightly and smoothed her dress around her ankles. "Ready when you are."

Luke gasped. There was a smear of blood in the dirt by her leg. "Poppy, are you bleeding?" He didn't mean for it to come out like an accusation, but it did anyway.

Her gaze traveled to the dirt, and she pursed her lips. "It's nothing. I've had more blood with a paper cut."

He studied her foot and nearly fell over. The black stocking on her right leg seemed to be saturated in blood. Why had he not noticed it before? "Let me see." *Ach,* he should have tempered his harsh tone. Poppy didn't like to be told what to do, even if it was for her own good. Stifling a growl, he marched to the five-gallon bucket that held about ten thousand nails. He overturned it, not caring that the nails spilled all over the ground, and set it upside-down in front of Poppy.

"Please, Poppy," he said, making his voice

soft and low. He had to reach deep for the humility to coax her instead of browbeat her. "I really think we should look at that leg."

Perhaps he caught her off guard. She didn't even open her mouth to argue as he took her hands and gently pulled her onto the bucket. He knelt down and motioned to her foot. "May I?" He'd never touched a girl's leg before, and it was probably all kinds of improper, but the only thing that mattered was Poppy's injury. He couldn't believe he hadn't noticed so much blood.

She stared straight ahead, as she had the day he'd looked at her hand. That emotionless expression seemed to be her brave face, and it made Luke's heart hurt. It must have stung something wonderful if she had to put on the brave face. He carefully pried first her shoe and then her stocking from her leg. She reluctantly nudged her dress slightly above her right knee to reveal a nasty gash just below her kneecap, an inch wide and at least a quarter inch deep. The heavy bleeding had stopped, but it oozed blood yet.

He eyed her in astonishment. She'd been kneeling on this for over an hour, hammering nails and pretending nothing was wrong. Again, he chastised himself for not noticing the blood.

"Poppy," he said breathlessly. "Why didn't you tell me?"

"I didn't want you to have an excuse to get me into the house."

He widened his eyes. "It's not an excuse. You're really hurt."

"You still would have told me to go in the house."

He scrubbed his hand down the side of his face. What would his *dat* say if he knew of Luke's negligence? "I'm sorry, Poppy. I should never have agreed to the race."

Her lips formed into a frown. "It's not your fault. I take the responsibility and the consequences for my own decisions."

"I'm supposed to be looking out for you. For all girls."

She seemed more concerned than annoyed. Luke didn't know if he'd ever seen that before from Poppy. "I didn't ask you to look out for me, Luke. I'm not helpless."

He drew his brows together. "But you're stubborn."

"So are you." She tilted her head to one side and twisted her lips upward. "It's not a bad quality."

Her expression drew a half smile from him. "So is it okay for me to stubbornly insist that we go tend to your knee?"

"I can stand the pain, Luke. Let's keep going on the pallets. Our chickens need a coop."

He grunted. "Stand it any longer, Poppy Christner, and you're going to need a blood transfusion." He stood and held out his hand. "I don't bite," he said when she looked as if she was going to resist him yet again.

She huffed her disapproval. "You just touched my leg in broad daylight. Nothing would surprise me." She gave in and put her hand in his, and he pulled her to her feet. Gasping in pain, she nearly fell over. She must really be hurting. Poppy wouldn't purposefully show him any reaction quite so vulnerable.

Besides that, she was trying to walk on one bare foot. She'd never make it to the house.

He didn't wait for permission or a debate. In one swift motion, he scooped her into his arms and walked quickly toward the house. She caught her breath, and her eyes nearly popped out of her head. "Put me down right now, Luke Bontrager."

"Don't even think about slugging me," he said. "I am not about to stand idly by and let your leg fall off, and I'd like to get to the house before dinnertime."

"My leg is not going to fall off, and I don't slug people anymore."

He marched toward the house with long and jolting strides. If she didn't want to fall, she'd have to hold on. It didn't work. She pushed against his chest with both her injured hands, and he nearly dropped her twice.

"Why are you doing this to me?" she said, and for the first time since he'd known her, he saw distress — almost alarm — in her eyes and felt her trembling in his embrace.

He halted abruptly, partly to spare her hands, but mostly because he'd never seen Poppy so undone. He placed her back on her feet, and she attempted to walk away from him. She could barely hobble. Not only did her knee hurt, but she'd been kneeling in the same position for an hour. She probably felt stiff as a board.

He reached out to help her, and she pushed his hand away. "You must really hate me," she said. He heard the sob in her voice even if she didn't show it on her face.

"Hate you? We don't like each other very much, but I don't hate you."

She inched her way toward the house, walking as if she'd never used her legs before. "And yet you're so eager to humiliate me in front of my family."

His mouth fell open. "Why would I want to humiliate you?"

"You know how foolish I would look if you carried me into the house like a baby. You always have to be better. You always have to win."

His irritation grew like a toadstool in the damp grass. Did she really think he'd try to hurt her feelings? He took a few steps to get in front of her. It didn't take much. She moved like an old man with two wooden legs. "Poppy, stop." She tried to go around him. "Will you stop for one minute so I can say something?"

She stopped, but he didn't know if it was because he asked her to or because she had lost the ability to walk.

He wanted to reach out and take hold of her shoulders so she wouldn't fall over. Something told him that would be a very bad idea. "Poppy, I would never purposefully embarrass you. We don't like each other, but neither you nor I are mean like that."

"You weren't trying to humiliate me?"

He slumped his shoulders. "I was trying to help."

She pursed her lips and looked away. "I don't need your help."

He pointed to her knees. "Oh, I'd say you

definitely need help. Most girls do not find it embarrassing to be carried when they are hurt." He flashed a cocky grin. "And if I'm the one doing the carrying, most girls would find it exciting."

She snorted her disapproval. "I've never met anyone as proud as you are."

He took a bow. "Stubborn and arrogant. My two best qualities."

"*Jah.* Your very best ones."

Luke huffed out a breath. "Poppy, you're obviously in a lot of pain. Why do you want to do this to yourself? It's no trouble for me to build the chicken coop. I've laid many a floor by myself."

"I want to learn," she said.

"Not a good enough reason with blood trailing down your leg."

She rolled her eyes. "Okay then. To prove I can do anything you can do."

He pinned her with a no-nonsense look. "You can't, and you're not going to prove anything if you faint from loss of blood."

"I won't faint."

"Maybe I'll faint."

She seemed to be biting back a tart reply. "I need to help you."

"Why?"

She lowered her eyes and stared at a spot on the ground just to the left of Luke's foot.

"You'll say it serves me right."

He tilted his head in an attempt to get her to look at him. "I promise I'll try to keep my mouth shut." No matter how much she irritated him.

She nibbled on her lower lip. "I think the chicken coop might be my fault, and I want to help rebuild it if I'm responsible."

"It wonders me why you would think that," he said.

"Boys don't exactly like me."

"That's no reason to chop down your chicken coop and tip over your beehives."

"Menno Kauffman kicked his dog, and I gave him a fat lip."

"Recently?" he said.

"Sixth grade. Marty Hoover picked on the little kids all the time. I got in my share of fistfights with him."

"Recently?" Luke asked again.

"Eighth grade. In fourth grade I shoved Alvin Lambright's face in the snow when he threw rocks at Rose." Poppy slumped her shoulders. "There's a long list of boys who would be very happy to see me get my comeuppance."

He shook his head. "Poppy, that was a long time ago. Alvin Lambright is married with two children, Marty Hoover lives in Nebraska, and Menno Kauffman has so many girlfriends, he wouldn't have time to take an ax to your chicken coop. They've all been baptized, Poppy. Why would they break their vows to get petty revenge for something that happened years ago? Not even Alvin Lambright is that much of a *dumkoff*."

Her lips twitched. "You think Alvin is a *dumkoff*?"

"He once left his boots in the oven to dry and baked them to a crisp."

The twitch became a grin. "I've never thought all that highly of Alvin. But even if it isn't my fault, you won't talk me out of helping."

"That wasn't my intention, even if I thought it would work. You won the race. I'll keep my word." He held out his hand. "If you don't want to be carried, will you at least let me offer an arm to lean on so you don't fall and injure your other knee?"

She grimaced and wrapped both arms around his. "Only until we get up the porch steps."

"Do you want me to give you a stiff shove into the house?"

They found another dead mouse on the porch. Luke picked it up and tossed it into the bushes.

"That's my job," Poppy said.

"You'd end up in a heap if you tried to bend over."

Poppy opened the front door, and Luke followed her into the house. The kitchen and sitting area were one big room, with a large wooden table directly in front of him as he walked in the door. The honey-colored wood floor had seen some wear. There were dents and divots everywhere, but the floor itself had been laid tight and straight. Being a carpenter, he noticed things like that.

Even at nine in the morning, the great room felt warm and muggy. All the windows were open, and a slight breeze teased the curtains back and forth. An elegant white cat with yellow eyes and a flat pink nose lounged on the window seat to Luke's left. The cat regarded Luke with something akin to disdain before turning away and turning up its nose. Luke was obviously beneath the cat's notice, but he wasn't offended. He hated cats.

Poppy's Aunt Bitsy sat at the table jotting things down in a notebook. Some of the folks in the district whispered behind their hands that Bitsy Kiem was odd and not to be trusted. She did have some unusual habits, like wearing earrings and coloring her hair strange shades of green and pink, but Luke knew Bitsy as the no-nonsense woman who'd come to their house every week when his *dat* had cancer and helped his *mater* with chores and baking. Her apple pie had been the best treat in the world to a boy who had been asked to carry the weight of the farm on his very small shoulders.

As far as he was concerned, Bitsy could wear earrings and tattoos all day long.

She looked up from her notebook and propped her chin in her hand. "I told Rose not to feed you."

Luke didn't even attempt to guess what she meant. "Poppy's been hurt."

Bitsy frowned, scooted her chair out from under the table, and stood up. "Again?"

"It's not bad, B," Poppy said, her voice betraying the pain she felt.

Bitsy bustled over and pinched her fingers around Poppy's ears. "What happened, little sister? Are you all right?"

"Her knee has a big gash in it," Luke said. He wasn't about to let Poppy talk her *aendi* out of the emergency room.

Bitsy folded her arms across her chest and eyed Luke with suspicion. "Every time you come around, Luke Bontrager, my Priscilla gets hurt. This is becoming a very bad habit. What did you do this time?"

He swallowed past the big lump in his throat. "We had a race."

91

Poppy nudged Luke aside. "It was my fault. I was going so fast I fell at the finish line."

"Did you win?" Bitsy asked.

Poppy bloomed into that smile Luke found sort of interesting. "*Jah.* I'm faster."

"Then it was probably worth it," Bitsy said, eyeing Luke as if Poppy had put him in his place but good.

He clenched his teeth. Poppy hadn't proven anything except that she had better shoes to run in.

Bitsy pulled a chair from the table and pointed to it. "Sit, Poppy, and let's have a look."

Poppy obeyed her *aendi* without arguing or rolling her eyes. Why was it always such a battle between him and Poppy?

Bitsy pulled the hem of Poppy's dress past her knee. New blood mixed with the old.

"You're going to need a tetanus shot," Luke said.

"It wonders me if you've been to medical school, Luke Bontrager." Bitsy didn't seem to care that lockjaw was a horrible way to die. "You think you know so much."

He wasn't about to back down just because Bitsy questioned his intelligence. "She could die without a tetanus shot. And she'll need stitches yet."

Bitsy simply twitched her lips and knelt down to get a closer look at Poppy's knee. She pressed her thumb lightly around the gaping wound and pulled the skin this way and that to ascertain how deep the cut went. "How bad does it hurt?"

"Not bad," Poppy said, hissing at her aunt's touch.

Why did she have to be so brave? Most girls would have made a terrible fuss. It wasn't bad to make a fuss. It was what girls did.

"Let's clean it up," Bitsy said. "And though I don't want his head to get any bigger, Doctor Luke is right. It's very deep."

Poppy glanced at Luke. "It looks worse than it is. I just need a Band-Aid and a little bit of antiseptic spray. I'll have a nice scar in a few weeks."

"You won't even be able to bend your knee," Luke said.

"Ever again?" Bitsy asked, with mock innocence.

Luke could be just as bullheaded as the Christners. "She needs stitches."

"You don't have to talk about me like I'm not in the room," Poppy said.

"Why should I talk to you? You won't listen."

Poppy narrowed her eyes. "The last time I

listened to you, we spent hundreds of dollars at the emergency room, and my hand wasn't even broken."

"I'm not the only one who thought it was broken," Luke said, his blood almost to the boiling point. He just wanted to build a chicken coop. Was that too much to ask? He looked at Bitsy and made one more attempt. "Will you see to it that she goes to the doctor?"

Bitsy studied him as if she were looking at a horse to buy. "I think you two can work that out between yourselves."

You two? Did she mean him and Poppy? Poppy would argue with him about which way was up if she had a mind to. They couldn't work out anything between themselves.

Bitsy went to the other side of the butcher-block island and pulled a metal bowl from the cupboard. She ran some water in the bowl, grabbed a washrag and towel from a drawer, and took the hand soap from the counter. She put her supplies on the floor next to Poppy's chair and knelt beside her. Starting at the bottom, she scrubbed the blood from Poppy's leg while Luke tried to decide where to fix his gaze. He wanted to make sure Bitsy washed Poppy's knee properly, but he wondered if he should have been staring so faithfully at her exposed leg. He didn't want her to think he had any interest in it.

When Bitsy washed the cut, it started bleeding hard. Luke filled another bowl at the sink, and Bitsy squeezed the clean water onto the wound to flush it out. Cleaning it made it look that much worse. Wouldn't Poppy consider getting stitches?

He didn't need to ask. The set of her jaw told him all he needed to know. Poppy was immovable.

He heard the words come out of his mouth before he had time to think. "I could glue it back together for you." Why not? He'd glued his lip back together once. If she refused to get stitches, super glue was a *gute* second choice.

Poppy eyed him suspiciously. What had he done to make her so doubtful? Dan said he was grumpy, but he was only ill-tempered when people deserved it.

Poppy always deserved it.

Oh. Well. Okay.

Maybe he'd given her reason to be wary. He did, after all, just ask for permission to touch her knee, and he'd acted pretty grumpy about it.

"I thought you wanted me to get stitches," she said.

"It's plain you aren't going to follow my advice, and that knee needs something. I glued my lip together before. Remember?"

"You glued your lip together?" Bitsy said. She looked to the ceiling. "Lord, where are You hiding all the smart boys?"

Bitsy had a reputation for talking to *Gotte* right out loud. At least Luke knew right where she stood with heaven. He grinned and pointed to the tiny scar on his upper lip. "I glued a cut closed. It might work on Poppy's knee, Lord willing. Do you have super glue?"

Bitsy nodded. "Any Amish *fraa* worth her salt keeps super glue on hand. You never know when you'll have to glue something back on, like the cat's tail."

Luke studied her face to see if she was joking. He couldn't tell. He glanced furtively at the cat, but its tail, if it had one, was tucked underneath its body. "Okay then," he said. "If you agree, Poppy, I'll see what I can do about your knee."

"Will I still be able to help with the chicken coop?"

He thought about telling her no, but he suspected that if he said no to the chicken coop, she'd say no to the glue. "After I put you back together, you shouldn't bend your knee or the cut will tear apart."

96

"I can hammer boards with one leg out straight."

Of course she could. She'd do it standing on her head if she had a mind to.

He tried not to growl. "You can still help with the chicken coop if you promise not to do anything to rip the wound open."

Poppy frowned as if she wanted to argue but couldn't decide if she should. "I promise." She dabbed blood from her knee with Bitsy's towel. "What do I need to do?"

Luke felt like smiling, but Poppy would probably take any show of happiness as gloating. "Bitsy has cleaned it out well."

"I'm glad you approve, doctor," Bitsy said.

He ignored Poppy's unsympathetic *aendi.* "It needs to be as dry as possible." He scooted a chair in front of Poppy. "Prop your leg on this, and keep your knee straight."

Bitsy rummaged through a drawer for the super glue while Luke washed his hands. After taking the glue from Bitsy, he positioned himself on the floor next to Poppy's leg, and she handed him the towel.

She leaned in to watch him work, and he caught a whiff of that pleasant honey-and-vanilla scent she always seemed to carry with her. Today the vanilla had a slight hint of cinnamon that made him remember that wonderful-*gute* apple pie with cinnamon. He loved cinnamon. And apples. And pie. Poppy Christner pie.

He cleared his throat and concentrated on the slow work of drying the moisture from Poppy's wound, trying his best not to hurt her in the process. He occasionally glanced up to check her expression, but all he saw was fascination in her eyes. If he was hurting her, she didn't care.

"Well," Bitsy said, returning to her place at the table. "Do your best, and don't glue your fingers together."

"I'm more likely to glue my finger to Poppy."

Bitsy frowned. "I'm not letting you hang around here just because you're glued to my niece."

Luke kept a straight face. "I don't mind sleeping on the floor on a sleeping bag."

Poppy looked at Luke, cocked an eyebrow, and twitched her lips as if she were trying not to smile. It was the most adorable look he'd ever seen from her. His heart hopped in his chest like a startled grasshopper.

"Don't worry, young man. If you need to be detached from Poppy, I can cut off your finger. I'm good with a meat cleaver." She casually jotted something in her notebook as if she hadn't just threatened him with a sharp object.

Luke chuckled, though he didn't doubt Bitsy might seriously consider cutting off his hand just to be rid of him.

Once he dried Poppy's cut, he took the lid off the glue and carefully pressed the two edges of the cut together. He ran a thin line of glue along the jagged skin and then went across the wound again with another layer.

Keeping the wound pressed together with his fingers, he glanced at Poppy. "Don't be alarmed. I need to hold on to your knee like this for a few minutes."

"Don't get fresh," Bitsy said, not even looking up from her notebook.

Luke forced his lips together to keep from grinning. It didn't work. "I've never heard the bishop preach against boys holding on to girls' knees."

"That's because you missed church yesterday," Bitsy said.

Luke shook his head. "I was there. Erna King fell asleep and slipped off the bench in the middle of the minister's sermon. You gave her a hand up. The minister didn't say anything about knees."

Bitsy nodded. "Okay, then. You have my permission."

He looked at Poppy. "Do I have your

permission?"

Was she blushing? Probably just flushed from the pain. Then again, a boy she didn't like very much had his hand on her knee.

"Why do you have to hold it?"

"It needs to dry completely so I can apply another coat. Every *gute* carpenter knows you have to let the bottom coat dry or you'll mess up the paint."

Poppy regarded him with her brilliant green eyes. "Okay. Just don't get your germs on my cut."

"I washed my hands," he said, before falling into an uncomfortable silence. He didn't have anything to do but sit on the floor with his hand on her knee and try to look busy.

Poppy must have felt the awkwardness creeping between them. She gave him a half smile. "*Denki* for fixing my knee. I don't like the hospital."

"Neither do I."

"The last time I was a patient in a hospital was at my own birth," Bitsy said. "It was not a good experience."

"You remember when you were born, B?"

"*Jah.* But I can't remember what I had for breakfast yesterday."

Poppy craned her neck to look at her aunt. "What are you writing? You've been at it all morning."

Bitsy set her pencil down and leaned back in her chair. "We're going to need a little extra money for Lily's wedding. Especially if we want fireworks."

Luke nearly choked on his laughter. "Does Lily want fireworks?"

"*Nae,*" Bitsy said. "I'm going to surprise her." She pointed a finger at Luke. "Don't tell."

Luke closed his mouth and shook his head. Not in a hundred years. The look on Dan's face when Bitsy started lighting things on fire at the wedding would be worth keeping the secret for.

Poppy leaned over to look at the notebook. "How are you planning on making extra money? Are you writing a cookbook?"

Bitsy folded her arms. "I thought I should come up with something that will make more money than a cookbook. Something that will be an instant success. I'm writing a Mennonite vampire romance. Vampires are very popular right now, and the Mennonites are such *gute* people." She tore the half-written page out of her notebook and crinkled it into a ball. "But it's a lot harder than it sounds. I can't decide if my conflict should involve a werewolf or Mr. Darcy."

Luke looked at Poppy. He must have had the same puzzled look on his face that she did. "What is a vampire?" Poppy said.

Bitsy waved away the question with a flick of her wrist. "It's a skinny teenager who can't get a tan, no matter how long he sits out in the sun."

Bitsy had lived as an *Englischer* for several years. When Poppy's parents had died, Bitsy had come back to the community to raise her nieces. She knew things that Luke couldn't even begin to guess.

"It sounds like a wonderful-*gute* book, B," Poppy said.

Luke couldn't say if it sounded *gute* or not. Some of the things that appealed to *Englischers* made no sense to him. A thin boy, a wolf, and Mr. What's-His-Name didn't seem like much of a story. "If the wolf chased the thin boy and tried to eat him, that might add some excitement to it."

Bitsy shook her head. "Never give an author writing advice. You don't want to mess up my creative flow. Isn't that right, Farrah Fawcett?"

The cat, who up until now had sat nearly motionless, lifted its head and mewed softly.

"Farrah Fawcett?" Luke said.

"That's our cat's name," Poppy said, smiling at Luke as if she didn't dislike him so much. "She's named after one of Aunt B's favorite movie stars."

As if she knew they were talking about her, Farrah Fawcett eyed Luke like he had a foul smell hanging about him — much the same look Poppy often gave him. Well, Poppy had never liked him, and what did he care for the opinion of a cat?

"She doesn't look like much of a hunter," Luke said. "But Poppy says she leaves a mouse on your doorstep every morning."

Bitsy smirked. "Farrah Fawcett would never stoop to chasing mice. Billy Idol kills enough mice for the both of them."

"Billy Idol?"

"Our other cat," Poppy said.

Luke examined the line of super glue on Poppy's knee. "This looks dry. I'm going to apply another coat."

As he picked up the tube of glue, he heard what sounded like a low-pitched moaning on the other side of the front door.

Bitsy raised her eyebrows. "That's our other cat." She ambled to the door and opened it.

A black-and-white cat stood on the welcome mat with one paw propped on a dead mouse. Luke wasn't exactly sure how a cat could manage to sneer, but that cat looked as prickly and mean as a porcupine with a splinter. No doubt it had seen its share of fights. The top of one of its ears was split in half, and one eye only opened halfway. It was a very ugly cat. Luke felt kind of sorry for it.

"*Cum reu,* Billy Idol," Bitsy said, motioning for the cat to come into the house. "Dan Kanagy brought him over two weeks ago. I've promised to give him a chance, but I haven't promised to keep him."

"He's taken care of our mouse problem, B," Poppy said.

Billy Idol crept into the house as if expecting to be shoved into a bag and taken to the ditch to be drowned. Farrah Fawcett took one look at Billy Idol and, showing more life than she had since Luke had been here, leaped from the window seat, padded quickly across the kitchen floor, and disappeared up the stairs. Apparently, Farrah Fawcett was not fond of the new cat either.

"We get a mouse or a bird on our porch two or three times a day. I think he expects us to eat them for supper," Bitsy said.

Keeping her leg still, Poppy held out her hand. "Come here, Billy Idol, and I'll give you some love." Billy Idol bared his tiny teeth, and Poppy giggled. "He's a ferocious hunter, but a very disagreeable pet. He won't want to be your friend."

"That's okay," Luke said. "I don't like cats."

Bitsy grunted. "Neither do I."

Billy Idol sniffed the air and pinned Luke with a glare made all the more menacing by the fact that one of his eyes didn't fully open. He padded closer and nudged his scarred nose against Luke's knee.

Luke faithfully pinched Poppy's wound while he sat cross-legged on the floor. "Go away, cat," he said.

Poppy's unfriendly, vicious, ugly cat mewed pathetically and leaped into Luke's lap without even asking permission. Luke nearly jumped out of his skin as the cat settled in and made himself comfortable.

Poppy's jaw dropped open. "He's never done that before." She turned to look at her aunt. "Did you see that, B?"

Bitsy tilted her head to look at the cat. "Maybe he likes Luke because they're both so ornery."

Luke would have protested, but he was too busy trying to get the cat off his lap without touching the mangy thing. He nudged the cat with his elbow, but Billy Idol didn't act as if he even noticed. "Don't sit on me, cat."

Billy Idol rested his head on his paws and closed his eyes.

Luke growled in helpless frustration.

Poppy looked as if she were about to burst

into laughter. "You've made a new friend. Or is Billy Idol your very first friend?"

"I have friends," Luke protested in mock indignation.

"Imaginary friends don't count."

He made a face at her.

"Billy Idol wants you to take him home," Bitsy said.

"I would never tear him from his loving family," Luke said. With his free hand, Luke lifted Billy Idol by the scruff of the neck and set him on the floor as far away as he could reach. Billy Idol scowled and crouched as if he might try to jump on Luke's lap again. Luke held out his hand to guard his lap from intruders. Billy Idol sat on his haunches and peered at Luke with a mixture of menace and outrage in his expression. At least that's what it looked like to Luke. Who knew what any stupid cat was thinking?

Luke took a last look at Poppy's cut, which seemed to be staying together, and slipped his hand off her knee. "I think you're cured. Try not to bend your knee for a few days. The glue is a poor substitute for stitches."

Poppy jumped to her feet too quickly, but at least she seemed to take some care with her knee. "I'll be careful."

"You should probably reglue it every day or so yet." He stood up, being careful not to step on the cat sitting next to him. "I should get to that chicken coop."

"*We* should get to that chicken coop," Poppy said, as if she were itching for a fight.

Luke stifled a groan. He had been hoping against hope that Poppy would decide she preferred sitting in a comfortable chair in the kitchen to sitting on the hard ground hammering nails. "I don't mind getting started if you'd like to rest for a few minutes," he said.

"I'm plenty rested," she said through gritted teeth.

"You need to bandage your knee first," he said through clenched ones.

She limped to the super glue drawer and pulled out a box of Band-Aids. Standing at the counter, she methodically opened three and stuck them over her hospital-worthy gash. Luke had no doubt that was as good as he would get.

He did his best to unclench his teeth. Poppy would gloat for days if she realized how much she irritated him. Better to keep his irritation to himself. "Okay then. Let's go."

Poppy, then Billy Idol, followed Luke out the front door.

He tried to bury his aggravation.

He wouldn't be able to shake either one of them.

CHAPTER SEVEN

"I had a wonderful-*gute* time tonight," Dinah Eicher said as she climbed into Luke's buggy. "But it was so hot, I almost melted."

"*Jah,*" Luke said, climbing in beside her. "I'm glad they made ice cream."

Dinah smiled at him as if he were the smartest person in the world. "Was the ice cream your idea?"

He smiled back. After the glares Poppy Christner had given him today, it was refreshing to have a girl gush over him. "*Nae.* Aunt Miriam wanted ideas for eats to serve at the gathering. Both Joe and I suggested ice cream."

"You're not giving yourself enough credit. You probably saved all *die youngie* from heat stroke."

At least Dinah knew how to appreciate a boy's efforts instead of accusing him of arrogance because he wanted to help people.

He picked up the reins and prodded the horse down the road. Many of *die youngie* had taken a van over to Shawano to watch the fireworks and then gone back to one of the ministers' homes for ice cream. Luke had been looking forward to taking Dinah home after the fireworks all day. Poppy Christner did her best to cut down his self-assurance; Dinah did nothing but build it up. She didn't question his motives or call him stubborn, and she would never challenge him to a race. A sweet, delicate Amish girl would never dream of doing that.

He frowned. How had he let Poppy talk him into a race? Not only had he gotten beat, but Poppy had been hurt, and she'd practically bled to death before he had even noticed.

Dinah Eicher would never let herself bleed to death.

A smile tugged at his lips when he thought of Poppy, so stubborn and so annoyed, practically drag herself to the house rather than accept help from him. That girl was as tough as a whole wagon full of crowbars. And she hadn't made a peep when Luke tended to her cut. Still, he wished she didn't have such a hard time letting him help. It would have made his life a whole lot easier if he didn't have to talk her into things that were for her own good.

"Did you hear that the Christners' chicken coop burned down?" Dinah said.

"It didn't burn down," Luke said, glad that whoever had chopped the coop into pieces hadn't thought of taking a match to it. The barn could have easily caught fire along with it. "Someone came in the middle of the night and took an ax to it."

Dinah's eyes got wide and moist. "Who would do such a thing? I'd be terrified if I were Bitsy, living out there all alone with no man to take care of her. It gives me goose pimples just thinking about it."

He should have kept his mouth shut. News like that scared the girls out of their wits. Luke was sure that deep down Poppy Christner was scared too, even though she would never show it. As long as the girls didn't know about such terrible things, they would be spared the worry that was the man's burden to carry.

"I'm building them a new chicken coop," he said. "No harm done."

"You're building them a new coop?"

"I have two free days this week."

Dinah batted her eyelashes in the perfect mixture of modesty and admiration. "It's *wunderbarr* that you would help that poor family out of the goodness of your heart.

No one is as kind and strong as you are, Luke."

He pressed his lips together. Poppy Christner had chastised him for being conceited, and maybe he deserved it. It was pride, pure and simple, to brag about helping his neighbors.

Dinah practically melted into a puddle right there in the buggy as she gazed at him with those trusting baby-blue eyes. He certainly preferred baby-blue eyes to the emerald-green ones that flashed with fire every time he opened his mouth. Was it so wrong to enjoy the sight of Dinah's face lit up in admiration?

"I can't take credit for the whole thing. Dan Kanagy helped me this afternoon, and even Poppy hammered a few nails."

Dinah glanced sideways at Luke and worried the ends of her *kapp* strings. "Why would she do that? I'd be too nervous to pick up a hammer."

That's because Dinah was soft and feminine and delicate, like a girl should be. "I tried to tell her I didn't need her help, but she wouldn't take no for an answer."

Dinah pursed her lips and gazed at Luke. "Poppy's always been strange that way. It's like she wants to be one of the boys."

Luke drew his brows together. He'd rather

be stepped on by his horse than admit it, but Poppy, with only one good leg, had been a great help. She'd never be as good as he was at swinging a hammer, but she kept up with him just fine and never complained once about her knee or her hand or the heat. The Christners didn't have a man around to help them out. He should be more understanding of Poppy's insistence that he teach her to build a chicken coop. She might never have a husband to take care of her.

Luke fingered the stubble on his chin. Poppy would get a husband all right. She might be contrary, but she was also very pretty to look at and made an irresistible apple pie. "I don't think Poppy wants to be one of the boys. I think she wants to prove that she is good enough as a girl."

Dinah studied Luke's face and blinked rapidly, as if she were trying to fan up a breeze. "That's downright prideful, if you ask me. A girl shouldn't want to be better than anyone, especially a boy." Dinah widened her eyes indignantly. "And surely she doesn't think she's better than you at anything."

Luke smiled. Poppy thought she was better than he was at everything, except maybe heavy lifting. She'd challenged him to a race to prove it.

Misguided or not, Poppy would never wilt like a flower in the heat.

A blaring car horn sounded behind them, and Luke pulled as far to the right as he could. The driver revved the engine and passed Luke, leaving only inches to spare between his fiery red car and Luke's buggy. Luke huffed out a breath as he slowed the horse considerably so he wouldn't be forced off the road into the ditch. Most drivers were courteous and did their best to share the road with the buggies, but sometimes someone in too big of a hurry would set Luke's heart racing with their wild driving.

The car disappeared down the road, its radio turned up so loud that the bass line probably rattled every house in the vicinity. Luke guided his horse Cody back to the center of the lane just in time to hear another car come barreling down the road behind him. This one had a loud engine that rumbled like a tornado. The car's brakes squealed as it came up behind Luke's buggy, and the driver laid on his horn as if he were trying to move the buggy with the sheer force of noise. Fearing he'd be plowed over, Luke held his breath and pulled the horse hard right. Dinah screamed as the buggy pitched wildly back and forth. It rolled down a shallow embankment and into the equally shallow ditch.

The driver passed him on the left, slowing down long enough to yell an obscenity at Luke, then followed the other car out of sight. For sure and certain, the angry teenager had just lost a race.

Luke took a deep breath and let his heart slow to a gallop. Thanks be to *Gotte,* the buggy was undamaged and Dinah was unhurt. Cody would be able to pull it back onto the road. Dinah's blue eyes were as big as dinner plates. With one hand she clutched the back of the velvet seat and with the other she held on to the dashboard for dear life. Was she breathing?

"Are you okay?" he said.

"I'm . . . I'm going to be . . ." she said breathlessly, before she gagged and threw up all over the inside of his buggy.

She'd eaten a lot of strawberry ice cream.

CHAPTER EIGHT

"This is a big mistake," Aunt Bitsy said as she pulled back the curtains and watched Dan walk across the yard. "There's no reason that we have to feed Luke Bontrager tonight. Poppy's honey apple pie was bad enough."

"But, Aunt B," Lily said, "he's worked for two days straight on our chicken coop. The least we can do is feed him dinner."

Poppy glanced out the window to see Dan disappear around the side of the barn. She had wanted to stay out there until she and Luke had completely finished the chicken coop, but an hour ago, she'd needed to make bread for dinner. She'd come into the house reluctantly, even when Luke assured her that there wasn't much more that needed to be finished up and that he'd be happy to do it himself. Of course he'd be happy. He would have been happy if Poppy had never insisted on helping him in the first place.

Then again, she wasn't entirely sure about that. This morning, after telling her that she didn't have to help, he didn't so much as peep when she limped right past him and picked up the hammer. Perhaps he had simply resigned himself to the fact that she wouldn't be talked out of helping. He had still treated her like a nuisance, but he had also taken care to teach her how to square the corners and level off the floor. Maybe he planned on taking credit for her *gute* work. It wouldn't have been the first time a boy had done that to her. Then again, Luke didn't seem the deceitful type.

He had been genuinely irritated that she was on the ground hammering nails with a sore knee, but then he had started calling her Stumpy, and she figured he wasn't really mad at her. They'd had a lighthearted conversation about wood floors and freak carpentry accidents. And when Poppy hit her thumb with the hammer, he hadn't even suggested that she go into the house and lie down.

All in all, it had been a *gute* day. Poppy wasn't too proud to admit that she enjoyed stealing glances at Luke Bontrager. Although he could be disagreeable, he was also very nice to look at. She frowned to herself and finished cutting the bread. She didn't usually give place to such frivolous notions.

"Luke is done with the chicken coop, Aunt Bitsy," Rose said, taking the meat loaf out of the pan. "It's not likely we'll see much more of him even if we feed him tonight."

Aunt B fingered her red-and-green poinsettia earring. She had told Poppy she wore the Christmas ones out of season just to make her life more exciting. "Mark my words, little sister, that boy will be harder to get rid of than the smell of skunk from a wool coat."

Lily poured a bottle of chow-chow into a bowl and set it on the table. "We can't very well invite Dan without inviting Luke."

Aunt Bitsy gave an indignant harrumph. "Of course we can. We have to put up with Dan because he's your fiancé, but I'd just as soon toss Luke out on his ear. He's pushy and too sure of himself. I can't abide a boy who is sure of himself."

Lily laughed and pulled a stack of plates from the cupboard. "He's confident, Aunt B. And smart. Dan likes him. He must have some *gute* qualities yet."

"He saved Poppy's hand," Rose said. "And he glued her knee back together. And he built us a new chicken coop."

And he had a nice smile, even though Poppy rarely saw it. But the smile wasn't near enough to make up for his arrogance.

Dan walked into the house with Luke following close behind. "I fetched Luke just like you wanted," Dan said, glancing at Lily, then Poppy, and grinning from ear to ear as if he were about to burst with a secret.

"Well, wash up then," Aunt B said, not even pretending to be happy that Luke and Dan were here for dinner.

Dan led the way down the hall to the bathroom. Luke took off his hat and wiped the sweat from his brow. "How is your thumb?" he said as he passed Poppy.

She held it up, pretending it didn't hurt something wonderful. The nail already looked a light purplish red. "It's fine," she said. It didn't look any worse than the bruise across the back of her right hand or the swollen cut across her knee.

What had happened to her? A week ago, before Luke decided to interfere in her life, she hadn't a scratch on her.

When Dan and Luke came back into the kitchen, Dan fetched the glasses and silverware and helped Lily set the table. Luke, on the other hand, made himself comfortable on the sofa. Billy Idol, who'd been lurking upstairs on the lookout for mice, appeared and leaped into Luke's lap. Luke raised his hands as if the cat had a dread disease and then tried to brush Billy Idol off like a piece of lint. Billy Idol didn't budge. Luke stood up in hopes of forcing Billy Idol to tumble. Billy Idol only scowled and dug his claws into Luke's trousers.

Luke winced in pain and gave up trying to shake the cat. He sat back down on the sofa and let Billy Idol snuggle into his lap.

Aunt B propped her hands on her hips and glared at Luke as if he'd brought a live chicken into the house. "Young man, no one lounges around in my house when there's work to be done."

Luke, being his own predictable self, spread his arms and settled deeper into the sofa. "I don't do women's work," he said, as if expecting everyone to sympathize with him. As if he had no idea how completely wrong he was.

Lily and Dan stopped setting the table to stare at him. Aunt Bitsy's glare became positively lethal. Rose eyed Luke with something akin to horror on her face. Poppy smirked and cocked an eyebrow. After a pleasant day learning how to build a chicken coop, she'd almost forgotten how much she disliked him. As soon as her knee got better, she'd have to challenge him to another race, just to keep him humble.

"You're too good to help us get dinner on?" Poppy said, almost hoping he'd dig a hole so deep for himself that he wouldn't be able to climb out.

Luke shook his head. "*Nae,* but I'm a man. Men do the hard work and let the women do the easier chores."

Even Billy Idol must have had enough of such talk. He twitched his whiskers and jumped off Luke's lap.

Dan broke the uncomfortable silence by laughing out loud. He put his arm around Lily's shoulder and gave her a squeeze. Lily smiled at him as if she were in on whatever secret he was keeping. "Don't believe a word of it, Poppy. For sure and certain, Luke is just plain lazy."

Luke didn't seem the least bit offended. What would it take to ruffle those peacock feathers of his? "I just spent two whole days building a chicken coop."

"With my help," Poppy insisted.

Luke glanced in her direction, and his lips curled slightly upward. "With Poppy's help."

He seemed sincere, as if he actually appreciated her help. Or maybe he'd just decided she hadn't been a complete nuisance. Why did that casual grin set her heart fluttering like a moth to a lantern, especially when she didn't even like him?

"It was very nice of you to build us a new chicken coop," Rose said.

"You won't help with dinner," Dan said. "Sounds lazy to me."

"I'm not lazy." Luke leaned forward and propped his elbows on his knees, revealing the hard muscles of his arms. *Nae,* those weren't the arms of a lazy man. He might be a hard worker, but he was still conceited.

If Luke was to be brought to the depths of humility, Poppy would have to be the one to do it. She'd made Marty Hoover cry in the sixth grade. She could surely teach Luke Bontrager a lesson.

She took the watermelon from the counter and set it on the butcher-block island. "You're afraid you'll be outdone by a girl."

A spark flashed in his eyes. *This* was the way to ruffle Luke Bontrager's feathers. "I'm not afraid of anything."

She pulled two knives from the knife block and held them in the air like umbrellas. "If you think women's work is so easy, why don't you cut this watermelon just to show me how it's done?"

"You can cut a watermelon all by yourself with no help from me."

Poppy smile archly. "I bet I'm faster."

"I'll bet you're not," he said.

"Would you like to find out?" She pointed one of the knives in his direction.

"Nae," he said. "I don't have to prove it."

"Then you're afraid because I beat you in that race."

"I was wearing my boots," he said, but he didn't seem exceptionally bitter about losing to a girl. He stood up, came around the island, and took one of Poppy's knives. "You forget that I'm a carpenter. I can cut a watermelon faster than you can get rolled up in a car window."

"We'll see." Poppy sliced the watermelon down the center and gave Luke half. She pulled two cutting boards from the drawer and handed him one.

"We'd better move out of the way, Rose," Aunt B said. She gazed up at the ceiling. "Dear Lord, we know Luke is a proud young man, but please see to it that he doesn't chop off his fingers." She looked at Poppy and shrugged. "If I had known you were going to challenge Luke to a race, I wouldn't have sharpened the knives this morning. I'm afraid there's going to be blood."

"Don't worry about me. I work with very dangerous tools," Luke said, with that aggravating air of confidence. "It's Poppy you

123

should be worried about."

Poppy kept her smile to herself. Luke Bontrager would be cut down to size same as the watermelon.

Dan said "go," and he and Poppy's sisters and Aunt B watched intently as Luke sliced his watermelon with a vengeance. Poppy turned her watermelon cut-side-down and sliced the rind off from top to bottom like peeling an orange. It was a trick Mammi Sarah had taught her, and it proved twice as fast as cutting the rind off each individual slice.

Luke saw what she was doing, but he was too far into his own cutting to change course, so naturally he tried to distract her. "You're going to lose that nail, you know. If you hadn't insisted on helping with the chicken coop, you wouldn't have hammered your thumb flat and you'd still have ten perfectly good fingernails and a leg that bends correctly." He chopped wildly at his watermelon, making juice fly in every direction.

Poppy grinned as his desperation seemed to mount. "If you had agreed to my helping in the first place, you wouldn't have been humiliated in that footrace. It hurts to lose, doesn't it?"

"You should know," he said.

Poppy finished cutting while Luke wrestled mightily with the rind of his last slice. She'd beaten him with two bad hands and a smashed thumbnail. Dan and Lily cheered, and Rose nearly clapped her hands. She must have thought better of it, because at the last second, she folded her arms and stared out the window as if nothing out of the ordinary were happening in the kitchen. Tenderhearted Rose wouldn't gloat, not even at Luke Bontrager.

Luke hurried to finish his watermelon, got overzealous on the last cut, and sliced right through the knuckle of his left index finger. He growled in frustration, and Poppy only knew it hurt because a grimace traveled fleetingly across his face.

"Are you okay?" she said, trying to suppress her elation at besting Luke once again. He'd cut himself. Probably not the best time to give a victory cheer.

He grabbed the nearest dish towel and wound it tightly around his finger. "Right as rain," he said, pressing the towel to his finger with his other hand.

"Put pressure on it," Poppy said.

"That was my favorite dish towel," Aunt Bitsy murmured. "I should have asked for protection for the towels in my prayer."

Poppy watched in alarm as a wide spot of

125

blood seeped through the towel. "Do you need stitches?"

He frowned and raised an eyebrow. "If you don't need stitches, then I don't need stitches."

It didn't seem as if he would die. Poppy smiled. "I won."

"Don't get used to it," he said, with a deep huskiness to his voice. "It will never happen again."

He narrowed his eyes and pressed his lips together in a tight line, as if planning a strategy for the next contest. He obviously didn't like to lose, but the good-natured glint in his eye surprised her. She'd expected him to be a sore loser, especially to a girl.

"I wouldn't be too confident," Poppy said.

His smile nearly knocked her over. "You might have won, Poppy Christner." He lifted his hand with the towel attached. "But this gets me out of kitchen duty."

"It doesn't get you out of anything," Aunt Bitsy said. "There's lots of things you can do with one hand."

"As long as it's man's work," he said with a grin.

B looked as if she might be ready to sell him to a band of traveling nomads.

"No need, Aunt B," said Lily, pulling a chair from the table. "We're ready to eat."

Poppy slid the watermelon into a bowl and set it on the table. Aunt B sat at the head of the table with Rose to her left and Lily to her right. Dan sat next to Lily and Poppy sat next to Rose. That left the other end of the table for Luke. It also meant Poppy would have to hold his hand during the prayer.

Could she trade places with Rose without being obvious?

Nae. Rose was skittish enough around boys. She might break into hives if she had to sit next to formidable Luke Bontrager. She might faint if she had to hold his hand. Poppy clenched her teeth. She would have to be the tough one.

They always had two prayers at mealtime. Aunt B said the first one out loud while they held hands, and then they bowed their heads in silent grace in the proper Amish tradition. Poppy's grandparents often admonished Aunt B about her unconventional praying, but Aunt B insisted that two prayers were always better than one. It was hard to argue with that, even for her grandfather, Dawdi Sol, and he argued about everything.

Aunt B held out her hands for Rose and Lily. Rose in turn wrapped her fingers around Poppy's hand, and Poppy reluctantly reached out her bruised hand to Luke. She tried to act as if she absolutely did not care that she had to make contact with him. Dan was the fortunate one. He simply took hold of the dish towel wrapped around Luke's finger.

Luke took her bruised hand as if he were reaching for one of his tools — without a fuss and without emotion. Holding hands with a girl obviously didn't unnerve him one little bit. He probably did it all the time.

"Is this okay?" he said, giving her hand a light squeeze. "You still look pretty sore."

Poppy felt the heat creep up her neck for absolutely no reason whatsoever. Her bruise ached, but her hand didn't particularly hurt when Luke took it. It felt rather more like a tingling sensation that trickled up her arm. "I'm fine," she said without meeting his eye. She didn't want him to suspect that his touch was comfortable and unnerving at the same time. He wouldn't see a moment of weakness from Poppy Christner.

Aunt Bitsy didn't waste time or mince words. She often started her prayer before anyone was ready. "Dear Heavenly Father," she said. Everyone quickly bowed their heads and closed their eyes. "We are grateful to be all together — not so grateful that Luke came by, but he did build us a new chicken coop and we owe him dinner. Since he is here, we ask that You strike him with a good dose of humility and give him more sense than to cut his finger again."

Poppy felt a little tug on her hand from Luke's side. Did Aunt B's plain way of speaking offend him? He hadn't seemed to crave Aunt B's approval before. Why would he start now?

"Lord, will You please forgive the person who chopped down our coop and give him a severe case of poison ivy to remind him of his wickedness?" Aunt B paused. She often reconsidered halfway through her prayers. "If the poison ivy is too much, could You at least send a few mosquitoes to plague him? If it was good enough for Pharoah, it is good enough for him. Please also bless me to think up a plot for my vampire romance. I need to pay for this wedding. Amen."

Poppy didn't even raise her head. As expected, Aunt B grunted in frustration and raised her voice to heaven once again. "And please bless this food to our use. Amen." She always forgot to bless the food the first time.

Poppy opened her eyes long enough to steal a glance at Luke. Most of the men in the district, including those as young as Luke, would have seriously disapproved of Aunt Bitsy talking to *Gotte* out loud, and any number of them would have given her a stern lecture on the spot. Luke, on the other hand, wore an unremarkable expression, as if Aunt B hadn't just said a very un-Amish prayer and censured him right in front of *Gotte* and everybody at the dinner table.

"Now you can all say your own prayer," Bitsy said.

Poppy again bowed her head. The silent prayer was how Aunt Bitsy ensured that her nieces learned how to be proper Amish girls. It had been their *mater*'s dying wish. Poppy closed her prayer and looked up.

Rose frowned, and her eyes were scrunched and soft like they always got when something troubled her. She wore that look more and more often these days. "Aunt Bitsy," Rose said. "Poison ivy can be very serious. People have ended up in the hospital."

The lines around Aunt B's mouth softened. "Oh, Rosie. *Gotte* will give that boy, whoever he is, just what he deserves in His own due time. I don't really have any say in it."

"Maybe he's had a hard life," Rose said. "Maybe chopping down chicken coops and scaring our chickens is the only way he can find happiness."

Fire leaped into Luke's eyes. "A man finds

happiness in behaving like a man, not in hurting other people and their chickens." He glanced at Rose and cleared his throat. "I'm sorry. I don't mean to sound harsh. You have a *gute* heart."

A light pink tinted Rose's cheeks. "I hope you found happiness in building the chicken coop."

Luke nodded and took the meat loaf plate from Poppy. "I like working with my hands."

"You have done us a very good deed, and we think you are *wunderbarr,*" Rose said.

Dan chuckled. "Be careful, Rose, or you'll undo Bitsy's prayer. How is Luke ever going to learn humility if you call him *wunderbarr?*"

Luke leaned back and grinned. "Bitsy thinks I'm proud because she doesn't know me well." He inclined his head in Aunt Bitsy's direction. "I forgive you."

Aunt B always wore an I'm-barely-putting-up-with-you expression for Luke. "*Denki* from the bottom of my heart."

Lily giggled. Poppy hid a smirk behind her hand. Luke had not the least desire to impress Aunt B, and B had not the least desire to befriend Luke. It was almost fun to watch them bait each other.

Luke pretended that Aunt B was sincere and showed off his nice white teeth when he smiled. "You're welcome."

Dan helped himself to a piece of Poppy's nut brown bread. "You can't use that excuse on me. I know you better than just about anybody. You're arrogant, grumpy, and you've been hit one too many times in the face with a hammer."

Luke laughed and scooped a mountain of mashed potatoes onto his plate. "You're just jealous because I'm handsomer and smarter than you."

"There's no one handsomer than Dan," Lily said, looking at Dan as if he were a cupcake with sprinkles on top. Poppy's insides felt all soft and mushy. Would she ever love someone the way Lily loved Dan?

Not likely. There weren't many boys she could tolerate, let alone one she could love. Most of them were like Luke Bontrager, proud and oh so superior. She hadn't trusted a boy since she was seven, when a boy's vindictive lie had gotten her a whipping from Dawdi Sol.

Luke had said she'd never get a husband because she was stubborn. Dawdi used to tell her she'd never marry because she refused to act like a girl. She flinched. She could still feel the sting of Dawdi's hickory switch.

Luke paused between hearty bites of

potato and looked at Poppy. "You okay?"

She immediately straightened and skewered a piece of watermelon with her fork. "I'm fine."

He frowned. "You really should take that thumb to a doctor. And get a tetanus shot."

She merely gave him a glare and took a bite of corn. Luke was in the same boat she was. For sure and certain, no one could love him just the way he was. It gave her a small measure of comfort and made her feel worse at the same time.

She studied Luke out of the corner of her eye. She was only fooling herself to think that Luke would remain a bachelor. He was certainly handsome enough to catch a wife, while she was as plain as a fence post — he'd told her so himself. And while she hated to admit it, Luke did have some *gute* qualities, like the kindness he showed to Rose and his good-natured determination not to be offended or cowered by Aunt Bitsy.

It didn't matter how abrasive or proud Luke was, he would get a wife — someone sweet and pretty and biddable like Treva King or Dinah Eicher. Not someone like Poppy Christner, who refused to keep her temper and spoke her mind and made a boy teach her how to build a chicken coop against his will.

"You're the one who needs a tetanus shot, Doctor Luke," Aunt Bitsy said. "You practically cut your finger off. For someone who is too good for women's work, you don't do it well."

"I'm not too good for women's work." Luke grinned at Aunt B and held up his finger with the towel wrapped around it. "But this is *Gotte*'s way of telling you that I am not fitted for it."

Dan snorted. "Don't let him fool you, Bitsy. He's only saying that because he lost the watermelon-cutting contest."

Aunt B pointed her fork at Luke as if she were going to hurl it at him. "Luke Bontrager couldn't fool me if I were blind and hard of hearing."

Luke raised his hands in surrender. His towel flapped in the air. "I'm not trying to fool anybody. Poppy won fair and square, but I won't be caught off guard next time. That was a clever watermelon trick."

Poppy very nearly flashed a smile but thought better of it. Luke didn't really think she was clever.

Luke helped himself to two pieces of Poppy's nut brown bread, spread a thick layer of butter over each of them, and took a bite as if he hadn't eaten in weeks. "This is wonderful-*gute* bread."

"Poppy made it," Lily said, as if Luke would care who baked the bread.

Luke turned his dark eyes to Poppy. "I know. I finished the chicken coop so she could come in early. This bread is worth all the work I had to do myself."

Poppy willed her pulse to slow down. One nice word from Luke wasn't going to affect her in the least. "I think what you mean to say is that you wish I would have been baking bread all day instead of bothering you outside."

"*Jah,* that's probably what I meant." He took another bite. "I'd build three chicken coops for a loaf of this bread."

"You would not," Poppy protested.

"You don't have to do that," Lily said. "Poppy made an extra loaf. You're welcome to take it home."

Aunt B scrunched her brows together. "We can't risk sending food home with him. He's sure to come back if we do, and I won't stand for it."

"I know how much you like my company, but I think I can safely promise you never to come back," Luke said, stuffing a bite of meat loaf in his mouth and savoring it like it was his last bite of food ever. "Unless you need something else built or I have to rescue

Poppy again. But I'll sure miss this bread."

"That's a piecrust promise, Luke Bontrager," Aunt B said, waving her fork so hard that Poppy was sure it would fly out of her hand. "Just look at Dan. We fed him once and he kept coming back, no matter how hard I prayed."

"I've never needed rescuing," Poppy said.

"I was happy to do it."

Poppy ground her teeth together. Luke Bontrager was as aggravating as a garden full of bindweed in the springtime.

Luke ate like a starved man. For as tall and muscular as he was and as hard as he worked, he probably ate that way at every meal. "*Denki* for dinner," he said. "The potatoes are creamy, and the meat loaf is delicious."

"Poppy helped with the meat loaf," Lily said.

Poppy glanced sideways at her sister. "I grated the carrots and chopped the onions. It's Lily's recipe and Rose's special sauce."

Luke trained his eyes on Poppy as his lips twitched upward. "The carrots are well grated."

A pleasant warmth overspread her face. She gritted her teeth and pushed it away by pressing her fingers against her cheeks. She refused to behave like silly Dinah Eicher, who swooned every time Luke looked at her. Poppy never swooned, especially not over a boy.

"It doesn't take much to grate carrots," she said.

Luke raised his eyebrows. "I'd probably lose half the skin on my hand."

"And bleed all over the kitchen," Aunt B added. She had a very low opinion of Luke's abilities.

Luke finally looked away from her. Poppy's breathing returned almost to normal. "It wonders me if Joann would like the recipe for your sauce, Rose."

Rose smiled, not the least bit disconcerted that Luke looked at her. So why was Poppy feeling so skittish? Luke didn't frighten her at all.

"Are you going to the animal shelter tomorrow?" Luke said. "You could give her the recipe when you see her."

"Jah," Rose said. "For sure and certain."

Luke had two sisters. Joann, age fifteen, and Dorothy, age thirteen. Luke's sisters and Rose rode the bus together every Wednesday afternoon to volunteer at the animal shelter in Shawano. At the ripe old age of twenty, Rose was like a mother hen when she got together with Joann and Dorothy.

Luke polished off the last of the meat loaf on his plate. Poppy had never seen anyone eat with the appreciation Luke showed his dinner. He had probably tucked away half of the food on the table. "This whole meal is wonderful-*gute.*"

The lines around Aunt B's mouth were as deep as canyons. "Well, don't get your hopes up."

Lily had been blessed in her choice of boyfriends. Always so helpful, Dan jumped up after dinner and began filling the sink with soapy water. Aunt B insisted that Luke, in spite of having only one good hand, help clean up too. He groaned about having to do women's work, flapped his towel-wrapped hand like a wing, and made a big show of struggling to lift his plate from the table, but he did his share and made everyone laugh. That is, everyone but Aunt Bitsy. Aunt B would never allow Luke to coax so much as a smile from her lips. She kept a watchful eye just in case Luke shirked his duties.

After dishes, Aunt B folded her dish towel and propped her hands on her hips. "Now, Poppy, I'd like to inspect part of the chicken coop."

"Which part?" Luke said, doing an unsatisfactory job of wiping down the table with his one good hand. He left several crumbs.

"The part that you built," Aunt B said. "I trust that Poppy's part is well made, but if you build like you cut watermelon, it might not pass muster."

For the first time since he'd walked into the house, determination settled into the lines of Luke's face, as if Aunt B had thrown him a challenge. Poppy had seen that same look on his face several times in the last two days. She hadn't really considered it before, but Luke took immense pride in his work.

"Then let's go have a look," he said.

Poppy furtively swiped a rag across the table to pick up leftover crumbs before they filed out behind the barn, where the brand-new chicken coop stood. They had built it raised from the ground, and it looked as if it would withstand a tornado and a flood.

Luke had made a clever latch for the door from some leather and a wooden peg. He unhooked the peg, and the door swung downward and rested on the ground, serving as a ramp for the chickens to get into the coop. "You pull up the ramp at night so foxes and dogs can't get in."

Aunt B stuck her head inside the coop. "Was that your idea, Poppy?"

Poppy shook her head. "None of this was my idea. Luke had it all figured out. I just took directions."

Luke acted as if she'd handed him three loaves of nut brown bread. "Poppy is a fast learner. And she is very *gute* with a hammer."

"Of course she is," Aunt B said.

Poppy wasn't sure she deserved such praise, even though it pleased her that a boy would offer it to her. She had forced her way into Luke's project and snapped at him for showing concern for her safety because she hated being treated like a helpless female. Then, earlier today, she had smashed her thumb with the hammer, just as Luke had feared.

Luke stepped back to let Poppy's sisters take a look inside. "We put in ten roosting boxes in case you get more chickens. Dan put some leftover shingles on the roof."

"Watertight," Dan said. He smiled at Rose. "And Josiah helped too."

Luke stood back and folded his arms, his face betraying nothing amiss. Josiah hadn't been allowed to hammer one nail, but it was clear that Luke would never tell Rose.

Poppy smiled to herself. Why hadn't she realized it before? Luke and Dan were trying to nudge Josiah and Rose together, but Josiah seemed like the cautious type. It might take years.

Josiah wasn't timid. He talked to girls at gatherings and *singeons,* and he and Poppy had had a normal conversation last night while he moved pallets for Luke. Josiah must have known how easy it would be to scare Rose away. He relied on his friends to prime the pump a bit.

Lily finished her survey of the inside of the coop. "We can't thank you enough for rebuilding our chicken coop."

Luke shook his head. "No need. I wanted to help."

Aunt B brushed some sawdust off her fingers. "No one can accuse me of not giving credit where credit is due. You and Poppy have done fine work, and we appreciate it. Now I'd appreciate it if you'd go home and forget you ever ate Poppy's meat loaf."

Luke cocked an eyebrow. "That will be impossible, but I'll do my best."

"I only grated the carrots."

"You're very *gute* at grating," Aunt B insisted.

"And hammering," Dan said.

Poppy ran her index finger lightly down the side of the chicken coop and noticed some screws that hadn't been there three hours ago.

She quit breathing as her chest tightened

with irritation. Had Luke taken a drill to her work? What about all his talk about her being a good hammerer?

Luke retrieved a small hand broom from his toolbox. "I need to brush off the floor and then I will leave. *Denki* for dinner. My *mamm* is always happy to have me eat somewhere else."

"So are we," Aunt B said.

Luke simply curved his lips upward. Aunt B had yet to offend him.

Rose was not cooperating with Aunt B's plans. "Won't you at least stay for ice cream? It's honey cinnamon."

Luke hesitated and glanced at Poppy. "I really like cinnamon."

"Then you'd better stay," Lily said. "It's one of Poppy's best recipes."

"I'm not as good a cook as either Lily or Rose," Poppy said. "Don't expect too much."

Luke eyed her as if he didn't believe a word she said. "I'll never forget your apple pie in a thousand years, and you made that bread. I think you could make sawdust taste good."

"She can," said Rose, almost eagerly.

Luke didn't need more convincing. For as enthusiastically as he ate, he was probably starving all the time. "Okay. I'll sweep out fast and come in."

Everyone but Poppy headed back to the house. Aunt Bitsy called over her shoulder, "And, Luke, you turn the crank on the ice-cream maker. It only takes one hand."

Poppy hung back as her family walked away, intent on giving Luke an earful of her displeasure. With his left hand still wrapped in a towel, Luke leaned into the coop and swept out the leftover wood shavings.

"Did you think I wouldn't notice?"

He jerked up his head in surprise and conked it on the top of the door frame. Hissing, he rubbed the back of his skull vigorously. "Poppy, I thought you'd gone in."

"You said I was good with a hammer. Were you lying or just trying to impress Aunt B?"

He leaned against the chicken coop, still rubbing his head. "I don't think I could say anything that would impress your aunt."

"So you were lying?"

He studied her with one eye closed. "Lying about what?"

She pointed to a screw just above his head. "You drilled the corners after I hammered them. You pretended that I've been a big help when really you've just been putting up with me. You can't bear to let a girl be good at 'man's work,' can you?"

143

He folded his arms across his chest, frowned, and rolled his eyes as if barely tolerating her. "Has anyone ever told you that you tend to overreact?"

"Don't blame me. You're the one who took a power drill to my work."

"The corners are stronger with screws instead of nails. Your hammering was fine, but I made it extra secure with screws. I wasn't trying to offend you."

"You should have let me do it."

His sigh came out more like a grunt. "I noticed you wiped the kitchen table after I'd already done it. Should I have been offended?"

"You cut your finger. I wanted to help you out."

"You have a bruised hand, a wounded knee, and a smashed thumb. I didn't want you using a power drill."

"Because I'm a girl," Poppy said. "And you think I'm stupid." She'd heard it over and over again from Urius Beachy. *You're just a stupid girl, Poppy. Go in the house and make a quilt.* Even though she had been only seven years old, it was an insult she would never forget.

"It's not because I think you can't do it. You did a better job on the wood than Josiah Yoder ever could. It's because I didn't

144

want you to drill a hole in your foot."

"You think I'm stupid enough to drill a hole in my foot?"

He sighed again. "You're not stupid. You're a girl, and like it or not, girls aren't as strong as boys. You won't take no for an answer, Poppy, and I had to protect you from yourself."

She plunked herself down on Luke's massive toolbox. "I don't understand where your thinking comes from. Dorothy and Joann seem like very capable girls, and your *mamm* isn't weak or helpless."

He bowed his head and shook it slightly. "My *mamm* is one of the strongest people I know, man or woman. But I don't want her to *have* to be strong. She endured so much when my *dat* had cancer. She worked late into the night trying to take care of our farm. If I can ease her burden and protect her from ever having to go through that again, I will."

Poppy rested her chin in her hand. "It seems you've put yourself in charge of saving the whole world."

He studied her face, then sat down next to her on the toolbox. "I can't save the whole world, but if you did things my way, you'd be so much happier."

She turned to him, ready to give him a

piece of her mind. He flashed a half smile, and she surrendered a grin. "The world does not revolve around you," she said.

He ran the back of his hand along the stubble on his chin and chuckled. "I truly believe everyone would be happier if they did things my way, but I know I *shouldn't* believe it."

"At least you're honest enough to admit that."

His arm brushed against hers as he propped his elbows on his knees. Her heart skipped a beat. She'd have to get that checked at the doctor.

"I'm sorry I drilled without your permission. I wanted to make sure the coop was completely sturdy."

"I'm sorry I've been such a nuisance."

"I'm sorry I called you a nuisance. You were a nuisance, but I'm sorry I called you one."

She saw the glint of a tease in his eye and cuffed him on the shoulder.

"I barely felt that," he said.

"Ha, ha," she said, resolving to smack him harder next time. "I'm sorry I rewiped your table."

"I don't mind. I didn't do a very *gute* job."

They smiled at each other. It felt like a truce. They sat in silence for a few moments watching as the sun disappeared behind the trees. Poppy scolded herself for sort of enjoying the feel of his arm lightly brushing against hers, but she didn't pull away.

"*Denki* for building us a chicken coop."

"*Denki* for helping me," he said.

He didn't really mean it, but it was a nice thing to say all the same.

Poppy felt a nudge against her ankle. Billy Idol pressed close to Luke's leg, looked longingly at Luke's lap, and gave a gravelly meow.

Luke sat up straight, and Billy Idol took it as an invitation to jump into his lap. Luke nudged Billy Idol with his elbow. "Get down, cat."

Billy Idol dug his claws into one of Luke's suspenders and hissed menacingly. "Stop it, cat," Luke said, wrapping his good hand around the cat in an attempt to get Billy Idol off his lap. He would have had more success prying a burr from his hair.

Poppy couldn't help but laugh. "Maybe you'd have better luck if you called him by his name and asked nicely."

Luke pulled while Billy Idol clung. "Please go away, Billy Idol."

"He likes you," Poppy said.

"Everyone likes me but you."

Well. Maybe she liked him okay. She was

amused by the helpless way he wrestled with that cat.

Luke finally gave up and let Billy Idol get comfortable. "As you can see, Billy Idol adores me."

"I see that."

Billy Idol scowled at Poppy, rested his head on his front paws, and closed his eyes. Luke shook his head, resigned to his fate. "The new coop will keep Billy Idol from trying to kill the chickens at night."

"I hope we don't find it in shambles tomorrow."

A worry line appeared between Luke's eyebrows. "It wonders me if it isn't Paul Glick making all the mischief on your farm. Dan says he got wonderful mad when Lily broke up with him."

"He was mad as a bee with a boil. He threatened to have our family shunned."

Luke frowned harder. "Because Lily won't marry him?"

"He says we aren't following the *Ordnung,* that Aunt B is leading us down the path of wickedness. His plan was to marry Lily and force Aunt B out of the community."

Luke growled his disgust. "Paul Glick wouldn't recognize his own hypocrisy if it smelled like fresh manure on his boots. I really can't stand the sight of him."

The fiery indignation Poppy saw in his eyes made her heart swell with gratitude. She was starting to like that look. Poppy curled her lips. "Me either, and he was almost my sister's fiancé."

"How did you bear the thought of it?"

"Whenever he came over, I bit down hard on my tongue and folded my arms tight to keep from smacking him. He wasn't nice to Lily. Boys who treated her like that in school got a mouthful of my fist."

Luke pursed his lips in mock disappointment. "You never socked Paul?"

"Nae."

"Too bad. I would have liked to see that."

Poppy liked Luke more and more all the time. "I resisted the sore temptation many times."

His smile really was very nice when he showed it.

"Paul is spiteful," Poppy said. "But he's not the one who destroyed our coop. The trouble started long before Lily and Dan got together."

They heard a faint call from the house. Luke took the opportunity to brush the unsuspecting Billy Idol from his lap before standing and rewrapping the towel around his finger. "I'm supposed to turn the crank."

"Thank goodness you still have one good hand."

He laughed and picked up his large toolbox as if it weighed as much as a pillow. "If I didn't have hands, she'd make me turn the crank with my foot." They walked around the barn where his buggy waited with both doors wide open. He slid his toolbox inside with a slight grimace on his face.

"Is your finger hurting?" Poppy asked. "Or are you thinking about your embarrassing loss?"

He growled even as his lips held the hint of a smile. "*Ach,* you're so smug, Poppy Christner. But it's neither. My buggy smells bad, and I'm thinking of driving it into the lake and buying a new one."

Poppy stuck her head into the buggy and crinkled her nose. "Smells like someone got sick in here. You'll never convince a girl to ride with you with that smell."

"I'm hoping it will wear off."

"It will," Poppy said, stepping back and breathing in the fresh evening air. "But three or four years is a long time to wait."

Luke groaned. "Three or four years? I'm definitely driving it into the lake."

The desperate look on his face made her smile. "It wonders me why your buggy smells like throw up."

"A car ran me off the road the other night, and my passenger got a little shaken."

"Your passenger?"

He fingered his eyebrow. "Dinah Eicher, but don't tell anybody. She was wonderful embarrassed."

Poppy felt a taste of something bitter in her throat. "Oh. Dinah." Pretty, sweet, petite Dinah Eicher. Of course a little buggy mishap would scare her to death. Dinah was demure and obedient. The kind of girl Luke was eager to marry. The kind of girl eager to marry Luke.

Poppy swallowed hard. Well, Dinah could have him. Who wanted the aggravation of being shackled to Luke Bontrager?

"What have you done to try to get rid of the odor?"

"Dan helped me wash the inside with soap and water."

"We have a deodorizer that works wonders. Aunt B practically bathes Billy Idol in it."

He widened his eyes. "Do you think it will work? I don't want to have to drive it through a car wash."

Poppy was already halfway to the house. "I'll run in and get it. It won't hurt to try."

"Could you hurry? Bitsy will get testy if I

don't come in soon to turn the crank."

Poppy bounded up the porch steps and into the house. Bitsy was pouring salt into the ice-cream maker while Rose stirred the ice-cream mixture and Dan and Lily poured the ice into a bowl.

Bitsy looked up and salt spilled all over the counter. "Where's Luke?"

"He's outside," Poppy said, going straight to the cleaning cupboard to search for their deodorizer.

"Did he decide to go home after all?" Bitsy said, picking pieces of rock salt off the counter. "My prayers have been answered."

"I'm helping him with a bad smell in his buggy."

Lily smiled. "It's nice to see you and Luke cooperating."

Poppy narrowed her eyes. "Luke and I don't cooperate. We tolerate."

"He better not be trying to get out of turning the crank," Aunt B said.

"B, do you know where the deodorizer is?"

Aunt B inclined her head toward the front door. "It's on the windowsill, handy so I can spray mice odor off the welcome mat."

Poppy grabbed the spray bottle and took it outside where Luke waited patiently by the buggy. He had unwrapped the towel and was looking at his finger. When Poppy shut the door behind her, he quickly wrapped his finger up again. It didn't look good. There was lots of blood on that towel.

She swung the bottle in her hand. When she got close, she held it up for Luke to see. "I'm ready to spray. Show me right where it happened."

He pointed to the floor, the seat, the dashboard. Dinah must have really exploded. Poppy sprayed generous amounts of deodorizer everywhere, including the inside wall of the buggy. She wanted to be thorough.

Luke sniffed the air. "Now it smells like lavender and toilet cleaner."

"Don't worry. The bad smell will be dead by morning."

He fingered the towel around his hand. "That was wonderful nice of you, Poppy. I know how tempting it must be to imagine me driving girls home in a stinky buggy every night."

Poppy looked skyward as if thinking hard about that. "Very tempting. But I did it for those poor girls. There's only so much they should be asked to endure. I mean, they have to endure plenty already just having to ride with you."

"I'll make sure all those girls send you a thank-you card." His fingers found the edge of the towel again.

"How is your cut?"

"It would have been worth it if I'd won."

Poppy put her deodorizer on the seat of the buggy and held out her hand. "Let me see if it's still bleeding."

He put it behind his back. "It's not."

"Let me see."

"I don't want you to faint."

She cocked an eyebrow and scowled at him. "Really? You think I'm going to faint?"

He merely grunted and wrapped his good hand around his towel. "It's deep. I'll need a whole tube of super glue."

She resisted the urge to snatch the towel away from him. She might make it worse. "Can I have a look at it?"

"You didn't want me to look at your knee."

"That's because I knew you'd make me go in the house."

He grunted again. "I can't make you do anything, Poppy Christner."

She held out her hand. "I can't make you do anything either, Luke Bontrager."

She stared him down until he sighed, rolled his eyes, and unwrapped the towel from his finger. She took his hand in hers and examined his cut. It started bleeding. *"Jah,"* she said. "It's nasty."

He looked at her sideways. "You're not

154

going to faint."

She stifled her exasperation. "I don't even feel light-headed."

He nodded. "I'm impressed." She could tell by the light in his eyes that he was telling the truth. It would be better when he went home and never looked at her like that again.

She became very intent on studying his finger. He'd really sliced himself bad. "Why didn't you say something earlier? I would have helped you glue it before dinner."

He huffed out a breath. "I wasn't happy I lost. Dan and Bitsy would never let me hear the end of it. I'm a sore loser."

"You like to win," Poppy said, "but a sore loser would have thrown his watermelon against the wall."

"You've been spending too much time around Paul Glick," Luke said.

"What if I go back in and sneak out with the super glue? Dan's making googly eyes at Lily. He'll never even notice."

Luke glanced around him as if Dan and Aunt B might be lurking in the shadows. "Okay, but only because my whole hand aches something wonderful."

"That's what you get for trying to hold on to your pride."

He smirked. "*Denki* for the sympathy.

155

You're gloating because you won."

"*Jah.* I love to win. I would have thrown the watermelon against the wall if I'd lost."

He chuckled. "Bitsy would have made me clean it up."

"With one good hand and both feet." Smiling, she headed back to the house for the super glue.

"Poppy?"

She turned back. "What?"

The appreciative glint in his eyes almost knocked her over. "*You* wouldn't have thrown up in my buggy."

Nae. She wouldn't have.

But that look he gave her made her feel like fainting.

CHAPTER NINE

Luke climbed next to Dinah in his *dat*'s open-air buggy. His enclosed buggy smelled better since Poppy had soaked it with deodorizer, but he didn't want to give Dinah bad memories by making her ride in it.

The courting buggy would be less stuffy than the big buggy anyway on such a warm evening. Dinah would appreciate the wind in her face.

Besides, he wasn't taking any chances. If Dinah threw up again, she would be able to lean over the side and aim for the ground. And if she happened to hit the buggy instead, he wouldn't have to spend an hour washing it out. He could spray anything off the courting buggy with a hose.

Luke frowned. He had taken Dinah Eicher home a dozen times in his buggy, and she'd only thrown up once. He didn't expect any trouble tonight.

But it didn't hurt to be prepared.

He flicked the reins to get Cody moving. Dinah looked very pretty in an emerald-green dress and her white *kapp*. The color accented her blue eyes, like trees against the sky. What would a dress that color look like on Poppy Christner? With her bright green eyes, she'd look like a forest in the sunlight.

Luke sat up straighter and shook his head a couple of times. He was out with Dinah — pretty, mild, agreeable Dinah. He shouldn't even be able to remember Poppy's name when Dinah sat next to him, smiling like she always did, as if he were the sun and the moon.

Jah. Poppy should be the furthest girl from his mind.

He just couldn't seem to shake the green eyes.

"I like your dress," he said, because green was his favorite color. Or was it? He couldn't remember if it had always been that way or if the preference was a sudden thing.

Her smile was all honey and peaches. "My *mamm* made it. She's been making shirts and dresses for my brother and sisters for back-to-school next month."

They pulled up to Dinah's house, and Luke set the brake. "Do you want to come in?" she said, twirling her *kapp* string around her finger. "I made coffee cake."

Luke tried not to smile too wide. Of course he wanted to come in. A girl was interested when she invited you to come and sit. Then again, he hadn't expected anything less. Girls liked him. Dinah liked him. He knew what a catch he was — a boy with a strong back and a *gute* job and a handsome face. She'd probably agree to marry him right now if he asked.

Not that he would ask. He hadn't settled on Dinah Eicher just yet. Mary Shrock and Treva King were still in the running.

Dinah took him through the back door to the kitchen, where a plate of coffee cake and two glasses of milk waited on the table. He'd told Dinah last week that coffee cake was one of his favorite desserts, next to apple pie of course.

He smiled to himself. She had remembered. He liked that in a girl.

The kitchen sink was full to the brim with gray water. Dinah saw where he looked and nibbled on her finger. "I clogged the sink, and Dat won't be home for another half hour to fix it. Sorry it looks so bad. I almost draped a towel over it. I hope you don't mind."

"Do you want me to see if I can unstop it?"

She laced her fingers together and looked at him as if he were Moses on Mount Sinai. "Could you? Dat always fixes stuff like this. I'm so grateful to have a man who knows what he's doing."

"Do you have a plunger?"

Dinah looked positively baffled. "You mean like to do the toilet?"

Luke opened the cupboard below the kitchen sink to find a small kitchen plunger standing behind the dish soap. He pulled it out and held it up for Dinah to see. "This should do the trick."

He submerged the plunger in the dirty water, found the drain, and pumped the plunger up and down several times. In a matter of seconds, the water drained out of the sink in a rushing whirlpool.

Dinah's eyes grew wide. "*Ach, du lieva,* that was amazing. How did you do that?"

Luke felt a twinge of annoyance that Dinah was so easily impressed — and a bigger twinge of annoyance that Dinah didn't even know how to use a plunger. A plunger wasn't like a table saw or a hammer. It wasn't very likely that she'd injure herself with a plunger. Girls shouldn't be completely helpless around the house. Not much would get done if the husband had to come in from the fields several times a day to fix a drain or put propane in the lanterns.

Ach.

Maybe even sometimes they'd need to know how to use a power drill.

Maybe he should have given Poppy the benefit of the doubt. And instructions on how to use a drill.

Maybe it annoyed him that Poppy had been right.

Once he put the plunger back in its place, they sat at the table, and Dinah dished him a hearty piece of coffee cake with a delectable layer of cinnamon and brown sugar on top.

Poppy Christner smelled like honey and cinnamon. One good thing about her insistence that she help with the chicken coop was that while they worked together, Luke had often gotten close enough to catch a whiff of her.

Dinah eagerly watched him as he took a bite. The cake was practically swimming in cinnamon and dry as dirt. After putting down his fork, he took a healthy swig of milk and let the cake slide down his throat in one big lump. This was nothing like Poppy's nut brown bread, hot from the oven and slathered with butter. What he wouldn't do for a piece right now.

Poppy might be feisty, but she knew how

to use a hammer and how to cook. Luke would brave a hundred of her scowls for a bite of that bread. He'd put up with three lectures for a whole loaf.

He cleared his throat and picked up a fork for another bite. Why was he thinking about Poppy Christner again? Green eyes and cinnamon should not be distracting him. It didn't matter that Dinah didn't know how to cook. Dinah had plenty of other good qualities that Luke wanted in a wife. She could learn to cook. And use a plunger.

Maybe Poppy could give her a few recipes.

"It's wonderful-*gute,*" he said, stuffing it into his mouth to prove how much he enjoyed it. But then he had to swallow it, so he took another gulp of milk. He'd better eat at least one more piece to make her feel good. Was there more milk?

Dinah blushed. "I wanted to surprise you. I know how you like cinnamon."

She took a dainty bite, chewed slowly, and washed it down with a tiny sip of milk. At that rate, she'd have a lot of milk left over. Maybe she wouldn't mind if he drank hers.

"Do you have more milk?" he said. It would be better to ask than to get cake stuck in his throat and die on Dinah's kitchen floor.

Dinah went to the fridge and brought

back a whole gallon. It looked heavy, so he tried to take it from her. *"Nae,"* she said. "I'll do it. Your hand is hurt."

"Denki," he said. Poppy would have made him pour it himself.

After pouring, she set the milk on the table and sat down to finish her dry coffee cake. "What did you do to your finger?"

Luke studied his bandage. He'd nearly forgotten it was there. "I was cutting a watermelon and cut myself. Poppy Christner super-glued it back together for me."

Dinah didn't seem quite satisfied with that answer. She nibbled on her index finger and didn't take her eyes from Luke's face. "Poppy Christner glued it for you?"

"I was at her house to build the chicken coop."

Dinah frowned as if she didn't understand. "And then Poppy Christner made you cut watermelon?"

"They invited me to dinner after I finished the chicken coop."

Dinah spoke slowly, seeming to measure every word that came out of her mouth. "How nice of Poppy to glue your cut back together."

Luke wasn't sure why, but he sensed that he should measure his words carefully too. "It was deep."

"I would never make you cut watermelon. Men shouldn't do the kitchen chores."

"I wasn't being very careful."

Dinah nibbled on her fingernail and frowned with her eyes and her voice. "You should have come here. I could have taken care of you."

"Poppy doesn't mind the sight of blood."

Dinah stiffened in her chair and pressed her lips into a rigid line. "You don't think I can stand the sight of blood?"

"I didn't say that. Poppy was there and you weren't. It seemed easier to . . ."

Without warning, Dinah burst into thick, plump tears with a sob to go along with them. She covered her face with her hands and cried as if her heart would break. "You didn't want to let me help you," she wailed. "You think I'm a baby."

Well, I do now.

Luke froze. Dinah was crying over a cut finger and some super glue? Were girls really that sensitive?

Not all girls. Poppy might be a little rough around the edges, but she wouldn't cry like this over anything.

Or faint. Poppy was too sensible to faint.

He eyed Dinah in disbelief. He'd only eaten at the Christners' because they'd invited him. It hadn't meant anything. It

164

seemed unbelievable, but could it be possible that Dinah was jealous? How could someone so sweet and delicate be jealous of Poppy Christner?

Instantly, he knew the answer to his own question. Poppy had shocking green eyes and skin as smooth as fresh cream. She could hammer nails like a carpenter and cook like an Amish *mammi.* And she wasn't afraid to get her hands dirty or stick her nose into a buggy that smelled like vomit.

Of course Dinah was jealous.

Dinah's pitch rose the longer Luke sat there like a bump on a log. He should probably do something to demonstrate the depths of his compassion, but what he really wanted to do was throw his hands in the air and shout for Dinah to stop.

Nope. He wouldn't do that. He thought about his sisters. They got upset sometimes. He usually told them to buck up and quit whining. How did he comfort a girl in the depths of despair? Something told him he'd better try or Dinah might start attracting neighborhood dogs with her high-pitched wailing. He reached out his good hand and patted Dinah awkwardly on the head. "Don't cry, Dinah. I'm sorry I . . ." What did he need to be sorry about? "I should have asked you to glue my finger together.

Can you ever forgive me?"

The patting worked, or maybe it was the apology. Her crying gave way to loud sniffling and an occasional sob. "I see blood all the time," she said, with her face still buried in her hands. "I'm just as brave as Poppy Christner."

He spied a box of tissues on the counter and handed the whole thing to Dinah. She pulled four tissues from the box, dabbed at her face, and regained her composure as quickly as she had lost it. How could she turn it on and off so fast?

Sniffling one last time, she straightened her *kapp,* leaned her elbows on the table, and pinned Luke with a pathetic gaze. "I want you to come to me when you need your finger glued."

He nodded vigorously. Anything to keep her from turning on the water again. "I will. For sure and certain." Lord willing, he wouldn't need any skin glued together ever again.

She nodded and took to nibbling on her fingernail again. "I would never force myself on you like Poppy Christner does. I'm shy, and Poppy is pushy and quarrelsome."

Dinah's opinion rubbed him the wrong way, probably because he used to think of Poppy exactly the same way. Of course

Poppy was headstrong and spirited, but Luke didn't mind so much. Her eyes flashed like stars when she was angry and her temper flared out of fierce loyalty to her family. Luke and Poppy wouldn't ever see eye to eye on much, but she wasn't the hopeless, unpleasant girl he had thought. He had been very unfair to her. "Poppy and I are just friends."

Dinah's face turned even redder than when she'd been crying. "Friends? You don't want to be friends with Poppy. She's like a boy. She'll be a horrible nag to her husband."

He should have known better than try to smooth things over or say anything nice about Poppy. "Dan's my best friend, and he and Lily are dating, so we see each other sometimes. She's nicer than you think, and she makes really good nut brown bread."

Dinah's lips quivered before the dam broke. A sob escaped her lips, followed closely by a river of fresh tears. "I know I'm not as good a cook as Poppy Christner. You don't have to be so spiteful about it." She snatched the box of tissues off the table, covered her mouth with her hand, and ran from the room faster than Billy Idol could jump onto Luke's lap.

He sat in silence for a few minutes, wondering if she'd come back.

The date was probably over.

At least he wouldn't have to finish his coffee cake.

There wasn't enough milk in the whole world.

Chapter Ten

Dear Luke, I'm so sorry for how I behaved last night, especially after you fixed my sink. You are the most unselfish boy in the community and the most nicest and godly too. I won't be able to sleep until I know I have your forgiveness. Dinah

Luke stood by his wagon and read Dinah's letter. Nice, short, and to the point. *Gute* thing, because the team was waiting and he needed to get to the Johnsons'. Dinah must have stuck the note in his mailbox early this morning.

It was a *gute* thing she had been the one to apologize, because he wouldn't have had any idea what he needed to say sorry for. Now he could see her at *gmay,* and it would be as if nothing had ever happened.

He hated having to guess what girls were thinking.

At least with Poppy, he knew exactly what

she thought every minute. Most of the time, she was not thinking well of him. He smiled to himself. He liked getting under her skin a little — just to see her eyes flash with indignation.

Luke folded the letter and stuffed it in his pocket. Time to get to work. Yesterday, he'd laid half of the Johnsons' entry floor with a dark, beautiful mahogany. He loved working with the wood, smoothing his hand along a board sanded so fine that it felt like silk, making floor joints fit together so tightly that not even a drop of water would seep through.

Was it a sin to take satisfaction in doing a job well? Even Poppy would be impressed by the floor he'd laid yesterday.

Luke scrubbed his hand along the whiskers on his chin. What he meant was, even Dinah would be impressed by his floor.

He blew a puff of air from between his lips. Of course Dinah would be impressed. She gushed over everything he did, from every hit he made in a softball game to every word that came out of his mouth. She liked the way he chewed his food, the way he drove the buggy, the way he laced his boots.

As far as he knew, Poppy didn't like any of those things.

So why had Poppy's face come to mind

so readily just now?

Granted, it was a pretty face, with bright, intelligent eyes that flashed whenever he said something that provoked her. Even when she smiled at him, her full lips were always poised for a quarrel. He propped his foot on the wheel hub and grabbed on to the seat to pull himself into the wagon. What would it be like to kiss Poppy's lips? Would they taste like cinnamon?

His foot slipped off the wheel and he tumbled, only missing the ground because his hand found the lip of the wagon before he fell face-first into the dirt.

Why in the world had kissing Poppy crossed his mind?

He would never kiss Poppy Christner.

Not in a million years — no matter how soft or inviting those lips were, no matter how much her smiles and her scowls tempted him.

He would rather kiss Dinah . . . what was her last name?

Eicher. Dinah Eicher. The girl who had gotten her feelings hurt because she thought he'd insulted her cooking. The girl who forgave him the next day without his ever having to apologize. She was the girl he wanted to kiss.

"You okay?"

Poppy, looking very pretty in a maroon dress, a black apron, bare feet, and a nose sprinkled with freckles, came walking down the road with a basket hooked over her elbow.

He would not stare at her lips.

Would not stare.

He brushed some imaginary dust from his trousers and leaned his arm casually against the wheel rim. "I lost my footing. My boots are slippery." He trained his eyes on Poppy's forehead. She probably thought he'd gone a little crazy. "I'm going into town to finish laying a floor."

"I'm glad I caught you," she said, flashing him a really nice I-don't-hate-you-anymore smile. Helping a boy clean vomit out of his buggy could do that to a girl.

He gave her an equally pleasant I-never-ever-hated-you-and-I-am-not-staring-at-your-lips smile. She really did have a nice forehead.

"Even though Aunt B says I shouldn't feed you, I wanted to make sure you know how grateful we are to you for building us a chicken coop. Since you seemed to enjoy that bread the other night, I made you the same kind." She pulled a brown paper package from her basket.

He took the bread carefully, as if it might

172

crumble into a million pieces if he handled it roughly. "I think I'm going to cry."

She smiled even wider, forcing him to take a good look at those lips. "It's just nut brown bread. It takes minutes to make."

He tore open the brown paper wrapping. "I see you've already cut it into slices so I won't be tempted to bite into it whole and eat it like an apple."

She giggled. "*Jah.* I was afraid you might do that."

"Mind if I have some?"

She shook her head.

Remembering his manners just in time, he offered her the first slice. She raised her hand in refusal. "I couldn't be so cruel as to take one of your precious slices."

He looked at her with his puppy dog eyes. "Oh, *denki.*"

She giggled again.

He polished off three pieces in a matter of seconds while Poppy stood with her basket in her hands watching him eat. Then he carefully rewrapped the rest of the loaf and placed it in the bed of his wagon by his toolbox. "I'll save the rest for supper at the Johnsons'."

Might as well give her the peace offering he'd bought yesterday. He had stowed it in his toolbox thinking he'd take it to her house tonight after work. Now he wouldn't have to make the extra trip.

She was still smiling at him.

He wouldn't have minded the extra trip so much.

"I have something for you too," he said, jumping into his wagon and unlatching the massive toolbox that sat in his wagon bed. He pulled the white plastic grocery bag out of the toolbox, jumped from the wagon, and handed it to her.

"It's heavy. I got their lightest model. I mean, not that you're weak, but it's easier to work with if you have to put in a lot of screws yet."

She reached into the bag and bit her bottom lip. The uncertainty was kind of cute. "A drill?"

"Battery-powered. Includes ten drill bits. That should take care of all your drilling needs."

Her mouth curled into a cautious smile. "I didn't know I had any drilling needs."

"That's because you don't know all the things this drill can do."

She studied his face. "I . . . I thought you didn't want me to get hurt." She practically whispered, as if fearing to upset some sort of precarious balance between them.

"I don't. But a girl should know how to

fix things around the house. Just be careful with it, okay?"

She stared at the drill as if she'd never seen one before. "I didn't expect this. . . ."

"From me?"

A blush traveled up her cheeks. *"Jah."*

"I was wrong to not trust you with the drill."

She widened her eyes in mock surprise. "I'm going to faint. Luke Bontrager admitted he's wrong."

"You don't faint."

"Thank goodness."

He didn't blame her for being a little shocked. Two weeks ago, he wouldn't have expected it of himself.

Even Luke Bontrager could change his mind. "I'll teach you how to use it, if you want."

Her smile lit up her whole face, like a sunrise on a clear day. "I'd really like that." Then she groaned, and the smile disappeared as quickly as it had come. "I can't accept this, Luke. It's too much."

"I needed to make a big apology," he said.

"It's worth a thousand loaves of bread."

He stroked his hand along the stubble on his chin and grinned. "You could be right. You're welcome to bring me as many loaves as you think will make us even."

175

Poppy's deep, throaty laugh made his heart do a cartwheel. Who knew he could take so much pleasure in making Poppy happy?

"I'd promise a loaf of bread a week until the day I die, but I'm afraid your wife wouldn't take kindly to a strange old maid bringing you food."

"Old maid? Poppy, when you're an old maid, I'll eat my hat."

Her eyes grew wide, as if he had taken her by surprise, and then she seemed to lose some of her enthusiasm. "You said I was too stubborn to get a husband."

"I wanted to scare you into getting a tetanus shot."

Her smile returned with a touch of mischief in it. "I guess it worked then."

He narrowed his eyes. "What do you mean?"

"I told them I was worried about not getting a husband, so they gave me a tetanus shot after they X-rayed my hand."

Luke growled like a bear. "All those times I begged and begged you to get a shot."

She giggled. "I'd already gotten one."

"And you didn't tell me because . . ."

"I didn't want you to think I did it because you told me to. Your head is big enough as it is."

He threw up his hands and rolled his eyes. "Well. That's one less thing to worry about at night. Do you know how much sleep I've lost?"

"Just remember, I didn't do it because you told me to."

"*Nae,* Poppy, the only reason you got a tetanus shot is because I told you to."

"And because the doctor recommended it."

Luke thumbed his suspenders. "So you admit I'm as smart as your doctor?"

Poppy shook her head. "I knew I shouldn't have said anything."

Much as he enjoyed standing there gazing at Poppy with her basket hooked over her arm and her new drill clutched in her fingers, he needed to finish the entryway today. "Are you going into town?"

"*Jah.* I have three more loaves of bread to deliver, and I might look in on my grandparents."

He gazed longingly at her basket. "You have three more loaves?"

"Don't covet," Poppy said. "You've got your own loaf."

"I can drive you into town, if you want."

"As long as you don't try to steal my bread."

He slumped his shoulders. "Okay. But

don't forget who just gave you that very nice drill."

That smile could have blinded a bat. "I won't ever."

She wasn't even insulted when he offered his hand and helped her into the wagon. *Gute.* He hadn't meant it to be insulting. He slapped the reins to set his team in motion, and they lumbered slowly down the road toward town.

"It doesn't always have to be bread," Poppy said.

"What?"

"I don't always have to bring you bread. The cherries come on next week. There's a *wunderbarr* recipe for honey custard with cherries. Or honey cherry cupcakes."

"I'll eat whatever will make you feel better about using that fancy new drill."

"Okay. I will pull out my cherry recipes."

"I'm hungry already," he said.

"You're always hungry." She smiled at him as if she thought that was an endearing quality. His *mamm* would have disagreed.

The team hadn't gone a hundred yards down the road when Luke's sisters came racing toward them waving their arms and screaming hysterically. Luke's heart beat like a drum as he pulled the horses to an abrupt stop and jumped from the wagon.

Poppy set her basket on the seat and followed right behind him.

"Luke," Joann screamed, running at him like a madwoman. "Luke, Griff Simons threw four kittens into the ditch."

Griff Simons? Luke thought that *Englisch* troublemaker had gone to live with his mother in Ohio.

Dorothy grabbed his arm. She had a good grip for a thirteen-year-old. "They're going to drown," she screamed. She pointed down the road. "If we take the shortcut through the woods, we can save them."

Joann grabbed his hand and started dragging him toward the trees. He pulled against her. "Hold on. Hold on. What are you talking about?"

Joann screamed louder, as if he couldn't hear her loud and clear already. "We've got to save the kittens. They're in the ditch, and they're going to drown."

Whose kittens? And why did they have to save them?

Luke still resisted Joann's tugging. "Why did Griff throw them in the ditch?"

Without waiting for a full explanation, Poppy took Dorothy's hand, and they started running in the direction of the shortcut. "Show me where," Poppy said.

Joann didn't waste more time trying to

communicate with Luke. She took off after Poppy and Dorothy, heedless of the danger of trying to fish four kittens out of a ditch.

There was nothing for Luke to do but follow. He couldn't allow his sisters or Poppy to go in the ditch — especially since the kittens were no doubt already dead. "Joann, Dorothy, stop. Don't get in the water."

Luke had firsthand knowledge that Poppy was a fast runner, but the bare feet and that sore knee of hers should have slowed her down a bit.

Nae. She and Dorothy disappeared into the trees before the words were even out of his mouth. "No one goes in the water," he yelled, loud enough so even three girls charging through the woods would hear him. His chest tightened, and he ran with all his might. His sisters might heed his warning, but Poppy wouldn't. He had to get there before she jumped in.

He pursued them madly into the trees, over fallen logs and brush and down the steep slope to the ditch. He breathed out a deep, thankful sigh. Dorothy and Joann stood safely on the bank, squealing and pointing out rocks and sticks that looked like they might be kittens. He was frustrated but not surprised to see Poppy already knee-deep in the ditch searching for kitten corpses.

The fast-moving water in the ditch was shallow and muddy and couldn't have been more than six feet from bank to bank. Still, Poppy could slip and hit her head on a rock or get sucked into the culvert half a mile downstream. His pulse raced out of control. He wouldn't let her put herself in danger like that.

Creating a small avalanche of sticks and pebbles, he charged down the steep ditch bank and tromped into the water, boots and all. "Poppy, you're going to kill yourself," he growled, as he hooked an arm around her waist and pulled her toward the bank.

His sisters redoubled their screaming.

It came as no surprise that Poppy struggled against him. He just tightened his grip.

"Let go," she snapped. "You're going to make us both lose our balance."

She was right. Sliding his arm from around her, he took her hand and tried to pull her to safety. "You'll drown," he yelled, over the roar of the foamy water.

She pulled back and rolled her eyes. Rolled her eyes? At a time like this? "The water is three feet deep, Luke. Dorothy and Joann will be heartbroken if we don't at least try to find those kittens."

He growled. Poppy was going to get

herself killed. "I don't care about dead kittens."

"Luke!" Dorothy screamed. She pointed to the far bank about ten feet upstream.

An orange ball of fur no bigger than his fist clung to some exposed tree roots inches above the water. With another growl, he released Poppy's hand and slogged upstream. He reached out and snatched the waterlogged kitten from its lifeline. The ungrateful thing hissed and scratched as Luke let the water push him downstream to the opposite bank. He stepped up onto dry ground and handed the kitten to Dorothy.

Tears coursed down her cheeks. "You got one, Luke. You got one."

One was enough. Poppy was getting out. Now.

He reached down to pull Poppy out just as she leaned forward, glided into the water, and let the current take her farther downstream. She floated away with only her head above water.

"Poppy, stop! Stand up, and we'll help you out."

"I see something," she yelled back.

"Poppy, be careful," Dorothy called.

Luke, wearing waterlogged boots and a very bad mood, ran along the bank keeping his gaze glued to Poppy as she made her way down the ditch. His sisters followed close behind, squealing every time they thought they saw a kitten or every time Poppy's head came close to scraping a branch or rock.

If she didn't get out immediately, he was going to have a heart attack. Not a mild, I-ate-too-many-french-fries heart attack, but a groaning, rip-your-heart-out-of-your-chest kind of heart attack. If Poppy didn't die, he'd yell at her so loud, even Billy Idol would run away.

Then suddenly, she stopped and stood up in the middle of the raging current. The water came up to her waist. Luke jumped over a fallen tree, plowed right through a sticker bush, and got close enough to reach out his hand and snatch her from the water.

Thankfully, she reached out to him. He breathed a profound sigh that she would let him pull her out of the water. Instead, water cascaded off her *kapp* as she smiled and handed him two more soggy balls of lifeless fur. All that work and frustration for two dead cats.

He turned and handed them to Joann, who squealed with delight. She didn't know they were dead yet. It didn't matter. Mamm would say the journey was more important than the destination. Luke would say that the journey had his sanity hanging by a thread.

Reaching out her hand, Poppy took a step toward the bank. She squeaked in dismay as she slipped on something at her feet and fell into the water with a loud splash. Her sudden fall knocked the wind right out of him. She flailed her arms trying to find something to hold on to as the swift current carried her away.

Luke raced after her, dodging trees and underbrush, trying to hold her up with the sheer force of his gaze.

Find a foothold, Poppy. Grab on to a branch. Grab on to anything. Don't drown.

He soon outpaced his sisters by several yards. Dorothy cradled the live kitten in the crook of her elbow. Joann held her two dead cats like apples she'd just plucked from a tree. Their grip on their dearly-bought kittens made speed impossible.

His panic rose with his heartbeat. He couldn't see Poppy anymore. The trees were too thick, and the ditch twisted and turned like a snake. All he could see clearly was the little slice of ditch immediately to his left. He didn't pull his eyes from it.

"Luke!" Joann yelled.

He turned. Squinting downriver, Joann stood on a little piece of land where the ditch bank jutted out into the water. "Get to the bridge!" Joann said. "She's holding on at the bridge."

The bridge across the ditch was nothing more than a slab of cement with a metal handhold caked with rust. At least Poppy's tetanus shot was up to date. A thin tree branch whipped him across the face as he pushed it aside and threw himself toward the bridge only a few dozen feet ahead.

Heaving air in and out of his lungs, he stomped onto the bridge and spied Poppy just below him. She didn't look to be in serious trouble. She was standing up, with one hand holding fast to a sizable rock on the bank and one hand clutching the gathered hem of her apron. He almost passed out with relief until he saw the blood trickling from her forehead.

"Poppy! Don't move."

She looked up at him and bloomed into a smile. A smile! He would definitely lecture her up one side and down the other. "I got her," she said.

Got who? What was she talking about?

It didn't matter. Luke just wanted to get her safely on dry land.

He had told her not to move, so of course she did. She tried to pull herself out of the ditch, but she couldn't find purchase on the slimy rocks. Luke's heart stopped as she lost her footing, dipped lower in the water, but pulled herself up again.

"I said *don't move*."

"I think I'm going to need some help out," she said, not acting the least bit concerned that she could die at any minute.

Luke got down flat on his stomach and stretched his hand toward Poppy. "Take my hand."

Instead of letting go of her apron like any sensible girl would do, Poppy released her hold on the rock. She teetered precariously with her hand outstretched as the current took hold of her and nearly snatched her out of Luke's reach. With a loud grunt, he lunged forward and grabbed hold of her wrist just as the rushing water took her feet out from under her.

She cried out in pain as Luke felt a sickening vibration from her arm, but he couldn't let go. With her legs still in the water, she dangled over the bridge like a spider on its web. He swung his arm at Poppy toward the bank, and she reached out her leg and found a foothold on a boulder. She made a path of rocks her stepping-stones and tiptoed up the steep embankment, but Luke didn't let go until she was completely out of danger. She never let go of that apron.

Huffing and puffing and beaming from ear to ear, Joann and Dorothy reached the bridge just as Luke released Poppy's hand.

Joann, with a kitten still in each fist, threw her arms around Poppy, being careful not to squish the kittens — although Luke didn't know why it mattered since they were dead. Poppy winced before smiling a soggy smile and giving Joann a kiss on the cheek.

Dorothy was still crying. For joy or distress, Luke couldn't tell. "Poppy, you're bleeding."

Poppy blinked back the water dripping from her *kapp* into her eyes. "I'm okay. Just a little scratch on a stick."

"You saved the kittens," Joann said, giggling and gushing.

Luke frowned so hard his teeth moved back in his mouth. *He* had saved one kitten, the only one that was actually still alive.

Dorothy held up her kitten, which was mewling and carrying on like a newborn *buplie.* "*Denki,* Poppy. They would have died."

Some of them *were* dead. Luke clenched his teeth and praised *Gotte* that Poppy hadn't drowned.

But she wasn't okay, either. It was bad enough that the wound on her head practically sent him into apoplexy, but she held her arm close to her body as if it would break off if she moved it. He gritted his teeth all the harder. If she hadn't gone into the water, he wouldn't have had to fish her out.

And he wouldn't have hurt her. That thought felt like a punch to the gut.

Dorothy wiped her eyes with her free hand. It didn't do much good. The dry places were immediately soaked with new tears. "But we only got three of them."

Poppy, oblivious to how close she'd come to drowning or how furious the boy standing behind her was, giggled and opened her apron. The fourth kitten sat in the crook of Poppy's apron, blinking the water from its eyes and shivering violently.

Joann squealed. Dorothy squealed too, at a higher pitch. Poppy scooped the kitten into her hand, and Dorothy took the edge of her apron and rubbed it back and forth along the kitten's fur.

"Dry all of them," Joann said. "Mine won't move."

"I hurt my arm," Poppy said. "Here, Dorothy, take mine." She handed her kitten to Dorothy, and his sisters held a kitten in each of their hands while Poppy did her best to warm them with the edge of Dorothy's dry apron.

Any second now, Joann would realize her kittens were dead.

"Look, look," Joann said. "He wiggled his nose." She gasped. "And I can see this one breathing. Wonderful-*gute.*"

In disbelief, Luke stepped in for a closer look. All four kittens showed signs of life. Two were mewling softly; one even licked its paws. Great. What were they going to do with four kittens?

"Oh, Poppy, you were so brave. You didn't even care if you got wet," Dorothy said.

Poppy wasn't brave. She was *deerich* and foolhardy. Luke wanted to spit.

Poppy smoothed her finger along one of the kittens' heads. "The ditch isn't deep. I knew I'd be okay."

"But you're soaked."

Poppy grinned. "It's a hot day. Almost as good as going swimming."

It was a very hot day. Luke probably had steam coming out of his ears. "Let's go so we can get Poppy to a doctor."

Poppy didn't remove her gaze from the kittens. "I don't need a doctor. I just wrenched my shoulder. It'll be okay in a few hours."

"I'm taking you to a doctor," Luke muttered through clenched teeth.

She ignored him and started walking,

holding her arm stiffly against her side and gasping quietly whenever a step jarred her shoulder. Luke felt the pain as if it were his own.

Dorothy cradled both hale and hearty cats in her arms. "Why is Griff Simons so mean?"

They hiked along the ditch bank, with Joann leading the way and Luke taking up the rear, keeping a watch out in case Poppy decided to jump into the ditch again on a whim. "You girls stay away from Griff Simons, no matter what."

Griff Simons had been away a long time. Too bad he hadn't stayed away forever. Griff and his dad were *Englischers* in their mostly Amish community, and they kept a farm down the lane from the Honeybee Schwesters. Griff's mom had run off shortly after Poppy and her family had moved into the neighborhood, and Griff had been angry about his mom ever since.

Griff sometimes took his anger out on the local Amish folks, and before he had turned twelve, everyone knew his name and his reputation.

Luke was bigger and four or five years older, so Griff never gave him any trouble, but Griff used to lay wait for Luke's brothers and the Honeybee Sisters when they walked home from school. He'd call them names or pull the girls' *kapp* strings and throw rocks at them.

They had all done their best to avoid him, though Poppy or his brother Mark would sometimes end up in a fistfight.

The bullying lasted for a year or two, until Griff started junior high school and got a motorcycle and a girlfriend. Like Mamm always said, *Idle hands are the devil's workshop.*

"I thought Griff moved to Ohio to be with his mom," Poppy said.

Joann slumped her shoulders. "He's back."

"We were coming home from Aendi Ruth's house when we spied him down the road with the four kittens in his arms," Dorothy said. "We asked him if we could pet them, and he told us his dad had told him to throw them in the ditch. They didn't need any more cats."

"That's terrible," Poppy said.

Luke scowled. "Next time, stay out of his way."

Joann glanced back at Luke and pursed her lips. "I'm sorry, Luke. We started crying and asked him not to drown them, but he kept right on going until he got to the ditch and threw them in. We couldn't just let those poor kitties drown."

"Of course you couldn't," Poppy said.

They'd gone a lot farther than Luke thought. They walked for a good ten minutes until they made it back to the dirt road and Luke's wagon. His trousers were soaked and he'd be more than an hour late for work, but Poppy would hear his lecture no matter how late he was.

His sisters, on the other hand, were going to march straight home where it was safe, and Luke wouldn't have to worry about them.

"What are you going to do with the kittens?" Poppy said, taking the hem of her apron and swiping it down the side of her face. She managed to wipe away about half the blood.

"Do you want one?" Dorothy asked, not acting all that eager to part with one of her precious kittens.

Poppy curled her lips. "We've already got two cats. Why don't you keep them?"

Dorothy and Joann flashed matching smiles. "Okay," Dorothy said. "That would be wonderful-*gute.*"

Luke propped his elbow on his wagon. "Mamm is never going to let you keep four cats."

Dorothy stuck out her bottom lip. "Yes, she will, once we tell her how we saved them. She'll want them to have a *gute* home."

"Go along then," he said, more eager to get rid of them than to argue about the kittens. They were Mamm's headache now.

"What about Poppy's head?" Joann asked.

Poppy dabbed at her forehead with her apron. "I'll be all right."

"I'll see she gets home," Luke said.

Joann handed her kittens to Dorothy and gave Poppy a hug. "*Denki,* Poppy. I hope I'm as brave as you someday."

Not if Luke had anything to say about it.

His sisters walked away, chatting merrily about how they were going to take care of their cats. No one seeing them would have guessed that they'd been weeping and wailing half an hour ago.

Poppy grasped her limp arm with her other hand. "I should go home and take some ibuprofen," she said, clearly in more pain than she would ever show.

Pressing his lips into a hard line, he pulled his damp handkerchief from his damp pocket and handed it to her. She dabbed at the blood on her forehead. The cut was just a small scratch, but he'd first seen it when the water mixed with the blood, and it had looked like a seven-stitch wound.

Luke pushed his fingers into his forehead,

trying to rub away the anger that burned hot right behind his eyes. "Your feet are bleeding."

She lifted one foot and had the audacity to grin. "Sharp rocks. But at least I didn't ruin a good pair of shoes."

Something about the cavalier way she talked about her shoes made him snap like a willow switch. "Poppy Christner," he said, making his voice soft and menacing so she knew he meant business — so she would wipe that aggravatingly stunning smile off her face and feel a little bit of remorse for what she'd put him through.

She peered at him as if waiting for him to tease her about her wet dress or how funny she looked with blood drizzling down her face.

He was so furious, he thought he might explode. He'd be hanged if he let her make light of this. He scrubbed his fingers through his hair. "That was reckless and foolish."

She finally lost her smile. "Luke, it was a ditch as shallow as a kiddie pool."

"And yet your head is bleeding and you can't move your arm," he snarled. "You put yourself in danger. You put my sisters in danger."

She lifted her chin, and a hot, raging forest fire flared to life behind her eyes. "I would never, ever do anything to harm your sisters."

"What if they had followed your example and jumped in? What if Dorothy had hit her head on a rock? Did you think of that? It was foolish, Poppy. Stupid and foolish."

Her jaw dropped. "I told them to stay on the bank."

"So you didn't care if you drowned."

"I wasn't going to drown."

Luke growled until his throat felt raw. "You almost did. If I hadn't pulled you out . . ."

"If you hadn't pulled me out, I would have climbed out by myself. You're not so indispensable, Luke Bontrager, and I don't need you."

"And I don't need this aggravation." He jabbed a finger in her direction. "I'm done with you, Poppy. For good and forever."

"Done with me?"

"I won't save you from yourself anymore."

She scowled. "I never asked you to save me in the first place."

He folded his arms across his chest. "I should have known you'd be ungrateful."

"I should have known you'd be arrogant. What are you so angry about? Are you upset because a girl did what you should have done? What you were too chicken to do?"

He smacked his hand against the side of his wagon so hard, even Poppy jumped. "You don't know anything. You want to prove you're so tough, just like the boys." His voice shook. "You're a girl, Poppy. You're weaker and softer, and you're never going to be as good as the boys at anything."

She stepped back as if he had slapped her across the face. "I'll never be as good at being an idiot."

"Then quit trying."

She took a deep breath and glared at him with such contempt in her eyes, she might have made a weaker man fall over. "I hate you, Luke Bontrager."

"I hate you right back."

She turned on her heels, leaving her basket, her drill, and four loaves of bread sitting in his wagon. She wouldn't be able to carry all of it with one good hand anyway. "Don't follow me," she said.

I wasn't even going to try.

He leaned against his wagon and watched her limp down the road, not looking away until she stepped safely onto the footbridge that spanned the pond at the front of their property. He'd hate himself tomorrow if he didn't at least make sure she got home safe.

He knew how a girl should be treated, even if she didn't want the treatment. At least Dinah Eicher appreciated him. Besides, he preferred blue eyes over brilliant green any day.

Good riddance, Poppy Christner.

CHAPTER ELEVEN

Poppy was getting pretty good at doing things with one hand. She couldn't work the hives, but she could use the smoker. She couldn't knead bread dough, but she could stir the cake batter. She couldn't hoe, but she could pull weeds by hand from her garden. And her garden sorely needed some attention.

Ever since she'd caught her hand in a certain car window, the bindweed had been creeping toward the tomato plants, and oh, *sis yuscht,* they were stubborn weeds. Unless she pulled out the whole root, the pesky things reappeared after only a few days, and the roots were nearly impossible to kill. It tempted her to spray the whole garden with weed killer and start again next year. But Aunt B refused to allow anything poisonous near the bees. Better to be careful of the bees than be rid of the bindweed.

Despite being out on a bright, clear day in

July, Poppy felt gray and drab, as if someone had extinguished the sun in her little patch of the world. It felt like she couldn't catch her breath, and her heart ached with something deep and raw that she didn't want to put a name to.

She scooted farther down the row, picked up her trowel, and started turning over small piles of dirt. She certainly wasn't sad about Luke or anything he might have said to her yesterday. She couldn't care less what that boy thought or how he behaved. A boy that stupid and hateful had absolutely no power to hurt her — except for the fact that in his panic to pull her from the three-foot-deep ditch, he'd dislocated her shoulder.

You're never going to be as good as the boys at anything. She bit her bottom lip to keep from crying out. That's what Luke had told her. She didn't know why his words stabbed her in the heart. She'd heard them dozens of times from boys at school. In the few terrible months they'd lived with Dawdi and Mammi, Dawdi Sol had admonished her daily for trying to be better than the boys. Urius Beachy had been the worst of all. He had pulled her hair and kicked her in the shins just to prove that boys were better than girls.

You're just a stupid girl, Poppy. Gotte *loves*

boys more.

It didn't matter what Luke had said. Nothing any boy said bothered her anymore. She only felt down because she had an annoying bandage on her forehead and a sling on her arm. The yawning hole in her chest was because her shoulder hurt something wonderful. To her relief, the doctor said that a dislocated shoulder was a minor injury. She just needed to wear the sling for two weeks and be careful for a few weeks after that, and she'd be as good as new.

At least her shoulder would be.

Just the thought of wearing a sling for a couple of weeks made her testy. How could she work around the farm or help with Lily's wedding or pick the cherries that would be ready to harvest next week? How could she gather eggs from their nice, new chicken coop with only one good hand?

Her heart slammed against her rib cage and made her wince.

Never mind. She'd let Rose gather the eggs.

The chicken coop reminded her of Luke Bontrager, and she'd rather not have that unpleasant experience every morning.

At least the chicken coop was still standing after last night. The troublemaker had come back and torn all their laundry from the line. That seemed to be his favorite thing to do. They'd have to start hanging their clothes to dry inside the house if they didn't want double laundry every week.

Laundry. Another thing she couldn't do with one hand.

A lump grew in the pit of her stomach. The harder she thought about it, the more sure she became that the vandalism was her fault. Whoever was making mischief on their farm did it because they hated her.

Unfortunately there were a lot of boys on that list, Luke Bontrager at the very top. He was the only boy who had ever been brave enough to tell her he hated her right to her face. Maybe he had been the vandal all along.

Poppy quickly squelched that thought. Luke had been the arrogant boy on the playground who wouldn't let her play football, but he wasn't vicious or vindictive. More recently, he'd saved her hand from a car window and pulled her out of a ditch. She'd spent two whole days building a chicken coop with him, and he'd eaten dinner at her house. He had even put his arm around her. Twice. Not on purpose, of course. Luke would never voluntarily touch someone he found so repulsive, but he'd done it because he thought he needed to save her, even if he hadn't.

He might be aggravatingly confident, but he would never harm Poppy or her family. She knew that from the bottom of her heart.

The ache in her chest grew with every breath she took. It felt even worse when she breathed out.

Oh, *sis yuscht*. Was she crying? She swiped the back of her hand across her eyes and bit back whatever tears wanted to escape. Poppy didn't cry. No matter what Luke or Dawdi or Urius Beachy thought, she was the tough one, the strong one, the one who watched out for her sisters when their parents had died. The one who would fight to defend her family, no matter what.

And she would never, ever, cry over a boy, especially a boy like Luke Bontrager, who yelled at her and told her she was weak and thought he was smarter than a doctor.

Crying over Luke was silly, and Poppy was not a silly girl.

She looked up as she heard the buggy come down the lane. Aunt B was back from the library. Poppy quickly dried any hint of tears from her eyes with the handkerchief from her apron pocket. Aunt B would not suspect a thing.

She paused and studied the handkerchief smeared with two or three spots of dried blood. Where had this come from? It wasn't one of Rose's embroidered ones.

Ach.

Luke had given it to her yesterday right before he'd started yelling. Her eyes stung with tears that she absolutely refused to shed.

Silly, silly girl.

Aunt B waved to Poppy and parked the buggy next to the barn. After unhitching Queenie, she led her to the little pasture on the far side of the barn, which gave Poppy time to compose herself. Aunt B need never know that Poppy had made a fool of herself over a boy.

A stupid, mean, conceited boy.

Aunt B came around from the side of the barn, retrieved some books from the buggy, and strolled to Poppy's garden. "The tomatoes are coming along nice," she said, being careful not to step on the dandelions or Poppy's lettuce.

"I planted some cherry tomatoes this year. We might even get enough to sell."

"Wonderful-*gute*. Every little bit helps if we want special M&M's for the wedding."

Poppy cracked a smile. "Special M&M's?"

"I went online at the library. You can order M&M's with the bride's and groom's names on them. With the M&M's and the fireworks, Lily will be thrilled."

"Then I'll pray we get a *gute* tomato harvest. We've got to have M&M's."

Aunt B smirked. "Paul Glick will be righteously indignant about our wedding M&M's. I can't wait to see his face get all red and splotchy."

"Will Paul be invited to the wedding?"

"We can't very well leave him out. We're inviting the whole district."

Poppy pointed to the four books Aunt B cradled in her arm. "What did you get?"

After studying Poppy's face for a minute, Aunt B plopped herself down in the dirt and rested the books in her lap. "I'm doing more research for my vampire book. I'm having real trouble getting it to flow. I don't think Edgar and Isabella love each other that much, but I can't make Isabella fall in love with the ogre because the ogre is in love with Isabella's daughter. It's a mess."

Poppy smiled. "What books did you get?"

Aunt B held up the first one. "This is the best one of all. I found some money in it."

"Money?"

Aunt B leafed through the book and pulled out three one-hundred dollar bills from between the pages. "I was the last person to check this out, and I accidentally stored some of my savings in here."

Poppy laughed. "That's wonderful-*gute.*" Aunt B didn't trust her money in a bank, so she stored her excess cash all over the house. The Bible always had the most money in it. Aunt B thought her money was safer in the Good Book.

"I cast my bread upon the waters, and *Gotte* brought it back to me. But I'll need to be more careful about where I put my money. Who knows how much I've lost." She tapped her finger to her lips. "I think I better go back and check out a few more books." She looked up at the sky. "*Denki,* Lord, for leading me to this book today. I'm really eager to get those fireworks."

With the books still cradled in her lap, Aunt B leaned over and pulled a few weeds from Poppy's neglected tomatoes. "We need to take a hoe to this."

Poppy huffed out an exasperated breath. "I know. I can't get ahead of the weeds. The cherries will be ripe, the honey is almost ready, and I've got to make bread for the fellowship luncheon next week."

Aunt B lightly pinched Poppy's earlobes with her fingers. "We'll manage, little sister. Dan will help with the cherries and the honey. Your sisters can do the bread."

"I can't do hardly anything."

Aunt B frowned. "Well, it's not your fault.

You've been mashed and squeezed and stretched harder than a cockroach in a washing machine. And it's all Luke Bontrager's fault. Every time that boy comes over, disaster strikes."

Something sharp like a shard of broken glass lodged next to Poppy's heart. She held her breath and tried to ignore it. Superior, ill-humored Luke had no power to upset her whatsoever. "Then we can all rejoice that he won't be over again."

Aunt B tilted her head to get a better look at Poppy's face and propped her chin on her fist. She had a small tattoo of a pink flower on her wrist today. "What happened yesterday?"

Poppy drew her brows together. "I told you. I fished those four kittens out of the ditch and then Luke thought I needed to be fished out. I guess he pulled too hard."

"Did he say something stupid?"

"He always says something stupid."

"Something extra stupid?"

Poppy ran her finger along the strap of the sling. "He said I'm weak."

"That boy wouldn't know sense if it kicked him in the head."

Poppy swallowed hard as that shard of glass edged closer to her heart. "He said I'll never be as good as a boy." She tried to sound as if she couldn't care less. Not even Aunt B would know how those words had sliced right through her heart. Poppy had never told her about Urius Beachy. She didn't need to know about Luke. "He said he hates me."

Aunt B pursed her lips. "Luke's proud and hasty, but that's harsh, even for him."

"I said it first." Once she admitted it, she realized how ashamed she was. As a Christian, she was supposed to love everyone. But that wasn't the reason she felt so ashamed. She felt ashamed because it was a lie. She didn't hate Luke Bontrager. The only thing she wasn't sure about was to what extent she *didn't* hate him.

Aunt B nodded. "That makes more sense now."

Poppy massaged her forehead and groaned. "I shouldn't have said that."

"It sounds like he had it coming. Luke sticks his foot in his mouth so often, he should learn to hop."

"I made him pretty mad."

"It ain't your fault, little sister." Aunt B squeezed her ear again. "Ever since his *dat*'s cancer and his *mamm*'s accident, he's been a little intense."

When Luke was in seventh grade his *dat* had gotten a cancer that laid him low for almost two years. During that same time, Luke's *mamm* lost her foot in a farming accident. Being the oldest sibling, Luke probably had a lot of worries fall on his shoulders.

"I shouldn't have told him I hate him."

Aunt Bitsy narrowed her eyes and leaned closer. "Do you?"

Poppy stared down at the freshly-turned dirt. *"Nae."*

"I see."

"He gave me a drill. I thought maybe we could be friends."

Aunt B's eyebrows were in danger of flying off her face. "A drill?"

"He said he wanted to teach me how to use it."

"That's no casual gift, especially for Luke," Aunt B said. "He doesn't like girls using drills."

They turned and watched as Dan Kanagy, with a lovesick grin on his face, drove his open-air buggy down their lane.

Aunt B growled under her breath. "Doesn't that boy have something better to do than come over all the time?"

Poppy giggled. "Probably not."

"He eats all our food."

Not as much as Luke had.

Dan parked his buggy next to the sidewalk

and jumped down with a spring in his step. He was a boy in love, after all. "Poppy, Bitsy," he called. He reached into his buggy and pulled out a basket. Poppy's basket.

Ach.

She'd left it in Luke's wagon.

Dan charged across the grass, and Aunt B stood so fast, she nearly jumped out of her skin. "Dan Kanagy, don't trample my dandelions. Have you no shame?"

Dan merely smiled, bent over, and gave Aunt B a peck on the cheek. "I've come to see Lily," he announced.

"I never would have guessed," Aunt B said.

He glanced doubtfully at Poppy. "Luke asked me to return this basket. He said you left it in his wagon."

Poppy took the basket from Dan. The three uneaten loaves of bread were there as well as the loaf she had given Luke with the three pieces missing. He hadn't eaten another bite. The drill was also missing. He didn't like girls using drills. He didn't like girls at all.

What did she care if Luke never wanted to eat her bread again? And what did she need with a drill? She'd gotten along just fine without one for twenty-one years.

He'd told her he was done with her.

Well, she was done with him.

Without another word, she turned her back on Dan and Aunt B and fled to the safety of the house.

No one would ever see her cry over a boy — especially the boy who hated her so much he wouldn't even eat her bread.

She hated him right back.

CHAPTER TWELVE

Luke had been frowning for four days straight. Thanks to Poppy Christner, the expression was probably etched into his face forever. It was bad enough that Poppy had ruined a perfectly *gute* Friday. Now she invaded his thoughts every waking hour, putting him in a bad mood on a permanent basis. Why did he let a stubborn tomboy irritate him like that?

He stood in the checkout line at Walmart, gripping the handle of his shopping cart as if trying to squeeze all the water out of it. He'd done the right thing, getting his money back for that drill. It was sitting in Walmart's return bin, waiting to be put back on the shelf to be bought by some other boy who wanted to do something nice for someone who didn't appreciate it. Dangerous tools should be kept out of Poppy's hands. Someone could get hurt.

He squeezed the cart handle until his

knuckles turned white. If only he could get those green eyes or that look she gave him out of his head — a look of pain so deep he could have gone swimming in it.

The line inched forward. A hundred registers at Walmart and only two were ever open. The slow line only served to compound Luke's bad mood. His driver waited in the car, and the work piled up in his shop. How was he supposed to get any furniture built waiting in this eternally long line with Poppy sticking to his brain like a cocklebur?

He glanced to his right to see if there was another check stand open. *Ach, du lieva.* Poppy's Aunt Bitsy stood not ten feet away looking at a display of nail polish. She shouldn't have been there. Hadn't anyone told her that Amish women didn't wear nail polish? The second-to-last person Luke wanted to run into at Walmart was Bitsy Kiem. She'd probably give him a lecture right there in the checkout line, though Luke hadn't done anything to deserve it. He'd gotten after Poppy for risking her life. Bitsy should thank him for talking some sense into her niece.

He crowded his cart into the person in front of him and ducked behind the tall aisle of candy that divided the checkout rows. He didn't have to stoop very low to avoid being seen. If the cashier would go a little faster, Luke could get out of there without Bitsy being any wiser.

A voice from above his head gave him a start. "Afraid to show your face, Luke Bontrager?"

He looked up. Bitsy was poking her head over the display and looking at him as if she'd just caught a robber in the act. Had she scaled the candy display like a mountain? Or maybe she was standing in a cart. Bitsy never did anything predictable.

"Bitsy," he said. "You're going to fall."

"I'm quite secure, unless this conveyor belt starts moving." Narrowing her eyes, she propped her elbows on top of the display and smashed two packages of oatmeal cookies, individually wrapped. "You've really done it this time, Luke Bontrager."

He pretended not to know what she was talking about. "I think you'd better get down before they ask you to leave the store."

"Don't play dumb with me. Poppy came home in quite a state the other day. Wet, bleeding, and limping. You are a very bad influence."

Luke growled quietly. The cashier called someone for a price check. He'd never get out of here. "I told her not to go in the ditch. I got mad at her for risking her life.

213

I'd think you'd be grateful."

Bitsy looked up at the fluorescent lighting. "Dear Lord, these boys are as thick as the ice on Lake Michigan. Could You please send me something I can work with?"

Bitsy's ingratitude made Luke feel especially petulant. "There is no ice on Lake Michigan. It's summertime."

She puckered her lips to one side of her face and looked up at the ceiling again. "Dear Lord, these boys are as thick as the scum on Cobbler Pond. What is an *aendi* to do?" She eyed Luke. "It wonders me why you told my Poppy you hate her."

His stomach dropped to the floor. He shouldn't have said that, no matter how angry he had been. "She said it first."

"So now you're in second grade?"

Luke pressed his lips together and glanced around him. Several people stared at the crazy Amish lady standing on the conveyor belt. Others watched Luke as if he might suddenly decide he hated all Walmart shoppers. Holding his head up high, he pushed his cart closer to the man in front of him. "It was nice to see you, Bitsy," he said, lying through his teeth. Hopefully she'd take the hint that the conversation was over or at least take the hint to climb down from the counter.

214

She did neither. "I know your *mamm* raised you better than to yell at a girl."

He slowly hissed the air from his lungs and gave up caring what anyone else in the store was thinking. Most people thought the Amish were strange anyway. "She could have died. A woman should never put herself in danger. A man should be the one to do it."

Bitsy leaned farther over the display. The cookies flattened like pancakes. "Would you have let the kittens die?"

Luke didn't want to answer that. Nobody looked kindly on the thought of dead kittens, except maybe Griff Simons.

Bitsy shook her head. "All this talk about man's work and woman's work is really starting to irritate me."

To Luke's relief, someone in Customer Service started yelling. "Ma'am, ma'am. You can't be up there."

Bitsy looked in the direction of whoever did the yelling, groaned, and disappeared from sight. *Gute.* Luke wasn't really enjoying that conversation very much.

He started putting his purchases on the conveyor belt when Bitsy nudged her way up in his line, grabbed his shopping cart, and pulled it backward. Before he could stop her, she pulled the cart out of line and

215

pushed it down the aisle with amazing speed. She didn't run, but Bitsy Kiem could sure walk fast. Luke had no choice but to follow her. He'd spent a great deal of time filling that cart.

But he'd lost his place in line.

Ach. Bitsy proved almost as aggravating as her niece.

He eventually caught up with her. His legs were longer, after all. "Bitsy, what are you doing? Give me back my cart."

She held up her hand when he tried to take control of the cart. Would he get kicked out of the store if he wrestled Bitsy for his own shopping cart? Even if he managed to get his cart back, something told him crossing Bitsy would be unwise.

She turned two corners and stopped in front of the book display. "Hold this," she said, handing him a small bottle.

"What is it?"

"Black fingernail polish. All the vampires wear it. I'm doing some research for my book." She also sported a tiny glittering tattoo on her left forearm. Luke couldn't be sure, but it looked like a horse with wings. It matched the blue tint of her gray hair.

Bitsy took a Bible from the shelf. Luke raised an eyebrow. He didn't know they sold copies of the Bible at Walmart. She leafed through the pages until she found what she was looking for, handed him the open book, and pointed to a verse in Matthew. "Read this."

"Look, I know Poppy was upset, but I don't really have time to read the Bible with you right now."

"What makes you think Poppy was upset? She's not made of eggshells, and she couldn't care less what you think of her." She pointed to the Bible again. "I'm only concerned for your welfare, Luke. No girl will be able to stand you if you don't stop being such a clod."

"Dinah Eicher likes me just fine."

"That's because she hasn't gotten to know you yet."

She kept pointing, and Luke finally gave in. If he read the verses, maybe she'd release his kidnapped cart.

"Then shall the King say unto them on his right hand, Come, ye blessed of my Father, inherit the kingdom prepared for you from the foundation of the world: For I was an hungred, and ye gave me meat: I was thirsty, and ye gave me drink: I was a stranger, and ye took me in: Naked, and ye clothed me: I was sick and ye visited me: I was in prison and ye came unto me." Luke looked up. "That's wonderful-*gute,* Bitsy. Can I go now?"

Bitsy narrowed her eyes and pressed her lips together. "Have a little patience. According to that scripture, who will inherit the kingdom of God?"

"The people who serve their fellow man. They serve Jesus and don't even realize it."

She very nearly smiled. "Very *gute.* What kind of service did they do?"

Luke huffed out a breath. "Why are we standing in Walmart having this conversation?"

"Would you rather sit?"

He scrubbed his hand down the side of his face. One more minute of this, and he would take his cart back by force if he had to.

"What kind of service did they do for Jesus?" she repeated.

"They fed people who were hungry, gave clothes to people who didn't have any. Cared for the sick, took strangers in," he recited, hoping if he said the right thing she'd let him go.

She tapped her finger on the page he'd just read. "Women's work, Luke. They got into the kingdom of heaven by doing what you call women's work."

Luke frowned and studied the verses again. "I suppose they did."

"Do you think you're better than Poppy

because you're a boy?"

He thought of Poppy's determination to defend those weaker than herself, her reckless desire to jump in and help, no matter the consequences. Her refusal to back down to anybody, including Luke. "I'm not better than anyone."

She squinted at him. "But you think boys are better in general."

Luke nearly choked on the lump in his throat. Was that what Bitsy thought of him? "*Nae,* I don't."

"Of course you do. You talk about women's work like it's beneath you. You yell at girls for doing brave things. You think they're too stupid to use drills."

"I never said Poppy was too stupid to use a drill."

Her glare could have peeled the varnish off a newly laid wood floor. "In your anger, I think you did."

Deciding he'd rather sit after all, he lowered himself to a cardboard box stacked in a display of luggage in the middle of the aisle. "What if Poppy drilled a hole in her finger with that drill? I would be responsible. Me and no one else. What if she had drowned? It would have been my fault, and I don't know if I would have been able to live with myself." He swiped his hand across his forehead. "I can barely live with myself as it is."

Bitsy folded her arms across her chest. "You've taken burdens on your shoulders that aren't yours to carry."

"Maybe you don't know anything, Bitsy Kiem."

She huffed out a breath. "I know a whole lot more than you. You're too big for your britches. That's been your problem all along." She snatched both the Bible and the black fingernail polish from Luke's hands. She put the Bible back on the shelf, gave Luke an I've-given-up-on-you look, and walked away, leaving him in blessed, uncomfortable peace.

Thankfully, she left the cart. Wrestling Bitsy to the ground would not have been a pretty sight.

CHAPTER THIRTEEN

Perry Glick scowled as if he had a sour stomach. "Is this all you want?"

"Jah". Poppy pressed her lips together as she handed him a five-dollar bill. *"Denki,"* she added as an afterthought. No matter how much she disliked the entire Glick family, she should at least try to be polite.

Perry counted out her change so slowly, she wondered if he had fallen asleep. *Nae,* he wanted to irritate her. She could see it in the set of his jaw. It was only to be expected. Not only had Lily broken up with Perry's brother three weeks ago, but she had also sold all their honey to another buyer, severely cutting into the Glicks' profit margin. Paul had been as mad as a grasshopper on a skillet, and the Glicks tended to hold grudges.

It was probably a good thing Perry was the one working the cash register today. Paul might have yelled at her or called her to repentance for being a tomboy. Paul and Luke Bontrager both thought Poppy was a disgrace. How funny that even though Paul and Luke hated each other, they had one thing in common. They both hated Poppy.

Ever since Lily's breakup with Paul, Poppy and her sisters had done their best to avoid Glick's Amish Market. They either took a buggy to the Lark Country Store in Bonduel or hired a driver to take them to the Walmart in Shawano. But Poppy hadn't had time for either today. She'd only needed a few measly chocolate chips.

Perry sort of shoved the change into Poppy's hand. "I hope you Christners can live with yourselves knowing you cheated our family out of the honey."

Ach, Poppy would have loved to give Perry Glick a big piece of her mind. She had a feeling that the Glicks were circulating all sorts of lies about her family. They'd done the same to Dan's family for several years. But yelling at Perry wouldn't solve anything, and some cockamamie story about Poppy would be all over the community in a matter of hours. Perry would probably tell people that she had attacked him or punched him in the face. She'd punched boys before. People would be inclined to believe it.

She smiled her nastiest smile as she stuffed her money and the chocolate chips into her apron pocket. "Don't worry about us, Perry. We made a very nice profit on our honey this year. If you ever need some, you can find it at Carole Parker's store in Shawano. Carole says she's almost sold out already."

Perry's scowl was so deep, she'd probably be able to see it etched into the back of his head if he turned around. "Cheaters never prosper."

"I agree," she said.

She turned around and walked out, making a mental note that Rose should never be allowed to go to the market. She'd be upset for days.

Outside in front of the market, a little *Englisch* boy sprawled on the sidewalk, kicking and screaming as if he were being tortured. A woman, who must have been his mother, was also screaming. "Get up, you little brat. Get up now or I'll spank you so hard you won't sit down for a week. Get up!"

The woman yanked the boy by the arm and pulled him to his feet. Poppy flinched. The roughness made her shoulder ache in sympathy. The little boy screamed louder and tried to escape his mother's grasp. The mother retaliated by pulling her son close

223

and spanking him two, three, four times hard on the bottom.

Poppy held her breath. Her heart raced, and for a split second she thought of walking away. She didn't want a confrontation. She wasn't good in confrontations. But she'd never before stood by while a little child got hurt. This wasn't one of the *kinner* on the playground being picked on by one of the older kids. This was a little boy and his mother. What should she do?

Despite what Luke Bontrager thought, Poppy had learned by hard experience in school that she couldn't make things better with brute force or even a swift punch to the nose. Violence almost always made things worse.

With her heart beating in her throat, Poppy laid a gentle hand on the mother's arm. "Is there anything I can do to help?"

The mother snapped her head around to look at Poppy. "Don't you dare judge me," she said with rage and defiance blazing in her eyes.

"I'm not judging. I only wondered if you —"

Poppy didn't get another word out of her mouth. The mother drew back her hand and slapped her hard across the face. Poppy felt more shocked than hurt. Had a grown woman just hit her?

"Leave me alone," the mother shrieked as she marched away, dragging her still-struggling son with her.

That didn't quite go the way Poppy had hoped.

Her eyes stung and her cheek felt as if it were on fire. She put her good hand to her face, wishing it were wintertime so she could scoop up a handful of snow from the sidewalk and soothe the burning.

With her fingers pressed against her cheek, she made the mistake of glancing across the street at something in her peripheral vision. Luke Bontrager stood just outside the door to the harness shop with his fists clenched at his sides, staring at her as if she'd just shoved one of his sisters into the ditch.

She quickly looked away. If she ignored him, she wouldn't have to hear a lecture about how disgusted he felt that she had interfered in someone else's business and gotten herself slapped.

Not a very *gute* day in town today. She'd been accused by Perry Glick, slapped by an angry *Englischer,* and frowned at by Luke Bontrager.

It made her sick to admit it, but the frown hurt the worst.

Not a *gute* day at all. The angry mother,

with her son cradled in her arms, came walking back down the sidewalk, probably gearing up to slap Poppy across her other cheek. Her heart sped to a gallop. At least she'd get some practical experience at turning the other cheek.

Poppy took three steps backward. She should just walk away quickly. Turning the other cheek would really hurt.

The mother reached out her hand. "Wait, please. I'm sorry."

Not altogether sure she shouldn't turn and run, Poppy stood her ground as the mother got closer. To her surprise, every trace of anger had disappeared from the mother's face. "I . . . I'm so sorry," she said, her eyes moist with unshed tears. "I was angry, and you took me by surprise. I was just so angry."

"Okay," Poppy said.

The woman scooted her son farther up her hip. Her whole body seemed to tremble. "I have never slapped anybody before. Nobody in my entire life. I'm so, so sorry."

Poppy nodded and tried her best to smile with a swollen cheek and a wounded heart. "*Cum* sit," she said, putting her good arm around the mother's shoulders and leading her to the bus stop bench just a few steps from the market. They sat down together.

"I'm sorry to interfere where I maybe shouldn't have. I didn't mean any disrespect."

"Don't apologize. I'm grateful you tried to help. I lost control. I just needed a nice stranger to pull me out of it." The little boy whimpered softly and laid his head on his mother's chest. The woman glanced down at her son and began stroking his hair.

"I'm sure it's hard to be a mother sometimes," Poppy said.

The woman sighed. A single tear plopped on the back of her son's shirt. "It's not that. My son was diagnosed with autism yesterday."

"Oh," Poppy said. "I didn't know. I'm sorry."

"For the last twenty-four hours, I've felt like I've been in a trash compactor. The world is crushing me and all the dreams I've ever had for my son." Her voice cracked, and she buried her face in her hand. "There's no way out, ya know?"

Poppy gave her shoulder a squeeze. "That is terrible. I would have slapped me too."

She shook her head. "There is no excuse for that. I shouldn't have tried to take him out today. But I wanted to get out of the trash compactor for a few hours. My husband doesn't want to talk about it. He thinks if he ignores it, it will go away. But it's not going away."

Poppy gave her a sad smile. "There is a boy in our district who is autistic. We call him one of the special children. There is nobody anyone loves more. *Gotte* sent him to you for a reason. Maybe you have to find different dreams."

"I suppose I do." She stood up. Her son wrapped his arms around her neck and rested his head on her shoulder.

Poppy stood with her. "I can tell your son loves you."

"Thanks for stopping me before I did something I would have regretted."

"You're welcome."

The woman eyed Poppy's cheek and frowned. "Well, I did do something I regret."

"But I'm a grown-up. If slapping me kept you from slapping your son, I'm willing to be the one to take it."

"It won't happen again."

Poppy smiled. "I know. I can see it in your eyes."

She returned the smile. "Thank you. It's going to be okay."

"Yes, it is."

The woman carried her son to a car parked on the street, put him in, and buckled him up. She waved to Poppy before pulling from the curb and driving away.

Her cheek didn't hurt so bad anymore. Sometimes the heartbreak was just too hard to bear on one's own. That's why Jesus said to turn the other cheek. You never knew how much another person was hurting.

She looked across the street. Luke had disappeared.

It was turning out to be not such a bad day after all.

CHAPTER FOURTEEN

Why had he come? He wasn't in the mood for a gathering of *die youngie,* even if he got to see Dinah.

Luke wasn't in the mood for Dinah Eicher either. He wanted steak and potatoes, and Dinah seemed more like tapioca pudding and syrup. Would he be eating soft, mushy pudding the rest of his life?

He clenched his teeth. *Ach.* He was in a very bad mood. If he hadn't promised Dinah he'd be here, he would have found something better to do, like clip his toenails or play Life on the Farm with Dorothy or go down to the bridge and throw rocks in the ditch.

"*Ach,* Dinah, these are much better than Poppy Christner's cookies," said Mandy Schwartz, glancing at Luke as if she were talking to him instead of Dinah. "She doesn't put cinnamon in hers."

What did Mandy know? She was Dinah's

best friend. Of course she'd praise Dinah's cooking, even if she had to lie about it.

They sat under a tree at the park watching some of *die youngie* play volleyball and horseshoes. A haze of smoke rose from behind the restrooms. Somebody was trying out a cigarette.

Luke gave Mandy a half smile and took a swig of lemonade to wash down his rock-hard cookie. Dinah liked her coffee cake dry. She liked her pretzels dry and her muffins dry, but how hard would it be to bake a moist, soft chocolate chip cookie? What he wouldn't give for a melt-in-your-mouth caramel or a bite of Poppy Christner's nut brown bread.

He nearly choked on his dry and crunchy chocolate chip cookie rock. How could he be so disloyal to Dinah to think of Poppy at a time like this? Poppy's bread tasted delicious, but on principle, he'd never eat another slice. Poppy had to learn that she couldn't give someone a loaf of bread and then be reckless with her life. Someone had to teach her a lesson.

He frowned. Why did he feel so rotten about teaching Poppy a lesson? Josiah would say it was because he hadn't gotten his way. Dan would say it was because Poppy wasn't demure and submissive like most Amish

231

girls and that Luke sort of liked that.

What did Dan know? Luke didn't like that at all. What boy would like someone who spoke her mind and did dangerous things just to spite him?

He wished he were anywhere but here. Dinah would burst into tears if he started scowling.

"Do you really think my cookies are good?" Dinah gushed — again — looking at Luke instead of Mandy, as if he were in on the conversation.

"The best ever," Mandy said. "And it wonders me if Poppy Christner even knows how to make upside-down cake."

"Of course not. She's too busy trying to be a boy." Dinah and Mandy giggled as if that notion was the funniest idea in the world. Dinah took another bite of her cookie. How could she chew that thing without a drink of milk? "Don't you think so, Luke?"

"Huh?" he said, trying hard to put Poppy Christner's fine green eyes out of his mind. Why did Dinah want to talk about Poppy? He didn't — didn't want to talk about Poppy or worry about Poppy or feel guilty about Poppy. Something twisted like a drill in his gut. He'd said some horrible things, and no amount of wishing would lessen the guilt.

"Don't you think Poppy should get off her high horse?"

Why this fascination with Poppy Christner all of a sudden? Was it because he'd said something nice about her at Dinah's house the other night? Dinah and Mandy obviously steered the conversation with Luke in mind. What did they want him to say? He gave Dinah what he hoped passed for a disarming smile. "I think these cookies are wonderful-*gute.*"

"But are they better than Poppy's?"

"I've never tasted Poppy's chocolate chip cookies."

Not the right answer. Dinah's smile sagged, as if she were doing her best, but finding it difficult to keep pretending. "*Ach.* Well. I thought you knew. You've spent a lot of time at her house lately."

A lot of time? He'd eaten dinner with them and built a chicken coop. Something in the tone of Dinah's voice and the pinch of her lips told him the facts didn't matter. Dinah sensed some sort of threat, though for the life of him, he couldn't begin to guess how she'd gotten the idea that there was anything between him and Poppy Christner.

Luke stuttered on his reply. "Your cookies are delicious. They're made with so much love."

Another fit of giggles from Dinah and Mandy. Luke bit his tongue. He sounded stupid and insincere, even to himself. He was already sick of being here. Maybe he could take Dinah home early and get together later with Dan and Josiah. He might be able to talk Josiah into doing something with him, but Dan was a worthless friend now that he was engaged. He'd rather spend every waking hour with Lily Christner.

Luke understood it, but tonight he wasn't happy about it.

Maybe Dan and Josiah would come to the gathering. If Lily planned on coming, Dan would be here. If Lily came, she would bring Rose, and Josiah would be here.

Of course, Lily and Rose would bring Poppy.

Why did his heart clomp around his chest like a bull wearing boots at an *Englischer*'s square dance? Probably because Poppy made him so mad he could spit. Probably because she argued with him about everything.

Maybe Poppy wouldn't come. She wouldn't be able to play volleyball or croquet with one arm. Lord willing, she'd stay home and do something safe like bake bread or change all the batteries in her flashlights.

He most certainly didn't want to see her. He already had enough guilt to last a lifetime.

Jah, he definitely wanted to leave early.

Luke and Dinah sat on a picnic bench under a big, shady tree. Three of Dinah's best friends sat on the bench with them as well as a couple of boys from Luke's district. They were all very nice people.

He wished they'd all go away.

He'd rather be miserable by himself.

The muscles of his neck and shoulders were as taut as baling wire. He needed to get away from Dinah and get rid of some of his tension. "I'm going to play volleyball," he announced. Without waiting for Dinah's approval, he stood and walked away.

"Wait for me," Dinah chirped.

Groaning inwardly, Luke stopped long enough for Dinah to catch up to him. He didn't want to babysit. He wanted to get Poppy out of his head.

They joined the game already going on. At least ten players stood on each side of the net. It wouldn't be much of a game, but at least he'd be moving. Even in his pathetic mood, he smiled when he saw Josiah jog from the parking lot. Maybe Josiah could help him figure out a way to get rid of Dinah without hurting her feelings, and they could go night fishing or something.

Josiah waved, and Luke motioned for him to join the game.

"Hi, Josiah," Dinah said, ducking out of the way of a ball that came too close.

"Hello, Dinah," Joe said, "It's *gute* to see you playing this time."

"I love volleyball," Dinah said.

Luke didn't contradict her, even though he'd never seen her play in his life.

Josiah made a place for himself in the game between Luke and Dinah. "Is Rose here yet?" he said, out of breath and all smiles.

Luke grimaced as that bull in boots started stamping around in his chest again. "Rose? Is she coming?" Why was he reacting this way? For sure and certain, Poppy would stay home.

Josiah jumped up and hit a ball coming right at Luke's head. "*Jah.* Dan is driving the three sisters over tonight." He leaned close enough to whisper. "I might get a chance to talk to her."

"You have to make your own chances, Joe."

Josiah merely smiled. "I have a plan."

Luke intercepted a very hard serve from

Mahlon Zook, and it went straight up in the air. Unfortunately, Dinah wasn't inclined to look up, and it hit her in the head and knocked her over.

She gave a little squeak as she tumbled to the ground and landed on her *hinnerdale.* The game halted as two girls rushed to Dinah's side and clucked and worried themselves into a tizzy. "Are you all right, Dinah? Do you feel dizzy?"

"If you're nauseated, it's a concussion. Maybe you have a concussion."

Moaning softly, Dinah cradled her head in her hands and closed her eyes. "It's definitely a concussion."

Luke felt obliged to kneel next to her and paste a worried look on his face. He was Dinah's ride home, after all. He had to look concerned, even if he'd seen paper cuts more serious.

"Do you want some ice?" Josiah said.

Dinah held out her hand to Luke, clearly expecting him to help her up. He did. "Luke is all the help I need," she said. "Can you take me to the bench?"

Holding firmly onto Luke's arm, she limped to the picnic table where her friends waited to make a fuss over her. He helped her sit down and got her a cup of lemonade. Mandy straightened Dinah's *kapp,* and

Treva King squeezed her hand sympathetically. Dinah had enough sympathy, didn't she? He'd really like to get back to his game.

Dinah closed her eyes, as if the sun would make her concussion worse, and reached out blindly for Luke. "I think I'm going to faint. Could I rest my head on your shoulder, just for a second?"

Luke deflated. No more volleyball for him. Not when Dinah needed him so desperately.

Desperately.

Treva scooted over so Luke could sit next to Dinah. He sidled close and let her lay her head on his shoulder. He felt awkward with her leaning on him like this, but there was nothing to do but take it like a man. He stiffened and did his best not to move a muscle. He didn't want Dinah's head to slip off his shoulder and catapult her into the dirt.

She opened her eyes long enough to look at him. "*Denki,* Luke. You are a *wunderbarr* boy. My *mamm* always says so."

Her praise didn't give him any sort of thrill or even the mildest satisfaction. Her constant compliments made her admiration meaningless.

He did his best not to notice Poppy when she stepped out of the buggy with her sisters. Poppy Christner was just another

238

girl at the gathering. They didn't have to speak to each other. He had no trouble ignoring the royal-blue dress or the way it accented the color of her eyes. He could see the bandage that covered her cut, but from this far, he couldn't clearly see the freckles that dotted her nose or the dimple on her cheek or the obstinate smile that took his breath away, but it was hard to miss the sling over her arm or forget why she had to wear it.

He cringed with self-condemnation. The shoulder injury was no one's fault but his own. In his panic, he had yanked too hard when he pulled her out of the water. He'd been so angry and afraid, that he'd been reckless. No wonder she hated him.

He cleared his throat three times. He couldn't swallow, couldn't breathe, couldn't speak. She didn't hate him because he'd pulled her out of the ditch. It went much deeper than that.

Like Bitsy said, he acted too big for his britches.

His gaze followed her every move as she and her sisters and Dan left the parking lot and strolled into the park. She said hello to Mahlon and Moses Zook. Owen Zimmerman made her laugh. Ohio John Newswenger offered to take the plate of cookies she carried in her one good hand. Wallace Sensenig stared at her like an eager puppy waiting for a treat.

Luke clenched his teeth.

Poppy Christner hated him.

The thought made his bones ache.

Sensing Dinah's gaze on him, he glanced down. She studied his face with wide eyes and a puzzled frown. Turning her gaze in the direction he'd been looking, she stiffened like a slab of cement. "What's she doing here?"

"The whole district was invited."

She lifted her head and patted Mandy on the leg. "Look at how she positions herself so she's in the center of all the boys. She's such a flirt."

Luke and Dinah were obviously seeing two different things. The boys had sought Poppy out. She stood in a group with Dan and her sisters and four or five boys who were quickly devouring the cookies on her plate. Josiah caught sight of Rose, left his volleyball game, and made a beeline for the Christner *schwesters*. He snatched a cookie off the plate as an excuse for creeping up on Rose. Luke felt personally offended every time one of those cookies disappeared. Dan knew how much Luke liked Poppy's baking. If he were any kind of friend, he'd save at least three cookies for Luke.

Mandy, bless her, must have read his mind. "Look, Dinah. She brought chocolate chip cookies. We can prove to Luke that yours are better."

Dinah thought about it for a little too long. Was she afraid of Poppy's cookies? "Okay, I guess, if she'll even let us taste one."

Mandy jumped up from the bench, grabbed Dinah's hand, and pulled her along. It looked like the concussion was cured.

"Luke, come on," Dinah said as Mandy pulled her away. "You're the one who has to do the tasting."

Luke didn't want to be anywhere near Poppy. She hated him. He didn't see a conversation going well. Maybe he could snatch a cookie off the plate and walk away without having to say anything.

Poppy's smile could have lit up the whole sky. That is, until she glanced up and made eye contact with Luke as he, Dinah, and Mandy approached her little group. Her smile disappeared like a July snowman, and something painful flashed in her green eyes. She immediately turned her face away as if she hadn't seen him.

"Can we have a cookie?" Mandy asked.

Without waiting for permission, she grabbed three off the plate.

Dan slapped Luke on the shoulder. "Luke, *wie gehts*? I thought you might stay buried in that workshop until winter."

"I have an order for a table and some chairs."

Poppy wouldn't look at him, but she pursed her lips and lifted her chin like she was preparing for Luke to yell at her. Was that really what she expected of him? Talk about a punch to the gut.

Lily folded her arms and raised her eyebrows in Luke's direction, as if she sorely wanted to scold him. Rose frowned at him as if he'd thrown Billy Idol in the ditch. They'd been talking to Poppy. He'd never be invited over again.

Not that he wanted to be invited over.

Mandy handed him a cookie, and he bit into it before realizing how foolish it was to do so. How would he break the news to Dinah that everything Poppy made was better than Dinah's baking? Just as he expected, Poppy's cookie was soft and sweet and practically melted in his mouth. He could have eaten the entire plateful. He finished it off before Poppy could tell him he couldn't have it.

Dinah took a bite and pinched her lips

together in indignation. It was hard even for her to go on pretending that her cookie tasted anywhere near as *gute.* "Why, Poppy Christner, I believe you have stolen my cookie recipe," she said, in a sickly sweet tone she usually saved to scold her little sister.

Rose put her hand over her mouth and giggled softly. Lily disguised her smirk with a smile.

It was clear Poppy didn't want a fight, even if Dinah had just accused her of stealing. The light in her eyes dimmed, and she breathed out a weary sigh. "It's a high compliment that you think my cookies taste like yours. Yours are delicious."

Dinah wasn't appeased. She propped a hand on her hip. "Who gave you my recipe? No one has permission to use it but me."

That wasn't such a bad thing. The fewer bad cookies in the world, the better.

Poppy looked more resigned than angry, but she cocked an eyebrow and stared at Dinah as if to silence her for good. "If you don't want me to use your recipe, you shouldn't put it on the back of the chocolate chip bag."

Dan threw back his head and laughed. Owen and Wallace were too polite to laugh, but they both widened their eyes and tried not to smile. Dinah's jaw dropped to the ground. No one won a battle with Poppy.

Not even Luke.

His heart pounded an uneven rhythm. He didn't mind so much.

Dinah glanced resentfully at the faces in the circle. Dan, Owen, and Wallace grinned like cats. The Honeybee Sisters were poised for Dinah to pounce. "How did you hurt your arm? Were you acting like a boy again?" Dinah said, sprinkling her overly sweet voice with a little nastiness.

Luke tensed at the insult behind the question. Dinah shouldn't treat Poppy that way. She'd been very brave.

His own stupidity punched him in the mouth and knocked the wind out of him. He'd given Poppy a lot worse.

Lily lifted her chin. "She saved four kittens, Dinah. Griff Simons tried to drown them in the ditch, and Poppy fished them out."

Poppy glanced at Luke and frowned. "Luke told me not to."

Dan grinned. "But you didn't listen. Smart girl."

Luke wanted to smack his best friend upside the head.

Wallace took another cookie from the plate. Hadn't he had his share already? "I heard Griff was back. Did he hurt you, Poppy?"

"*Nae.* Luke pulled my shoulder out of place when he helped me out of the ditch."

The boys hovering around Poppy eyed Luke as if he'd broken all the rules of the *Ordnung.* "Luke," Owen said. "What were you trying to do? Drag her halfway to Iowa?"

Luke stuffed his hands in his pockets. "I feared she might drown. That's why I told her not to go in."

Dinah nodded, her lips puckered in a smug pout. "There, you see? If Poppy hadn't been such a silly goose but done what Luke told her, she wouldn't have hurt her shoulder."

Poppy's eyes danced with defiance. "I never do what Luke tells me."

She'd never looked prettier. He forgot how to breathe.

"You saved those kittens," Ohio John said. "No one can fault you for that."

Poppy gave Ohio John a beautiful, knock-your-hat-off smile. Why was John hanging around Poppy's cookies? Everybody knew he had a wheat allergy.

"I think it's very selfish of her to jump in the water and expect Luke to risk his own life to save her," Mandy said. She and

Dinah nodded to each other.

Luke cleared his throat. "I didn't risk my life. I just got wet."

Poppy's eyes darted to his face. He'd surprised her. She'd been expecting an attack.

"Dinah," Dan said, grinning as if it were Christmas morning, "I know you're very protective of Luke, and I'm sorry you're offended, but are you saying you would have let the kittens drown?"

Every eye zeroed in on Dinah. A blush traveled up her neck. "If Luke had told me to stay out of the ditch . . ."

"Would you have pushed Dorothy in and made her swim for the kittens?" Lily said.

Dinah pulled herself up to her full, indignant height of five feet two inches. "For sure and certain not."

Poppy almost knocked Luke over with her gaze. "Even if you think I behaved poorly, I can't regret doing it."

At that moment, Poppy looked so fierce and loyal and beautiful, he didn't regret her doing it either.

He held his breath as the world spun like a dust devil around him. What had he done? What if Poppy had not been there that day? Joann or even little Dorothy would have jumped in. Neither of them was anywhere near as strong as Poppy. They would have gotten hurt, or worse.

Dorothy and Joann were home safe, playing with their new kittens because of Poppy Christner. And he'd yelled at her for being brave enough to act instead of panic. If Poppy hadn't been there, Luke would have let those kittens die to keep his sisters safe, and they'd probably cry and sulk and give him the silent treatment for weeks.

His heart throbbed with regret. Why, oh why had he gotten so mad?

Because headstrong, independent Poppy Christner had wounded his pride. She hadn't cared for his opinion, and he'd been offended, pure and simple. He'd been mad that she put herself in danger, but Poppy never thought about the danger if someone needed her help. Even someone like the little *Englisch* boy in town.

From across the street, Luke had watched that mother become increasingly agitated with her son. He couldn't have done anything about it. It wouldn't have been appropriate for an Amish man to accost a woman in the street, even if she did need help.

And then Poppy had appeared like an angel from heaven and got a slap in the face for her trouble. That's how Poppy was. If she thought she could help, she charged in, regardless of the consequences. Luke had to hold himself back from marching across the street and pulling Poppy into his protective embrace. Seeing her sitting on that bench with the *Englisch* woman had nearly cracked his hard heart. Poppy might be foolhardy, but she was also good and strong and un-afraid.

He winced as his own words came back to him. *You're a girl, Poppy. You're weaker and softer, and you're never going to be as good as the boys at anything. Ach.* He'd taken back the drill. That must have felt like a slap in the face.

To his horror, he realized he had meant it to hurt her.

He felt thoroughly, nose-in-the-dirt ashamed of himself. He, who prided himself on protecting women and treating them with respect and kindness, had yelled things at Poppy that he wouldn't say to his worst enemy. His emotions reeled as if he'd been hit in the head with a shovel.

Oh, *sis yuscht.* He'd told her he hated her.

He knew one thing for certain.

He didn't hate Poppy Christner.

He wanted to get down on one knee right there and beg for her forgiveness, but study-ing the determined set of her jaw and the fire that burned hot in her eyes, he despaired of ever getting another crumb of kindness from her. He'd never be able to make up for how cruel he'd been.

Sweat beaded on Dinah's lip as she realized that only Mandy and Luke agreed with her. That is, she believed Luke agreed with her, but he had very recently changed his mind. She huffed out her indignation. "Poppy wants to be like the boys when she should be content with the place *Gotte* has put her."

Josiah kept his eyes glued to Rose. "No one is as brave as Poppy. *Gotte* put her here to bless our lives."

Rose practically burst out of her skin smiling at Josiah.

Dinah folded her arms. "There's a difference between being brave and being foolish. Isn't there, Luke?"

He glued his gaze to Poppy's face and prayed she'd see the remorse in his eyes. *"Jah,"* he said. "I'm the fool."

Disbelief flitted across Poppy's face, and Luke nodded to reassure her. *I'm sorry, Poppy. Will you give me another chance to be the godly man I should be?*

For a brief moment, it looked as if she might let her guard down, but then Dinah opened her mouth and Luke lost hope.

"What do you Honeybee Schwesters know about anything? No one believes anything you say. You cheated Paul Glick, you stole my recipe, and you're mean to Luke."

Cheated Paul Glick? Who was circulating that rumor?

Luke clenched his teeth so hard, pain shot down his neck. Paul Glick, of course.

Dan and the Honeybee Sisters frowned and glanced at each other. Dinah's outburst hadn't surprised them. Poppy had said they'd been expecting something spiteful from Paul Glick.

"Paul Glick spreads rumors like most farmers spread manure," Poppy said.

An unhealthy shade of purple traveled up Dinah's cheeks. "You have some nerve showing your faces anywhere in town. We all know what kind of girls you really are."

In unison, Dan and Josiah stepped forward and stood between the Honeybee Schwesters and Luke, as if protecting Poppy and her sisters from further attack. Luke sort of stumbled backward. Didn't Dan and Joe know he'd rather be standing shoulder to shoulder with them than standing with Dinah?

"Luke," Dan said. "Maybe you should take Dinah to get a glass of lemonade."

"Dan, I'm not trying to . . ."

Dan placed a firm hand on Luke's shoulder and pinned him with a look of complete understanding. The tightness in Luke's chest subsided. Dan didn't blame Luke for Dinah's bad behavior. "I know." He glanced at Dinah. "It's okay."

"I need to talk to Poppy," Luke said, trying to catch her eye from behind Dan's big head.

"Just get Dinah away," Dan whispered. "She's embarrassed herself enough already."

Luke's desperation mounted. He had to apologize. Now. Poppy shouldn't have to go one more minute without knowing how bad he felt. "I've got to talk to Poppy."

Dan nodded. "Later."

Luke nearly growled. Dan had picked a very inconvenient time to be levelheaded. "Come on, Dinah," he said, turning around and marching away. "Let's get something to eat."

He heard Dinah and Mandy behind him, shuffling through the grass in an effort to keep up with his long strides. He tromped past the eats table to a bench on the edge of the park farthest from Poppy. He had to set Dinah straight.

He sat down and propped his arms on his knees. Dinah huffed out an irritated breath and sat next to him. "How could you just walk away like that? You're supposed to defend me from people like Poppy Christner. She stole my cookies. Doesn't that mean anything to you?"

Mandy plopped herself on the bench next to Dinah. "They shouldn't think they can come to a gathering after what they did to Paul Glick."

Luke thought he might bite through his tongue. *Oy,* anyhow. How had he gotten himself so tangled up? "The Honeybee Sisters didn't cheat Paul Glick," Luke said, trying to keep the anger from seeping into his voice. He should be over there asking Poppy for forgiveness, not sitting on this bench coddling poor, weak Dinah Eicher. "No one has done anything to Paul Glick that he hasn't done to himself."

Moisture pooled in Dinah's eyes. She blinked and a tear ambled down her cheek. "I'm your girlfriend. Don't you love me enough to believe me?"

Luke flinched at the word *girlfriend.* He nearly fell off the bench at *love.*

As sure as he was that he didn't hate Poppy, he felt even more sure that he didn't love Dinah Eicher. He harbored no deep emotion for Dinah at all. She was just a girl who was terrible at volleyball and got all bent out of shape over a plate of chocolate chip cookies.

It didn't matter that she never contradicted him, never scolded him for his arrogance. It didn't matter that she agreed with him without question, even when he was wrong. He found her annoyingly sweet, gratingly oversensitive, and hopelessly helpless.

A helpless girl was only attractive for about three minutes. She made boys feel strong and clever at first, but then her weakness became an irritation. What boy wanted a girl who wouldn't even attempt to hit a volleyball? Or couldn't plunge her own sink or super-glue a knife wound or pluck mice off the welcome mat?

He had thought Dinah was everything he wanted in a girl — sweet, demure, feminine — but here he was, sitting next to the girl of his dreams, wishing she would just go away and leave him be.

He stood to put some distance between himself and Dinah. He had to get to Poppy. The breakup with Dinah would have to be fast. He opened his mouth and clapped it shut again. No matter how big a hurry he was in, he should be as kind and considerate as possible. He'd been mean and hasty with Poppy, and he regretted it with every breath he took.

"Dinah," he said, sitting back down and trying to shape his face into something soft and sympathetic. He wasn't very good at it. He'd only ever been plainspoken. "Remember how I hurt your feelings at your house last week?"

Her bottom lip quivered. "I said sorry."

He held up his hand in hopes of preventing a flood of tears. "*Nae. Nae,* you didn't need to apologize. That was my fault. All my fault." He narrowed his eyes and pinned her with a serious look. "I'm like that. I am insensitive and conceited, and I make girls miserable. You do not want to date me."

Her lips curled upward. "Oh, Luke. You're so humble. That's one of the things I like about you."

Luke expelled all the air from his lungs. He was terrible at beating around the bush. "I'm not being humble. I'm trying to tell you that you and I don't suit, and I'm eventually going to end up getting on your nerves."

Dinah opened her mouth in disbelief. "That could never happen. I'm more loyal than that. *I* would have defended *you* against the Honeybee Sisters."

Luke lifted his hat and scoured his fingers through his hair. *Ach.* He'd have to break the news to her straight and with a hard heart.

Even if she cried about it.

"Dinah," he said, pinning her with a serious gaze and swallowing hard. "Poppy Christner's chocolate chip cookies are better than yours."

CHAPTER FIFTEEN

Was it time to go yet?

Poppy's cheeks ached from forcing a smile — a big, cheesy, I'm-not-crying-inside smile — all evening. She wanted to go home, get in her nightgown, eat a whole bowl of Rose's honey lavender ice cream, and daydream about what her life would have been like if Luke Bontrager hadn't saved her hand from that car window.

If Luke had minded his own business, her heart wouldn't feel like a tiny, black pebble.

She hadn't wanted to go to the park at all. Going to a gathering when Luke Bontrager might be there had sounded as fun as getting a tetanus shot. But there was nothing else she could do. If she wanted to show him that his words hadn't felt like shards of broken glass against her skin, she had no choice but to go.

A strong girl would smile and laugh and pretend Luke's dark look didn't pierce her right through the heart.

Which it didn't. Luke Bontrager could go jump in the ditch for all she cared.

She was glad she had joined the others at the park, if for no other reason than to show Luke that she wouldn't be bullied. Not every girl swooned at his very presence. Her only regret was that he and Dinah Eicher had gotten their hands on two of her precious cookies.

Poppy thought she might be able to breathe after Dan told Luke to take Dinah and go, but her eyes involuntarily followed him and Dinah as they walked away and sat on a bench at the opposite end of the park.

"Don't worry, Poppy," Wallace said. "I don't believe a word of what Paul Glick says about your honey."

Owen shook his head. "Neither do I. It was just a misunderstanding — that's what Dat says."

Poppy wanted to reassure Owen that it wasn't just a misunderstanding, but she kept her mouth shut. The Glicks gossiped freely about the Christners, but the Christners didn't feel right gossiping about the Glicks, no matter how badly Paul had cheated them.

"We hope the gossip will die down," Lily said. "No good can come of it."

Owen and Wallace and Ohio John were all real nice boys. Wallace had eaten four of her cookies. Owen smiled at her the way Dinah Eicher smiled at Luke. Neither of them sparked any interest. Wallace made her feel like yawning.

"What are the Bontragers going to do with the kittens now that you've saved them?" Owen asked.

"I don't know," Poppy said, trying hard not to glance in the direction of a certain young man and his demure girlfriend. "They require a lot of care yet. They aren't weaned. Maybe they'll keep them."

Rose nodded. "Or try to find *gute* homes for them."

Poppy studied Rose's face. Rose wanted one of those kittens. Aunt B would never agree to that. She already had two cats too many.

Luke and Dinah, with Mandy looking on, didn't seem to be having a pleasant conversation. Dinah puckered her face, and Luke took off his hat and ran his fingers through his hair. He put his hat back on his head and dropped his hands to his side. Dinah looked as if she were crying, though from this distance Poppy couldn't be sure. She didn't see any tears.

Luke turned his back on Dinah and

marched in the direction of Poppy and her sisters. Didn't he want to avoid her as much as she wanted to avoid him? She watched for a few tense seconds, hoping he might turn suddenly and go to the eats table. *Nae.* He made a beeline for Poppy.

She held her breath as he approached. She couldn't force one more smile. Couldn't hide the pain in her eyes for one more second. It was cowardly, but she had to get away. "Lily, I'm going to the bathroom."

She turned and strolled toward the small building at the edge of the park so that Luke would never suspect she was running away. He'd gloat if he knew he'd scared her off.

"Poppy, wait."

Her heart sank. She shouldn't have strolled, but it was hard to do much more with this sling on her arm. Was he purposefully trying to torment her?

Of course. He enjoyed making her miserable.

Her pride was already as low as it could go. She quickened her pace in hopes of escaping into the bathroom before he caught up with her. She had beaten him in a race once.

Not this time.

"Poppy, please stop. I need to talk to you." He blocked the path to the bathroom with his broad shoulders and thick arms.

She stepped off the path and made a wide circle around him. "There is nothing you have to say that I want to hear."

"Come on, Poppy," he said, with a tinge of desperation in his voice. He was probably dying to chastise her for putting poor, innocent Dinah in her place. He wouldn't get the chance.

"I have to go to the bathroom."

"What are you afraid of?"

That stopped her in her tracks. "I'm not afraid of you, if that's what you're hoping."

"I don't want you to be afraid of me." He grunted in frustration. "Poppy, get off your high horse and talk to me."

"My high horse? You've got a very long list of my faults, Luke. I already know what you think of me. But I'm not going to change just because my very existence offends you."

He winced. "I didn't mean it that way."

Poppy swung open the metal bathroom door. It hit Luke in the foot before slamming shut behind her. She heard him groan on the other side of the door. He wouldn't dare come in.

She leaned against the far wall next to the sink and tried to calm her racing heart. It was a typical park bathroom with metal toilet seats and cinder-block walls that magnified every sound. If she stood still enough, she could probably hear her own pulse. Let Luke call her a chicken or a horse or whatever farm animal he thought she resembled. She wouldn't talk to him. One more nasty look from him and she would disintegrate into a puddle of tears. Better to hide than to bawl like a baby in front of Luke. Wouldn't he love to see her break down.

She stood in the bathroom for a good fifteen minutes listening to the sound of her breathing echo off the walls, straining her ears for any clue that Luke still lurked outside. Lord willing, he'd given up and found some other girl to pester, some other girl to yell at and humiliate.

She poked her head out of the door. No sign of him. She would find her sisters and tell them she needed to go home. They'd agree without question. She and her sisters stuck together, no matter what.

Glancing around, she walked about ten feet from the bathroom door when Luke sneaked up behind her and stationed himself between her and the bathroom. She couldn't escape that way. She scowled at Luke and marched in the opposite direction.

He jogged to catch up to her. "Poppy, you

know how persistent I am."

"I'm more persistent."

He frowned with his whole face. "But I'm more desperate, and I don't mind playing dirty to get you to listen to me."

She kept on walking. "I already told you, you don't scare me."

Luke ran a few feet ahead of her, cupped his hands around his mouth, and yelled, "I've touched Poppy Christner's knee, and I don't care who knows it."

They were too far away for any of *die youngie* to actually hear what he said, but she grabbed his sleeve and yanked him to a halt. "What are you doing?" she hissed.

"I'm trying to get you to listen to me."

It wasn't the threat of everyone knowing about her knee that finally made her stop. His eyes spoke of desperation, as if he was at the end of his rope and she was the only person who could keep him from falling. Her heart flip-flopped. She was seeing something that couldn't possibly be there.

She propped her good hand on her hip and stared him down. "I'm listening."

He closed his eyes for a second, as if saying a prayer of thanks, and breathed a deep sigh. *"Denki."*

"What do you want, Luke?"

He pinned her with a serious gaze. "I

made sure Dinah knows the truth about Paul Glick."

"Who cares if a gossip like Dinah Eicher talks about us?"

"Paul's rumors aren't harmless."

"It wonders me why it matters to you."

He frowned as if frustrated that she didn't know. "I hate him too, remember?"

Jah. Well. Luke also hated *her.* It didn't make her feel any less rotten.

Luke reached out as if to take her hand, but she was not about to let him touch her. She slid her good arm behind her back. An apology flashed in his eyes. "I'm not very good at this," he said.

"At what?"

He stumbled over his words and pressed his fingers into his brow. Poppy had never seen him so uncertain before. What game was he playing? "The other day, that day in town when that *Englischer* slapped you . . ."

Anger flared to life inside her. Luke had waited outside the bathroom for fifteen minutes to scold her about the *Englischer?* "I don't care if you think I'm foolish. That little boy needed my help."

"That's what I'm trying to tell you. You were right." Were his hands shaking? "I'm sorry about everything."

She narrowed her eyes. "What are you

talking about?"

He looked as if his heart were broken and he couldn't find any of the pieces. "I'm sorry I yelled at you. I'm sorry I gave you back your bread and took your drill. I'm sorry I called you weak."

Every word he said poked her like a straight pin. *Jah,* it still hurt.

"I'm sorry. . . ." His breath caught in his throat. "I'm sorry I said I hated you."

"I said it first."

"Only because I provoked you." He rubbed the back of his neck. "Jesus said not to get angry. But I got mad anyway, because you make me so mad, Poppy."

Another poke with a pin. "I already know what you think of me, Luke. You can't hurt me with it."

He growled and looked up at the sky. "What I'm trying to say is that I said things because I was angry, but I didn't mean what I said."

"You did mean it. I got the message when you kept the drill. Poppy is a weak, stupid girl. She doesn't deserve a man's drill."

Irritation traveled across his face. "Poppy, stop picking a fight and listen."

Poppy pressed her lips together. Let him blame everything on her. He wanted to ease his guilty conscience by pretending his rudeness was her fault. After all, she was proud and stubborn and full of error. She could withstand his attack, and then Lord willing, he'd go away and leave her alone.

"I shouldn't have kept the drill. I admit it. I wanted to make you suffer like I suffered. You put me through five minutes of sheer terror."

Go ahead, Luke. Make it out to be my fault yet. "I was thinking of your sisters and the kittens." Why did she try to defend herself? It didn't matter. It wasn't as if he'd ever listen to a girl.

"My sisters could have been seriously hurt."

The heaviness in her chest became unbearable. She laughed bitterly. "*Ach.* I might have killed them."

"*Nae,* Poppy. You saved them. They would have gone in." He stepped close enough that she could feel his breath on her face and see that his *kaffee* brown eyes sparkled with flecks of caramel and chocolate. Her heart was not supposed to be doing somersaults. "That's what I'm trying to tell you. I'm sorry for treating you like I did, for the yelling and stomping. I wish I could take it back."

For a brief moment, she softened. He seemed so remorseful.

He gave her a half smile. "You're just too pigheaded to believe me."

He was still playing a game with her heart. She swallowed a sob and took a shuddering breath. "I suppose it shouldn't surprise me that you think I look like a pig."

He practically bared his teeth. "Are you misunderstanding me on purpose?"

"*Jah,* because it's all my fault."

"It isn't. I'm just as stubborn. Dan is always telling me so."

It suddenly became as clear as the air after a rainstorm. "Dan put you up to this, didn't he?"

"Dan? I haven't said anything to Dan."

"He's afraid you and me at odds will hurt Lily. Or maybe Josiah is worried that our hating each other will risk his chances with Rose. It must have taken a lot to convince you to pretend to be sorry."

"That's not true."

She couldn't look into those eyes anymore. Turning her face from him, she stared at nothing. "Tell Josiah he needn't worry. Rose would never hold our relationship against him. And nothing could pull Lily and Dan apart. Not even Paul Glick."

He took off his hat and pulled his fingers through his hair as if he were trying to yank it out from the roots. "Why are you so difficult?"

She felt as if he'd grabbed her shoulder and wrenched it out of the socket again. She very nearly cried out in pain.

This was the absolute last time she would allow Luke to hurt her. She squared her shoulders and raised her chin. "You have made it very clear what you think of me, Luke Bontrager. I'm bullheaded and ugly, boyish and contrary." Her voice cracked like a glass jar against the pavement. "I don't care that I'm not pretty and sweet like Dinah Eicher. And I don't care if *Gotte* loves you better because you are a boy."

"I don't want you to be Dinah Eicher."

She glared at him. "Go away and leave me alone."

"*Ach,* Poppy, don't go like that."

She ignored him and marched away. Thankfully, Luke didn't follow. She'd gotten rid of him.

If only it was as easy to pry him out of her heart.

CHAPTER SIXTEEN

Luke didn't even have the heart to pick up a knife and whittle a pencil. The hissing propane lantern was his only companion as he sat in the dim shadows of his workshop and tried to make sense of what had just happened.

He cradled his head in his hands and stared at the floor, lightly covered with sawdust. Sawdust was a permanent part of any wood shop. He'd sweep it out in the morning because he couldn't muster the energy or the desire to do it tonight.

How had he managed to make such a mess of things? One minute he was pouring out a heartfelt apology to Poppy, and the next minute he was accusing her of being pigheaded.

And somehow, he'd made things worse. Much worse.

The ache in his chest felt like an old scab that had been ripped off. Poppy would never talk to him again, and he thought he might lose the ability to breathe.

Dan poked his head in the wood shop. "Can we come in?"

Luke nodded. He wasn't in the mood for his friends tonight, even though he'd asked them to come over. Everything just felt too raw. Maybe he should tell them to come back another time, when he felt more like talking. Two or three years should be long enough.

Josiah and Dan strolled into his wood shop, an ample space Luke and his *dat* had built just off the road at the front of their property when Luke's carpentry business had started to make some money. Josiah ran his finger along the table saw, leaving a trail where the sawdust had been.

He should probably dust tomorrow too.

"I expected you a long time ago," Luke said, not even bothering to stand. His friends knew their way around.

Dan pulled an unstained chair from the stack of furniture Luke had sanded today. Josiah sat on a wobbly stool that Luke should have fixed three days ago. He'd been letting too many things slide since that day at the ditch.

"I had to take Lily and her sisters home," Dan said. "And I wasn't about to cut my visit short to come see you."

"I never could abide being around a man in love," Luke said, tempering his words with a weak smile.

Dan grinned. "You're the one who invited me."

Josiah, whose stool was taller than either of the chairs his friends sat on, towered above Luke and Dan like a sycamore. "So, Luke. What is the emergency? Did you call it off with Dinah Eicher?"

"Jah," Luke said.

Josiah frowned. "I was joking."

"I wasn't."

Dan nodded and rested his arms on his knees. "What happened?"

"It doesn't matter what happened. That's not the emergency."

"I'm listening," Dan said, as if he knew exactly what Luke would say.

"I need your help with Poppy."

"Poppy?" Josiah asked. "What happened with Poppy?"

"I don't know much," Dan said. "But I know she's really mad at you."

Luke blew out a puff of air. "I've really messed it up, and I don't know if I can make it right again."

Josiah scooted his stool closer. It scraped

loudly along the floor. "So tell us what happened."

"She jumped in the ditch to save those cats, and I got mad at her."

"We heard the story," Josiah said.

"I got really mad at her. I yelled. I told her she was weak and that she would never be as good at anything as the boys." He ran his fingers angrily through his hair. "I told her I hated her."

Dan and Josiah were stunned into silence. They stared at him as if he'd sprouted an extra ear.

He lifted his hands in a gesture of hopelessness. "Tonight at the gathering I tried to say I'm sorry and ended up accusing her of being pigheaded. I couldn't even apologize without offending her."

Josiah stood and paced, leaving little imprints in the sawdust where he stepped. "It's not that I don't care about you and Poppy, but do you think this will hurt my chances with Rose? I mean, if my best friend and her sister hate each other, maybe she'll think she should stay away."

"Poppy said it wouldn't hurt your chances at all."

"Poppy said that?"

"She thought you forced me to apologize."

Josiah narrowed his eyes. "She . . . she

271

knows about me and Rose?"

Luke leaned forward. "Everybody knows, Josiah. Your face is like a billboard."

"Does Rose know?"

Luke rolled his eyes. "Everybody but Rose. Could we talk about me now?"

Dan rubbed the whiskers on his chin and studied Luke's face. "So you were mean?"

"Really mean."

"And you feel bad because you're too obstinate and grumpy to make a decent apology."

Luke scowled. "Do you even like me or are you just pretending to be my friend?"

Dan chuckled. "I like you well enough yet. You're a good friend to have because when I see what a sorry state you're in, I always feel better about myself."

"That's not funny."

Dan wiped the smile off his face. "Why do you feel so bad? You and Poppy have had plenty of dust-ups before."

Luke groaned and slapped his palm against his forehead. "And the drill. I kept the drill. *Oy,* anyhow, how could I have been so stupid?"

Josiah looked at Dan. "What is he talking about?"

"I have no idea." Dan leaned forward and pinned Luke with an unwavering gaze.

"What it comes down to is this. You love Poppy Christner."

Luke forced a laugh. "Love her? Dan, that is the stupidest thing I've ever heard come out of your mouth. I don't love Poppy Christner. She's strong-willed and independent and has made it very clear she doesn't need a man. I like her, but I was really mean and now she can't stand the sight of me. I hate that she can't stand the sight of me. I want her to like me. I want her to be happy. I want her to smile at me and talk to me and help me build chicken coops. She's not like any other girl I know, and oh, *sis yuscht,* I love her."

He'd just been hit by a speeding freight train, and the blow would have knocked him off his feet if he'd been standing. Burying his face in his hands, he let the emotions pound into him.

He loved Poppy Christner.

And it hurt so bad.

Dan chuckled softly. "I tried to warn you. You should have been nice. She despises you."

"That's not helpful," Josiah said. "Can't you see he's in a bad way?"

Luke massaged the lines on his forehead. "Dan is speaking the truth. She hates me." He lifted his head. "But he doesn't have to be so smug about it."

Josiah furrowed his brow. "Poppy doesn't hate you. I can't imagine she hates anybody, except maybe Paul Glick."

"*Nae,* Josiah, she hates me. She told me so herself."

Josiah seemed to deflate as he sat on his stool. "Then there's no hope."

"Right," Luke said. "No hope. I feel better already. I'm so glad you came over."

"I don't think it's a permanent condition," Dan said. "If she were dead set against you, she wouldn't be so sad."

Luke frowned. "She's sad?"

"When I took her home tonight, she didn't say a word, and I can always get Poppy to talk to me, even when she's in a bad mood. She was definitely not happy."

"I don't know what to do. My apology went very wrong."

"You need something big." Dan eyed Luke as if trying to determine his commitment to something big.

"I'll do anything to get rid of this ache in my chest. I don't mind begging for forgiveness."

Dan shook his head. "She's already forgiven you. Despite all her protests, Poppy really does blame herself. She knows she's stubborn and strong-willed, but she doesn't think those are good qualities."

"Those are her best qualities," Luke said.

"The community bears part of the blame for how Poppy feels about herself. Bitsy and Poppy's sisters have done their best to build her up, but so many people, including her *dawdi,* have mocked her for being different. She truly believes she is undeserving because of who she is."

Luke swallowed the lump in his throat. "A beautiful, feisty girl who wants to help everybody."

"*Jah.*"

The ache flared into searing regret. How many times had he told Poppy she was stubborn? He hadn't meant it as a compliment. She'd never taken it as one. How many times had he teased her for being a tomboy or chided her for not being demure and submissive, like Dinah Eicher?

Yet it was Poppy he loved. He loved her determination and her bravery and her refusal to be cowed by what other people thought of her. Her refusal to be bullied by him. He massaged the lines in his forehead as if he could erase them. He felt lower than a snake in a well.

Luke could tell Dan was sort of tired of reminding Luke of all his faults. "She was starting to trust you, and you shoved her face in the dirt."

Ach. He'd never be happy again.

Dan reached out and placed a hand on Luke's shoulder. "I tell the truth because I'm your friend."

"The truth really hurts."

Dan tried to smile. "Now you know what the damage is, you can repair it."

Luke scrubbed his fingers through his hair yet again. "I can't. I've hurt her too deep."

"I saw that chicken coop," Josiah said. "I wouldn't have been able to fix it."

Luke looked sideways at Josiah. "You can't fix anything."

Josiah ignored the insult. "But you can."

He couldn't. He couldn't fix things with Poppy. Their relationship was like that demolished chicken coop. "No one could have put that thing back together."

"You had to start over," Dan said.

It was as if someone had lit a match in his dark life. "Start over?"

"Soften her up with something really big."

It suddenly felt easier to breathe. Trying was better than despairing. "Do you think I can make her love me?"

Dan waved that suggestion away. "Let's work on building a little trust first."

"What do you suggest?" Luke asked.

"I don't know," Dan said.

Luke smirked. "*Denki* for the help."

"I just know it has to be big, and you have to keep your mouth shut."

"How am I supposed to restore her trust if I keep my mouth shut?" Luke said.

"Every time you've opened your mouth, you've made it worse."

Luke grunted. "For sure and certain."

Dan made a fist and tapped Luke on the shoulder. "You're trying to win Poppy, not beat her, so don't make everything a competition and don't say anything about women's work, as if it's below you. The Honeybee Sisters do everybody's work. Believe me, you're not better than they are."

"Of course I'm not better. It's just that my *dat* always taught me that men are to do the hard work because women are softer and weaker."

"You might have more arm strength than Poppy, but that doesn't mean you should push her around," Dan said.

"I don't want to push anybody," Luke said, scowling. "And you're confusing me. All I want to know is how to get Poppy to love me."

"We'll help you if we can," Josiah said.

Josiah couldn't even work up the nerve to take Rose on a ride. He wouldn't be much help with Poppy. "Dan, you're always welcome at the Christners'," Luke said. "You can put in a *gute* word for me."

Dan frowned and folded his arms. "We've got our work cut out for us. Not only is Poppy dead set against you, but Lily and Rose don't take kindly to anyone hurting their sister's feelings. And after your wonderful-bad apology, Bitsy might never let you in the house again. She's not afraid to wave that shotgun around."

"If she shot me, I couldn't feel any worse than I do already."

Josiah nodded. "That's the spirit."

Luke's heart hurt so bad, he couldn't sit up straight. He wasn't in love with an ordinary girl like Dinah Eicher or Mary Schrock. This was Poppy Christner — a girl worth fighting for.

And he'd fight tooth and nail for her.

Even if she put up a fight.

CHAPTER SEVENTEEN

Aunt B's voice rang loud and clear in the orchard. "I got me a Chrysler, it seats about twenty, so hurry up and bring your jukebox money." Poppy loved hearing Aunt B sing the "Lob Song" or the other hymns they sang at *gmay*, but at home she often sang *Englisch* songs that the girls didn't know and couldn't sing along with. Poppy didn't mind. She was perfectly content to listen and try to figure out what in the world the songs were about.

Poppy looked down at her bucket with a few measly cherries at the bottom. It didn't help her low spirits to know that she was worse than no help at all. She quickly glanced around. Her sisters and Aunt B were hidden among the trees picking cherries on ladders. An empty ladder stood right next to Poppy's tree. If she climbed up a couple of rungs, she'd be able to reach so many more cherries. Balancing with one good hand couldn't be that hard. She glanced around again for good measure, then stepped up one rung and then another. She put her bucket on the top step, propped her injured arm on the next step down, and reached for a cherry.

"Poppy Christner," Aunt B called from the treetops. "Get down from that ladder. I won't have you singing with the angels in heaven just yet."

Poppy groaned, grabbed her bucket, and stepped down. "I only want to help, Aunt B."

"You'll be no help at all if you're in the hospital. Pick what you can reach with both feet on the ground."

Ach. She needed two good hands today. Even though it was a small orchard, it took Poppy, Aunt B, and her sisters the better part of three days to pick all the cherries. This year, without Poppy, it might take a whole week. She felt only slightly better knowing that Dan would come and help after milking. He couldn't give every waking hour to the Honeybee Sisters' farm. He had his own chores at home.

Poppy tried to hold a branch down and pick cherries off it at the same time. It didn't work very well. She got three cherries in her bucket and a scratch on her wrist.

She only needed to wear the sling for one more week. What would it hurt if she just slipped it off for a couple of hours so she could pick cherries? It wasn't as if she'd be doing somersaults through the orchard. She hung her bucket on a low branch and slid the sling strap over her head. She'd leave it off for a few minutes and see how it felt. No one would ever have to know.

"Poppy Christner, put that sling back on this minute."

Poppy threw her head back and sighed a long, plaintive sigh. She knew one thing with certainty. Aunt B had eyes in the back of her head. "Can't I try picking without it on?"

"Nope. The doctor said two weeks or he'd have to amputate."

"He did not."

"I'd rather not push our luck."

"We're Amish, Aunt B. We don't believe in luck."

"Speak for yourself," Aunt B called back. "I believe in luck, karma, and fortune cookies."

Poppy gave up trying to be sneaky and settled for picking all the cherries she could reach on her tippy toes. She placed the bucket on the ground and dropped the cherries in one by one. At this rate, she'd have half a bucketful by nightfall.

She did a very graceful pirouette on her toes, reaching for a cherry, when Luke Bontrager came walking through the orchard with a bucket in his hand and a doubtful look on his face. She lost her balance, and he grabbed her arm before she fell over. "You okay?" he said.

She brushed off her dress and tried to pretend he hadn't set her aching heart racing. "I'm fine."

He quickly released her arm, as if he'd done something wrong, but didn't let his eyes stray from her face. "Dan said the cherries were on, so I came to see if you could use some help."

"Is that you, Luke Bontrager?" Aunt B called.

Luke looked up to try to figure out where the voice came from. "Is that you, Bitsy Kiem?"

"Maybe. Or maybe it's your conscience calling you to repentance."

He gave Poppy a half smile. She wished she didn't like that smile so much. "I'm sure I need it."

The tree above Aunt Bitsy's ladder shook. "I know you do." A few cherries plopped to the ground below Aunt B. "Don't you have a job, Luke Bontrager? Or did you get fired?"

Luke glanced at Poppy, then up into the trees, obviously a little unsure about having a conversation with an unseen voice. "I carved out a little time today to help with the cherries. Is it okay if I help you pick?"

Of course it wasn't okay. Luke hated Poppy. Poppy hated him. They'd probably end up yelling at each other.

Aunt B paused for a good, long time. "Are you going to pester Poppy to get a tetanus shot or an X-ray?"

Luke didn't take his eyes from Poppy. It made her nervous. "No pestering. I just want to help."

"We don't need your help," Aunt B replied. "You can go home."

Lily picked at a tree to Poppy's right. "That's not true, Aunt B. We've got to get these cherries before the wind takes them, and Poppy's only got one *gute* hand."

"And you won't let her get on the ladder," Rose called from somewhere behind Poppy.

Poppy ground her teeth together. Her sisters were way too welcoming. They might have needed Luke's help, but Poppy didn't want it. She'd rather happily pick her measly amount of cherries than be miserable for weeks because of Luke. Or longer. Right now she felt so downhearted, she could see the misery going on for years.

Luke raised his bucket even though Aunt B couldn't see it. "I brought my own bucket."

"I don't know why you think that makes a difference," Aunt B said.

He turned to Poppy with a pleading look in his eyes. "I'd really like to help. It's my fault you can't use both arms."

His fault indeed.

What could she say? If she said no, her sisters would be stuck with the extra work. If she agreed to let him stay, it would be a rotten day.

She pressed her lips together. She was having a rotten day anyway. How much worse could Luke make it?

She didn't want to know the answer to that question.

"We'd be grateful for your help," she heard herself say, in a surprisingly polite tone. She wouldn't have to say a word to him. He wouldn't be forced to talk to her. She knew how unpleasant that must be for him.

His smile bloomed like a sunflower. "*Denki.* I can stay until supper time."

Aunt Bitsy rattled her tree again. "Just

watch yourself. Every time you come over, Poppy gets hurt."

His smile lost some of its luster. "I hope that won't happen again."

"Show him how to pick, Poppy," Aunt Bitsy said.

Poppy grimaced. She didn't even want to be in the same orchard with him. "You have to pick them with the stems," she said, showing him how to snap the cherries off the tree. "They stay fresher that way."

Luke nodded, climbed up Poppy's ladder, and started picking, just like that. He didn't yell at her or show disapproval of any kind.

But the day was still young.

Billy Idol sauntered into the orchard, stationed himself at the foot of Luke's ladder, and gazed up as if all the cat food sat at the top of the tree. Did Luke smell like catnip or something? Billy Idol placed his paw on the bottom rung, hesitated for a second, and climbed carefully up the ladder. Luke nearly fell as Billy Idol clawed his way up Luke's trousers and came to rest on the top of the ladder next to Luke's bucket.

"Go away, cat," Luke said.

Billy Idol hissed and scowled and stayed put. Poppy grinned. She wouldn't mind if Billy Idol gave Luke a little trouble today.

Poppy chose a tree at the other end of the

row. It wouldn't take her long. There was only so much she could reach before moving on. She could hear Luke and Lily having a conversation, with occasional help from Rose, but Poppy felt no obligation to join in. She had no interest in what Luke Bontrager had to say about anything.

It sounded as if Luke was grasping a branch and shaking it with all his might. What was he doing to their poor tree?

"You're going to break something," Aunt B said. "Don't be so rough."

"I want to be fast," he said, but the violent rustling settled down a bit. "I can hear the bees from up here."

Ten hives sat at the edge of the orchard, and they made a pleasant hum that could be heard from several feet away.

"They never rest," Rose said.

"I like the pictures of flowers painted on the hives," Luke said.

Aunt Bitsy climbed down from her ladder and moved it a few feet around the tree. "Rose painted all our hives."

"They're beautiful."

Poppy pursed her lips. She didn't care how agreeable Luke acted. It wouldn't last long.

"How are the kittens doing?" Lily asked.

Why did Lily have to bring up the kittens?

Every tear Poppy had shed in the last decade was because of those kittens.

"Dorothy and Joann couldn't be better mothers. They feed them by hand and brush their fur and keep them in their room to sleep," Luke said. "I hate cats, but my sisters have never been happier. Even Mamm tolerates them for my sisters' sake."

"Luke?" Rose said, and even from four trees away, Poppy could hear the timidity in her voice. "Aren't you glad Poppy saved them?"

Poppy hadn't the least interest in Luke's answer, but she held her breath and stopped picking so she wouldn't miss it.

"Glad?" Luke said. "My sisters would have been devastated if those kittens had drowned. I'm more than glad. I thank *Gotte* every day for what Poppy did. I lashed out at Poppy when I should have thanked her."

Poppy almost snorted out loud. Luke didn't mean any of what he said. He'd been furious. He blamed her for putting his sisters in danger. He surely hadn't changed his mind. He only said what he thought Lily and Rose wanted to hear.

She furrowed her brow. She'd never known Luke to be a liar. He always spoke his mind, even if what he said offended everybody.

"It's no excuse for how I treated Poppy," Luke said, "but I get anxious when it comes to my little sisters and other girls. I even get concerned for Poppy, who can take care of herself in any ditch in Wisconsin."

Lily climbed down from her ladder and poured her full bucket of cherries into the wooden box sitting in between the row of trees. "Maybe your *mamm*'s accident made you overly cautious."

Luke paused long enough that Poppy wondered if he'd even heard Lily's question. She squinted among the branches of his tree but couldn't see his face. "Maybe it did," he finally said.

Even with a cat sitting on his ladder and getting in the way, Luke proved to be a lightning-fast cherry picker. He finished two trees before Rose or Lily had even finished one. Leaves tumbled from his trees as he picked, as if he were stripping the branches instead of merely plucking off cherries. It's how she would have expected Luke Bontrager to pick. He dove in headfirst with any job he did and worked with every ounce of energy he had until the job was done. It was how he'd tackled the chicken coop. It was how he cut watermelon. It was even how he ate pie and how he pestered her with such persistence.

It took three hours for Poppy to pick every cherry she could reach. She refused to say a word to Luke, even when he hovered seven feet above her head picking the tree she was working on. Sometimes he talked to Lily and Rose; sometimes he kept quiet. He even whistled occasionally. But he didn't seem to mind her silence. He didn't seem to mind anything about her, even though he'd found plenty to say on that subject in the past.

The first time she had needed to empty her bucket, she'd realized that she couldn't do it by herself. She hated to ask for help, especially because Luke gloated when she admitted weakness, but she couldn't dump the cherries into the box with one hand. She had asked Lily to help her, but Luke had practically vaulted from his ladder before the words were out of her mouth. There hadn't been a hint of smug superiority when he'd emptied her bucket, but Poppy couldn't be comfortable. Every smile he gave her was like a stab to the heart, and her chest felt heavy, as if she'd lost something that she'd never get back.

She hated that she needed the help, but at least he didn't gloat, not even when he helped her two more times.

Poppy set her full bucket next to a half-filled box of cherries and brushed her hand down the front of her apron. Before she even stood up straight, Luke was off his ladder pouring her cherries into the box. She made the mistake of looking at him, and his smile stole her senses. She didn't like it. That smile made her want to let down her guard, to give Luke her friendship again. But that would be very foolish indeed. Was it supper time yet?

She turned away from him. To protect herself, she had to be strong.

"Aunt B," she said, pretending Luke wasn't standing three feet away from her, "I've picked everything I can reach." Luke watched intently as she tucked a lock of hair beneath the scarf tied around her head. "If I just stood on the bottom rung of the ladder, I could get more."

"You shouldn't be on a ladder," Luke said, before clamping his mouth shut and stuffing his hands in his pockets. He lowered his gaze and didn't utter another word.

Poppy's argument died on her lips.

Aunt B tilted her head so Poppy could see it below the branches. "No ladders." She stood up straight again so all Poppy could see were her feet. "We'll finish up. You can go clean toilets."

Poppy expelled a puff of air. Too bad she didn't need two hands to clean a toilet.

Luke was surely laughing at her. He'd probably never cleaned a toilet in his life. "Okay," she said with little enthusiasm. The only *gute* part about cleaning toilets was that Luke wouldn't be around. His presence made her whole body hurt.

"Luke, why don't you help her? You'd do very well with your face in the toilet."

"I'd enjoy that, but I have to go soon. I have a customer waiting for me at the shop." He smiled, no doubt ecstatic to be leaving the toilets to Poppy. "Can I walk you back to the house?" *Oy* anyhow, he was pushy.

"I know the way."

"Can I follow you?"

She didn't even answer, just tromped out of the orchard, not pausing to see if he would follow. She heard him fall into step behind her, with the cat meowing in step behind Luke. That cat was the only one who could tolerate Luke Bontrager.

Poppy turned on her heels and halted Luke in his tracks. She had to put a stop to this now, or she'd be on pins and needles forever trying to outguess exasperating Luke Bontrager. "It wonders me why you are here."

He smiled uncertainly. "Dan said you needed help with the cherries."

She narrowed her eyes. "That's your

excuse for being here. Why are you really here? Do you want to gloat or get another chance to yell at me? Because I'll tell you right now that I won't let you hurt me anymore."

She shouldn't have let her voice crack, and she shouldn't have said *anymore.* He didn't need to know that he had hurt her in the first place.

She squared her shoulders. He hadn't hurt her. Not really. Luke's yelling had been more of a nuisance than anything else.

He seemed immediately contrite. "I want us to be friends again."

She closed her mouth and searched his face. Wasn't he going to argue? "Why do you want to be friends?"

"Because I like you."

The Luke she knew would never admit that. "I don't believe you."

He lowered his eyes. "I know. I want to change that."

He seemed sincere, but she wouldn't trust his sudden humility. Luke had let her down before.

An idea lit up his face. "Race you to the house?"

She didn't even flinch. "We've already raced, and you lost."

"I know," he said. "You're fast."

What happened to *You'll never be better than a boy at anything?*

He jogged a few steps ahead of her, all the way to the lane in front of their house. "I brought you a present," he said. "I left it on the porch when I came out to the orchard."

Poppy felt her face get warmer than a woodstove during a cold spell. "Why?" She'd asked that question too many times to count.

He bounded onto the porch, tossed the body of a dead mouse off the welcome mat, and picked a white grocery sack off the floor. She knew what it was without having to look. Her heart felt as heavy and dense as a lump of coal. Was he mocking her?

"I want you to have this," he said. "I never should have kept it."

She took a deep breath and wrapped her arms around her waist. "I don't need your permission to use a drill."

His smile faltered. "I'm not saying you do. I thought it might come in handy."

"I know you feel guilty, but you don't have to be nice to me simply to make yourself feel better. I know what you think of me. You don't have to pretend."

He ran his fingers through his hair. "I'm not pretending, and you know it. Why won't you admit it?"

Poppy glared at him and dared him to contradict her. "Because I'm stubborn."

He didn't even hesitate. "I love that about you."

He loved that about her?

He held out the drill. She wouldn't touch it. "Please take it. I want you to have it."

She lifted her chin a little higher. "You said a girl should have a drill to fix things around the house. I went and bought my own."

His face fell so far, he had to scrape it off the ground. "*Ach.* I see. I suppose I deserve that." The plastic grocery bag made a crinkly sound as he clutched it in his fingers and pulled it close to his chest. "I guess Walmart will take it back again. Can I come back tomorrow?"

"Why tomorrow?"

"I want to help with the cherries again. And maybe I can teach you how to use your new drill."

Poppy didn't even blink. "I can read the instructions."

He stepped off the porch and shuffled his feet across the flagstones. Turning back, he nodded, bowed his head, and walked away as if she'd killed all his dreams.

She was definitely imagining things.

CHAPTER EIGHTEEN

Poppy blew a strand of hair out of her eyes and knelt on the floor. She found it impossible to lift a bag of wheat with one good arm. She'd have to get what she needed cupful by cupful. It took about eight cups of wheat for four loaves of bread. At least she could grind the wheat with one hand. Kneading might be a little trickier, but she was determined to pull her weight.

The wheat berries sounded like rain as she poured them into the bowl. It was too bad they had rain last night or they might have heard Queenie making a fuss in the barn or someone skulking around their farm. The troublemaker had sneaked into their barn last night and cut off Queenie's tail, right down to a nub. All of them, even Poppy, cried over the loss of that beautiful tail, and Poppy didn't usually cry over anything. But *Gotte* was *gute*. Whoever did it hadn't docked the tail, and Aunt B said it would grow back. Poppy was ready to sleep in the barn every night until she caught the mischief maker in the act of something. This vandalism had to stop.

The wonderful-*gute* news was that the cherries were done. Luke and Dan had helped her sisters and Aunt B finish the picking yesterday. They had even loaded them into Luke's wagon and taken them to market in Shawano. Poppy sighed. Now that the cherries were picked, he wouldn't come around anymore. That thought shouldn't have made her sad, but it did. Luke had behaved himself very well, picking cherries so fast no one could keep up with him, and letting Billy Idol climb onto his lap because it made Rose happy.

Someone knocked on the door, and Poppy's heart raced at the thought that it might be Luke. Luke or the mischief maker, come to attack Poppy while she was all alone in the house.

Please, Gotte, *let it be Luke.*

Had one of her prayers ever been answered so fast? Luke stood in her doorway smiling that devil-may-care smile that left her feverish and aggravated at the same time. If he was as handsome on the inside as he was on the outside, Poppy would have fallen for him years ago. A ribbon of electricity threaded up her spine. She didn't think he'd come back. How nice to be wrong.

Billy Idol sat at his feet on the porch, and Luke held a dead mouse by the tail, swinging it back and forth like a clock pendulum between two of his fingers. "I think Billy Idol has been playing a trick on all of us," he said, nudging the mouse closer to her so she could get a better look.

"I'd rather not," she said.

His eyes sparkled. "This mouse has a spot on its back exactly the same as the mouse I threw off the porch yesterday."

Poppy frowned. "What does that mean?"

He chuckled and looked down at Billy Idol, who scowled and hissed as if he was getting ready for a catfight. "It means that every time I throw this mouse off the porch, Billy Idol goes and brings it back. He's been deceiving all of you."

Poppy smirked and squatted to be closer to Billy Idol's scarred face. "You naughty cat. How many times have I thrown dead mice off the porch?"

"Don't be too mad at him," Luke said. "He wants to be accepted into the family. You might not appreciate his gifts, but he's trying real hard yet."

Poppy stood up and came face-to-face with Luke and his dark, brooding gaze.

Wasn't he standing a little too close? She cleared her throat. "Do you want to come in?"

"Nothing I'd like better."

She stepped way back so he would have room to enter without getting uncomfortably near. He held a strange handful of — was that hair? — in his other hand.

"What is that?" she said, putting her hand to the hair at the nape of her neck. After having done the dishes and dusting the furniture, she must have looked a sight.

He didn't seem to mind her stray hairs or the dust that smudged her apron. In fact, his gaze didn't leave her face. "Dan told me your horse's tail got cut last night."

"*Jah.* But it wasn't docked, so it will grow back."

"It makes me mad what people will do to animals."

"Me too," Poppy said. "It's one thing to take your anger out on three grown-up girls, but quite another to hurt the animals. They can't defend themselves."

A deep furrow appeared between his eyes. "I don't like the thought of them doing anything to harm you or your sisters either."

"Aunt B called the sheriff again, just so he knows, but he said he couldn't do much about it."

He took off his hat and ran his fingers through his dark, thick hair. Poppy held her breath. Why was she thinking about hair at a time like this? "What can I do to help you, Poppy? I wish I didn't feel so helpless."

"You're the least helpless boy I know," Poppy said.

His face spread into a grin. "I am?"

"You paint barns, you build furniture and chicken coops, you pick cherries as if you were born in a tree."

He pretended to be disappointed. "You found out my secret."

Poppy smiled. "I'm making honey custard with cherries if you want to stay for dinner," she heard herself say. Why had she invited him to eat? She wanted to get rid of him, didn't she?

The grin couldn't have gotten any wider. "You would let me stay for dinner?"

"If you're nice."

He nodded earnestly. "I promise to be nice."

"You still haven't told me what that is you're holding in your hand. Have you been collecting hair at the barbershop?"

He pulled his gaze away from her and set the thing on the table. "Dan told me Queenie's tail got cut, which I think is especially cruel to a horse in the summertime. She can't swish the flies off, and flies can be torture to a horse." He smoothed the hair with his hand. "This is a temporary tail made of horse hair. People buy them when they're going to show their horses at auction. We attach it onto Queenie's stubby tail, and she can swish the flies away. By next summer, her tail should be back."

Poppy fingered the ends of the hair. "I didn't even think about the flies."

"Only someone really spiteful would cut off a horse's tail."

Poppy lowered her eyes. She still had the nagging feeling that someone was out to spite her specifically. "Someone who hates me very much."

He frowned. "It's not your fault."

"You don't know that for sure."

He seemed to get closer though he stood perfectly still. "I'm not going to lie, Poppy. I'm worried about you."

The air around her felt soft and snuggly, like a warm blanket on a chilly afternoon. For probably the first time in her life, Poppy didn't take Luke's concern as an insult. It was kind of sweet, as if he really cared about her, as if Dinah Eicher weren't on his mind day and night. "If you can't help yourself, worry about Rose. Some nights, she's too frightened to go to sleep."

"She takes it hard like I do, but maybe for different reasons."

Poppy nudged his elbow and gave him a reassuring smile. "It would have been much worse if you and Dan and Josiah hadn't painted that barn door."

His lips twitched in embarrassment. "Bright orange."

"Your chicken coop made her very happy, and she feels better when you or Dan are here."

He curled one side of his mouth and looked at her sideways. "What about you? Do you feel better when I'm here?"

"You did pick all those cherries. I suppose I don't mind that Dan drags you along."

She meant it as a tease, but he acted as if she'd just handed him a whole plate of Rose's meat loaf with special sauce. "You don't mind? I think I'm going to cry."

She giggled. "I've never seen you cry."

He grunted and gave her a quick nod. "And you never will."

Billy Idol darted into the house before she shut the door. "Please don't worry. The troublemaker hasn't tried to hurt us."

"Yet."

"Don't say that. You're going to scare me."

He smiled. "I've never seen you scared."

"And you never will."

He clapped his hands together. "Enough spooky talk. What can I do to help?"

"Nothing. I need to make bread."

Luke's eyes lit up, and he spread his arms in front of him. "I've got two hands. I can help."

"It's women's work," she warned. That would keep him out of the kitchen. Picking cherries was one thing, but making bread? Dinah Eicher would never ask him to make bread.

"I want to learn," he said. "Are you afraid I'll be better than you at loafing?"

"You're not better than me at anything. And what, for goodness sake, is loafing?"

He chuckled. "You'll never know unless you let me help. But I warn you. I've got muscles of steel."

She wouldn't give him encouragement by smiling. "More like a head full of dough."

"All the better to make bread."

Poppy gave in and let Luke grind the wheat. She could have done it herself, even with only one hand, but she didn't want to waste all those muscles standing right there in her kitchen. Luke ground the wheat, measured the flour, soaked the yeast, and made himself extremely useful.

Once they mixed the dough, Poppy

floured the counter and directed Luke to scrape the dough out of the bowl to be kneaded. She glanced at him. "I think I can do this with one hand if you've got somewhere better to be."

He acted as if she'd just insulted him. "Somewhere better to be? There's nowhere I'd rather be."

Why did he sound so sincere? It was just bread, and she wasn't Dinah Eicher.

She pressed the heel of her hand into the dough and showed him how to press and roll. "Since this is just women's work, I'm sure you already know how to do it."

He winced and shook his head. "I am going to be eating a lot of my words." He dusted his hands with flour and pressed them into the dough. "You do this every week?"

She nodded.

"You probably could beat me in an arm-wrestling contest. This is really *gute* for my muscles. See?"

He flexed his arms as he pressed and rolled the dough, and Poppy had to look away to keep from grinning. Luke Bontrager was a peacock, pure and simple.

The sweat beaded on his forehead. "You should let me knead the bread every week. I feel my arms getting stronger."

Once the dough was to Poppy's liking, Luke rolled it into a ball and put it in a bowl. Poppy covered the bowl with a dishcloth and left it on the counter to rise.

They shared the sink to wash their hands, and Luke gave her first use of the towel. "I wish it was done already. Poppy Christner's bread is famous."

She shook her head. "This is Luke Bontrager bread. I'll only take credit if it tastes good."

"How long did you say it needs to rise?"

"About forty minutes in the bowl, then another forty in the pans."

"Have you got a Bible?" he said.

She pressed her lips to one side of her face. "You want to do some reading?"

"I want to show you something."

Poppy pointed to the table next to the sofa. Luke retrieved the Bible, laid it on the butcher-block island, and leaned his elbows against the counter. Poppy stood on the opposite side of the island wondering just what he wanted to show her.

He opened the book, raised an eyebrow, and pulled out a hundred-dollar bill from between Genesis and Exodus.

Poppy blushed. "Aunt B keeps her money in the books."

"All her money?"

"She doesn't trust banks."

Luke nodded. "My *dawdi* kept his money in a jar that he buried in the backyard. Once, he forgot where he'd buried it and spent two years digging up the yard looking for it. When he found the money, Mammi planted a daffodil bulb in every one of those holes. Their backyard bloomed bright yellow every summer."

"I suppose some good came out of it."

"After that, he kept his money in Mammi's cookie jar. She never made cookies again. It was a sad day for the grandchildren. Now you know why I like your cookies so much. I cried myself to sleep every night after Mammi stopped making cookies."

Poppy grinned. "We find money every time we open a book."

"My *dat* should do that. I'd read a lot more." He leafed through the pages, finding three hundred more dollars before landing in Matthew and turning his eyes to her. "I don't like admitting when I'm wrong."

"That's quite a surprise," Poppy said drily.

"I'm sure it is." He leaned his elbows on the island and gazed at Poppy as if she were the sun, the moon, and the stars. "I want you to know, Poppy, that I don't think I'm better or more important than you. I never did. The way I've acted and the things I said made you believe that. I don't think women's work should be done just by women or that men are more valuable."

She only had to look into those eyes to tell he believed it. Had he changed his mind, or had he always thought that way? She thought her heart might swell out of her chest. "Are you throwing out your entire personality then?"

He groaned. "Very funny. I have been stubborn and arrogant, haven't I?"

"I happen to think that stubbornness is a very *gute* quality, as long as you're humble about it."

"I agree," Luke said. "I'm still working on the humility."

Poppy placed her hand on the open page. "When you pick cherries and knead bread as well as you do, it's hard. I won't get my hopes up."

He stared at her until she felt a little awkward, as if he might go on staring until dinnertime.

"Did you have a scripture you wanted to share with me?"

He seemed to snap out of whatever daze he was in. "The truth is, I can't get enough of your eyes."

She moved back a little so he wouldn't hear her heart beating against her chest or feel the heat from her face. It had surely turned bright red. Luke had noticed her eyes? They weren't anything special — not interesting half blue, half green like Lily's or clear sky blue like Rose's — just green, like the weeds that grew in every pasture in Bienenstock.

He smiled and fingered the scar on his lip. "And I was hoping to find some money." He turned pages until he found what he wanted on the same page as a twenty-dollar bill. He pointed to a verse. "Bitsy showed me this. Did you know we need to feed and clothe people to get into the kingdom of heaven? I used to think it was women's work. Now it's just the work of *Gotte.*"

She squinted as if to get a better look at him. "You *have* changed. Or are you Luke's secret twin brother who doesn't get out much?"

Luke chuckled. "Only if you think you might like my twin brother."

She smirked. "Maybe. Is he arrogant and stubborn?"

"*Jah.*"

Poppy tapped her finger to her lips. "I'll think about it."

A shadow passed across his face, and he leaned over and cupped her cheek in his hand. "*Ach,* Poppy. Do you know how much

I regret hurting you?"

She felt as wobbly and soft as a tower of Jell-O. "I don't know."

"Boys aren't better than girls, and girls aren't better than boys. *Gotte* loves us all."

Poppy took a shuddering breath, as if she'd spent the last hour crying, and pulled herself away from Luke's touch. "Tell that to my *dawdi* or Urius Beachy."

"Urius Beachy? The goat farmer?"

Poppy nodded. Urius Beachy lived outside of Bonduel with his wife and two daughters on a modest farm where he raised a herd of goats. An unpleasant odor always wafted from his place, and Poppy sort of felt sorry for his nearest neighbors. She also felt sorry for his daughters. If they ever heard a *gute* or loving word from their *dat,* Poppy would be surprised.

"What about Urius Beachy?" Luke said.

Poppy shrugged. "After my parents died, my sisters and I lived with Mammi and Dawdi Kiem before Aunt B took us. I was only seven and Urius was ten, but he worked for my *dawdi,* doing odd jobs around the yard, mucking out the barn, tormenting me. I tagged after Urius every morning and tried to help him with his chores. Every day he told me that *Gotte* loved boys better than girls and that I was nothing. I don't know why I kept coming back for more. I suppose I hated to be cooped up indoors. My *dawdi* scolded me for not acting like a girl and said I'd never get a husband if I insisted on being so stubborn."

"Maybe he's sorry for that now."

"I wanted his approval. I didn't realize I would never get it. One day I found some new wood and rebuilt the three toolshed stairs that had been squeaking and tilting for months. I used a handsaw and the hammer all by myself."

Luke widened his eyes. "You were seven."

"I know, but I wanted to impress my *dawdi* and prove to Urius that I was just as *gute* as any boy. I guess I hoped to win both Dawdi's approval and *Gotte*'s love." Her throat felt thick, as if she might choke.

Luke took hold of her hand as if to keep her from falling. "You always had *Gotte*'s love."

She cleared her throat. The memory was fourteen years old, but today it felt fresh. She'd never forget the look on Dawdi's face. "I was excited to show Dawdi what I had done. I took him by the hand and led him to the toolshed, even though he was none too happy about the interruption. Urius was sitting on my new steps when Dawdi and I got there. Urius lied to Dawdi and told him

309

that he had repaired the stairs. When I insisted that I had done it, Dawdi called me a liar. 'A girl could never do such a fine job,' he said. Urius stuck to his story and lied right to Dawdi's face. Dawdi dragged me up my new stairs to the toolshed and gave me a whipping, but I wouldn't budge. I kept insisting I had repaired the stairs, and Dawdi kept hitting me." She flinched at the memory of Dawdi striking her again and again with the stinging leather strap. She didn't realize she'd been squeezing Luke's hand until her fingers cramped up. Sheepishly, she pulled out of his grasp. "I never gave in. Dawdi still thinks I'm a liar, and Urius still knows the truth. After that, Dawdi didn't allow me outside and made certain that Mammi taught me everything I needed to know to be a *gute fraa.* He said I was wicked for wanting to use a hammer instead of a needle."

Luke frowned, his eyes lumps of cold, hard coal. "No one should hit a child. I hate to think he could have broken your spirit."

"I won't back down if I think I'm right. I told Dawdi I didn't care if I ever got a husband." She smiled weakly. "Actually, I yelled it at him, more than once."

He hooked his index finger around hers. "I hate it that you got hurt, but I love that

310

you don't back down."

Love that she didn't back down? She didn't know what to say when he teased her like that. "You didn't used to like that about me."

He winced. "What did I know? I was a *dumkoff* with no sense and no brains."

She propped her chin in her hand and gave him a teasing smile. "Was? Like you mean a week ago?"

"I've come a long way in a short time."

She felt her face get warm. Why did he have to look at her like that? "*Jah,* you have."

He stared at her for too long. Embarrassed, she curled her lips and averted her eyes.

He cleared his throat. "To prove my sincerity, I'd like to help you weed the garden."

"I won't be much help. I've only got one hand."

He winked at her. She stopped breathing. "Don't worry. If you think I'm a fast cherry picker, you should see the way I weed."

"Do you know the difference between a weed and a tomato plant?"

"I think so."

She shook her head. "Not good enough. I'll do it myself."

"I really want to help you weed."

"Why?"

He glanced at her and then back down at Aunt B's Bible. "I like being with you. You're not boring like all those other girls."

Like Dinah Eicher?

"Because you like being yelled at?" she said.

"I like the way your eyes sparkle when you're mad at me."

She narrowed her eyes. "I have a lot to be mad at you about."

"*Jah,* I deserve your irritation, but I shouldn't enjoy it so much."

Rose walked in the door and set her canvas bag on the table. Her expression was stormy, as if there were permanent cloud cover across her face.

"Rose," Poppy said, feeling like she'd been caught doing something she shouldn't have been doing. Did being mushy around Luke count? "How was the animal shelter?"

Rose sat on the window seat and picked up Farrah Fawcett, who had been lounging there since Luke had come in. She snuggled her cheek against Farrah Fawcett's snowy white fur, closed her eyes, and frowned. "Such a pretty kitty. I love you, pretty kitty," she said. Her voice cracked in about three places, and it sounded as if she were about to burst into tears.

Poppy furrowed her brow and glanced at Luke. He returned her gaze with a worried expression of his own. "Did everything go okay today at the animal shelter?" he said. "Did Dorothy and Joann have a *gute* time?"

Rose pressed her lips together and forced a smile. "They have a pretty black dog that Norma at the shelter says will probably be adopted soon. Joann and I cleaned out the cages while Dorothy played with the puppies."

"Is everything okay?" Poppy said, knowing full well it wasn't. Maybe Rose was still stewing about Queenie's tail.

Rose deposited Farrah Fawcett back on the window seat, went to the sink, and washed her hands. With Rose's back to both of them, Poppy couldn't see her face. "I've been thinking, Poppy. I should spend more time at home. Lily is getting married, and our family needs me more than they do at the animal shelter. I don't think I'll go back."

Poppy's chest tightened. That didn't sound like an explanation. It sounded like a carefully prepared speech. "But, Rose, you love the animal shelter."

"I should be with my family."

Even though she felt puzzled and a little

irritated that Rose wouldn't give her a straight answer, Poppy tried to speak with a mild tone of voice. Rose's feeling were so easily hurt. She took hold of one of Rose's shoulders and turned her around. "Look me in the eye and tell me why you're not going back to the animal shelter."

Rose met Poppy's eye briefly before she sighed and dropped her gaze to the floor. "I told you. With Lily getting married, we need each other more than ever."

Luke had the sense to keep his face expressionless and his tone light. "What about Dorothy and Joann?"

"They're not going back either."

"Why?" he said.

"They want to spend more time with the kittens."

Poppy pulled her sister in for a one-armed hug and pressed a kiss to her forehead. She wanted to fix whatever made Rose unhappy, but she had to know what it was first. "Rose, you know me too well to think I'll settle for that excuse."

Rose kept her eyes downturned, and her lips began to quiver.

Luke stood up straight and took two steps around the island as if Rose's distress had moved him toward her.

"Please don't cry, Rose," Poppy said,

squeezing her sister's shoulder tighter. "Tell me what's wrong, and we can solve it together. Me, you, and Luke." She glanced in Luke's direction and gave him a half smile. He nodded back, his eyes alight with gratitude and determination. Her heartbeat surged like waves crashing against the shore. She'd never seen a more captivating expression.

Rose nudged herself away from Poppy and drew her hands across her eyes, wiping away any hint of moisture. "I'm not crying. I promise. I'm too old for that nonsense yet."

Poppy nodded. "Okay. But you're still upset. Did something bad happen at the animal shelter?"

Rose ran her hand along the kitchen counter and plopped herself down at the table. Poppy pulled out a chair next to her. She looked at Luke, giving him permission to sit as well. He took a chair next to Poppy. Billy Idol, who had been lurking underfoot, immediately jumped into Luke's lap. Under the circumstances, Luke didn't even protest.

"I don't want you to get mad. Promise me you won't get mad," Rose said.

Poppy propped her elbow on the table. "I'm not going to make a promise I might break."

"I don't want you to get into a fight."

"With whom?" Poppy said. Luke was the only one she had fought with recently. Did Rose expect a fight between them?

"Please, Poppy," Rose said. "No fighting."

Poppy shook her head. "*Ach,* little sister, you know you're going to grow old waiting for that promise."

Rose's eyes got moist again. "That's why I'm not going to tell you."

Poppy leaned back in her chair and growled. She nearly jumped out of her skin when Luke took her hand underneath the table and squeezed it.

"If she promises to do her best, is that good enough?" Luke said.

"Will you keep Poppy from fighting?" Rose said.

Luke frowned. "I always try to." He released Poppy's hand, leaving her breathless and a little woozy.

Rose nodded and fidgeted with a strand of hair at the nape of her neck. "Griff Simons met us on the road today coming home from the bus stop."

"Griff Simons?" Poppy said.

"And he's older and bigger and meaner."

She felt Luke tense beside her. "You, Dorothy, and Joann?"

Rose nodded. "We saw him come out of his garage and walked past as fast as we could. We should have run, but we didn't want him to think we were running away from him. He would have liked that. He called to us and asked Dorothy and Joann about the kittens and laughed when Dorothy scolded him for trying to drown them. He put himself directly in our path and told us we couldn't pass until I gave him a kiss. I grabbed Dorothy's hand and the three of us ran away as fast as we could."

Luke's calm demeanor grew into something more intense. He leaned forward, his eyes flashing with anger. "Did he touch you or hurt you in any way?"

Rose shook her head.

"What about my sisters?"

"He didn't touch us. He laughed when we ran away."

"I'm sorry he's back," Luke said. "His father never stirs up trouble."

Poppy reached out and took Rose's hand, as if the simple touch would keep her sister safe. "Why would anyone take pleasure in scaring three Amish girls?"

Rose sniffed back a tear. "So now you understand why we're not going back."

Fire pulsed through Poppy's veins. "So we have to huddle in our house because we're afraid of Griff Simons? It's not just the animal shelter. We walk down that road all the time. Are we confined to the farm because we don't dare pass Griff's place? It's not right."

"I wish I could take the buggy," Rose said. "That would solve all our problems."

Poppy sighed. "Until Griff started throwing rocks at Queenie. She'd take off and you'd get upended for sure and certain. Besides, Shawano is too far for a buggy. It's got to be the bus."

"Or not at all," Rose said. "I've chosen not at all."

Poppy pursed her lips. Not if she had anything to say about it. "It's not fair. You love the animal shelter."

"But I'd rather be safe than frightened out of my wits every Wednesday."

"Same goes for my sisters," Luke said. "They won't be going back."

Poppy glared at Luke. "We can't let Griff bully us like this."

Luke shrugged. "I won't allow my sisters to put themselves in any kind of danger, and it's not our way to involve the police. They wouldn't be able to do anything anyway."

Poppy's chair scraped loudly against the floor as she stood up. "I'm going over there. Griff Simons is going to hear just what I have to say about it."

"*Nae,* Poppy," Rose said, the panic rising in her voice. "This is why I didn't want to tell you. You promised not to get in a fight."

Poppy shook her head. "I never even promised I wouldn't get mad."

Luke grabbed her wrist and tugged her to sit. She didn't want him to yank her other shoulder out of its socket, so she sat down. Reluctantly. "This is foolish, Poppy, and you know it. You're not going to convince Griff of anything and you're very likely to get hurt."

She lifted her chin and stared Luke down, all two hundred plus pounds of him. "Someone has to stand up to him or this will never stop. I refuse to be intimidated by a teenager who thinks he owns the road."

Luke furrowed his brow. "I don't want to argue with you."

"There's nothing to argue about. I'm going over there."

He gave a low, frustrated growl. "I forbid it, Poppy. It's for your own good."

Poppy frowned. Just when she was starting to like him . . . "You forbid it? You're not my *fater.* Or my boss."

Rose placed a hand over Poppy's. "He's right, Poppy. You could get hurt, or you could make it worse. Griff would do something just because you told him not to."

Luke gave Poppy a stiff nod. "Listen to your sister. She knows what she's talking about."

Poppy folded her arms. She wouldn't let Rose and Luke talk her out of doing what was right.

Luke reached over and took her hand in plain sight of Rose, Billy Idol, and Farrah Fawcett. A warm sensation traveled all the way up her arm. She didn't want to, but she softened like butter on a hot day. "It was wrong of me to forbid you from doing anything," Luke said. "You are smart enough to make your own choices, but please don't go over there. Rose and I would both be sick if something happened to you."

Luke had never shown her the puppy dog eyes before. The puppy dog eyes were nearly irresistible. It was too bad he tried to persuade her instead of argue with her. She could dig in her heels when they argued. She had no defense against persuasion.

"And I'd be really mad at you," he said under his breath.

Poppy groaned. "There has to be something we can do. If Rose and your sisters stay away from the animal shelter, then Griff has succeeded and we've given him power over our lives."

Luke gave Poppy's hand a squeeze before

letting go. "Rose, can you go to the animal shelter anytime you want?"

"I suppose so."

"Every morning at six forty-five sharp, Griff's truck rumbles out of his garage and down the road, and he doesn't come back until three or four. I know because that truck of his is so loud, I can hear it in my workshop with the door closed. What if you and Dorothy and Joann went to the shelter earlier in the day and returned before Griff comes back? That works with the bus schedule, doesn't it?"

Poppy gave him a mock sneer. "*Ach,* I hate that I didn't come up with that idea myself."

Rose's eyes darted from Poppy to Luke and back again. "I suppose that might work. We could avoid Griff altogether."

Luke nodded. "For sure and certain. And Poppy won't have to take another trip to the hospital."

"I would have been fine," Poppy said, glad she wouldn't have to find out. She might be brave enough to fight a grizzly bear, but it was always better if she didn't have to.

Aunt B burst in the door. Her eyes went wide as she caught her breath and clutched her chest. "What is that creature on my table?"

Poppy giggled and ran her hand along the

strands of the fake horsetail hair. It looked like a long, hairy, lifeless cat. "It's a new tail for Queenie to help her keep the flies off. Luke brought it over."

Bitsy eyed the tail suspiciously before nearing the table and running her black-polished fingernails across it. "It's long."

"And pretty, ain't not?" Poppy said.

Aunt B lifted her eyebrows and widened her eyes. "I've just had an epiphany." She practically raced to the glue drawer and pulled out her trusty notebook and a pen.

"What's an epiphany, Aunt Bitsy?" Rose said. "Do you need a doctor?"

Aunt B stood at the island and furiously scribbled notes into her book. "*Nae.* I'm right as rain. What if my vampire falls in love with Rapunzel? Instead of climbing up her hair, he could jump into her tower and jump out with her in his arms. Vampires are very strong, you know."

As usual when B worked on her book, Poppy had no idea what she was talking about. She seemed excited about it, though, and that was all that really mattered.

"I thought you said vampires were skinny," Luke said. "How can he be strong without any meat on his bones?"

Aunt B paused long enough to look up and frown at him. "Never give a writer advice, Luke Bontrager. It's unwelcome, and it inhibits the creative flow."

Luke blew out the air between his lips. Poppy giggled. When it came to Aunt B, Luke should probably keep his mouth shut.

CHAPTER NINETEEN

It was too late to still be up, but Luke had spent a lot of time at Poppy's house this week, and he still had an order of chairs that needed to be stained by morning. The propane lantern hissed as he touched up the last chair.

The fatigue had been worth every minute of sacrifice. He smiled to himself. Poppy was coming around.

He was pretty sure she didn't hate him anymore, and he was pretty sure he loved Poppy better than his own heart. Well, not pretty sure.

Sure and certain.

He'd marry her tomorrow if she'd have him.

Luke's frown felt as if it cut a deep trench in his face. She didn't hate him, but could he convince her to say yes? He'd made a lot of mistakes with Poppy. Maybe too many to make good on.

Then again, he'd been allowed to help with the bees today. The beehives were the most prized possessions on the Honeybee Farm. It gave him some hope that Poppy trusted him enough to let him work the hives.

He scratched the small bump on his wrist that Poppy had insisted on spreading toothpaste over. He'd gotten stung three times today, which according to Poppy was a very bad thing, not only because it hurt but because the bees died after they stung him. Bitsy was downright hostile about his bee stings and scolded him for killing her bees. He didn't get an ounce of sympathy from her.

He had worn an old sweatshirt that zipped up the front, gloves, and a beekeeper's veil, which was a hard, wide-brimmed hat with netting draped over the top of it. Poppy had worn a sweatshirt and jeans with her pants legs stuffed into her long stockings.

Even though it was very un-Amish, Luke quite liked Poppy's beekeeping outfit. It didn't really matter what Poppy wore — she was still the prettiest girl he'd ever laid eyes on. The bishop approved of the outfit for beekeeping, but Paul Glick still threatened to have the whole family shunned for wearing pants.

Luke scowled. Paul Glick had given Poppy and her sisters nothing but trouble. Still, he couldn't be too irritated with Paul Glick. His and Poppy's mutual dislike for Paul had given them something in common — at least a place to start their relationship. He had to give Paul the credit for that. Poppy's righteous indignation over Paul was one of the first things Luke had liked about her.

After being closely connected to Poppy for several days, Luke had decided that she was not so much stubborn as she was fiercely loyal to her aunt and sisters. She couldn't be talked out of anything if she thought she could save her family from pain or injustice.

Would Poppy ever include him within that circle of loyalty? His heart skipped a few beats. Maybe she already had. She had scolded Billy Idol on Luke's behalf today when Billy Idol tried to scale Luke's trousers. It wasn't much, but it was something.

At least Poppy had agreed to stay away from Griff Simons. No matter how badly he had scared Rose, Poppy could see the wisdom in keeping away from him. Lord willing, Griff would go off to college or join the military and only plague their neighborhood for a few more weeks. If not, Luke didn't know what they'd do.

He'd pray for college.

Someone tapped on his workshop door. He opened it, and Poppy seemed to catapult into the workshop as if she'd been fired from a cannon. She wore her royal-blue dress and her hair tied up in a scarf. Her feet were bare. She must have been in a hurry. Hair poked out in every direction from the unruly braid that sat half in, half out of her scarf. Her green eyes looked almost wild, and he could practically hear her heart pounding.

He took her by the shoulders and led her to a stool. "Poppy? Is everything okay?"

She wouldn't sit. "I almost caught them."

Luke's stomach dropped. He knew exactly whom she'd almost caught. Couldn't Poppy use even a grain of caution? "Who?"

"The two boys who have been tipping our beehives and pulling our clothes off the line."

"Poppy, you've got to be careful."

She didn't even listen. "I was lying in bed and thought I heard something, so I threw on my clothes and tiptoed outside with a flashlight. The two of them were spray-painting our barn door again."

He was going to die of a heart attack. "You didn't try to stop them, did you?"

She seemed more excited than frightened.

"I got real close and shined my flashlight in their faces. One of them cried out, and they dropped their spray-paint cans and ran away. I chased them behind the barn, but I didn't have shoes and it was too dark to see anything." She was panting for air by the time she finished her story.

Luke scrubbed his fingers through his hair as the familiar anxiety and desperation and irritation warred with each other in his chest. Did love always feel this rotten? "Poppy, they could have ambushed you in the dark." He shuddered at the possibility. She'd be the death of him.

She gazed at him with wide, innocent eyes, as if that were the strangest notion in the world. "They wouldn't have done that. They were too scared to do anything but run."

"You shouldn't have even left your house." An icy hand wrapped itself around his throat. "Poppy, you put yourself in terrible danger."

Poppy finally caught her breath. "I did not." She bloomed into a devious smile. "I got a good look at one of their faces."

"Who was it?"

"I don't know, but it wasn't Paul Glick and it wasn't Griff Simons." She smiled even wider. "And it wasn't one of the boys I punched in school. Isn't that good news?"

"Only like chicken pox is better news than measles." She wasn't wearing her sling, so he gently wrapped his fingers around her forearms and nudged her to sit on the stool. "You must promise me that you will never do that again."

She acted as if he'd insulted her. "Of course I won't promise. I got a *gute* look at one of them. It's only a matter of time before we catch them and make them stop pestering us forever."

He covered his eyes with one hand. "But not you. Promise me you won't be the one to catch them."

"I *will* be the one to catch them. You can be sure of that."

He wanted to shake some sense into her. Instead, he sat down on an unfinished dining room table and gazed at her in resignation. "So, did you come over to make sure I wouldn't get a wink of sleep tonight?"

"I need your help. They painted *Get Out* on the orange barn door, and it's got to be painted over before Rose wakes up in the morning. Griff Simons scared her so bad on Wednesday, and I don't think she could bear another fright like that."

Luke rubbed the whiskers on his chin. "If Rose's anxiety is anywhere near as high as mine, she's in a bad way."

"You and Dan and Josiah painted the barn the last time they spray-painted it. I was hoping you could help me again."

Luke could be smart when he wanted to. "All right. I will help you paint it on one condition."

She narrowed her eyes. "What condition?"

"You must promise me that you won't try to catch those boys. If you hear them outside the house, you'll stay inside where it's safe. Maybe the bishop will approve a cell phone, and you can call the police."

Her mouth fell open. "I've already told you. I won't make you any such promise. I'm going to catch them."

He had to stand firm for her own good. "Then I won't help you with the painting." He had her between a rock and a hard place, but she'd come around. She would do anything for Rose.

"Fine," she said, standing up and marching to the door. "I'll paint it myself."

"You don't have any paint."

"Walmart is open twenty-four hours. I'll hike to the phone shack and call a taxi."

Frustration rumbled in Luke's chest like an underground volcano. It wasn't an idle threat. Poppy wouldn't think twice about walking to the phone shack in the middle of the night. She would have tried even Job's patience. He got to his feet. "Okay. Okay. I'll get my paint and brushes and come over."

It irritated him that her smile seemed to make everything all better. "*Denki,* Luke. I will meet you out there in a few minutes."

He held up his hand. "I'll only do it if you go back into your house and go to bed."

"But you need help."

"Dan and Josiah will be more than happy to help me again. Dan would move mountains for Lily, and Josiah would swim oceans for Rose. They won't be hard to convince."

"I still want to help," Poppy said, squaring her shoulders as if she were gearing up for a fight.

He sighed and gave Poppy a defeated look. "Do it for me because I'm such a nice person to paint the barn for you, and I would feel so much better knowing you're safe inside, tucked into your comfy bed instead of running around the countryside chasing beehive tippers."

"I'll be perfectly safe if I stay close to you, Dan, and Josiah."

He gave her the stink eye. "You won't be safe because I will be tempted to throttle you."

She grinned. He must not have been very

intimidating. "You're the one who's not safe. I've half a mind to throttle you."

"As long as you stay in the house."

"You're no fun, Luke Bontrager."

"And you're going to give me an ulcer."

CHAPTER TWENTY

July was not a *gute* month to be a beekeeper. Some of Poppy's hair had escaped from the scarf around her head and stuck to the back of her neck. Sweat trickled down her back and she longed to scratch it, but there was little she could do about it except work faster. To protect herself from the bees, she wore the traditional veil, a long-sleeved zip-up sweatshirt, jeans, canvas gloves, and long socks. She felt as if she were swimming in a pot of boiling water.

Aunt B had given her permission to go without the sling this morning. She'd worn it three days longer than the doctor had recommended because Aunt B wanted to be sure it was healed. It felt wonderful-*gute* to have two hands again. She'd volunteered to check the hives. They wouldn't pull honey again for almost two months, but they inspected the hives every few weeks just to make sure they were healthy and the queen was still laying. Nobody liked the job in the middle of July.

Poppy used her hive tool to pry another frame from the super. Bees covered practically the entire brood chamber, but she could see uncapped chambers with larvae inside. The queen had been busy, and the mite population looked low. She inserted the frame back into the super, being careful not to smash several bees in the process. She always smashed a few. There were just too many not to kill some.

Rose handled the hives better than any of them. Maybe she was more patient. Aunt B said it was because Rose had a way with animals of all sizes. She loved them, and they responded to her.

Except for Billy Idol. The only person Billy Idol didn't despise was Luke Bontrager. But how that had happened, Poppy would never be able to understand. Poppy couldn't help but smile when she thought of Luke's dislike for cats and Billy Idol's insistence that Luke be his best friend. Last night, Billy Idol had sharpened his claws on the table leg and then climbed into Luke's lap while he ate ice cream. Billy Idol hissed and snarled at Luke the same as the rest of the family, but he didn't stray far from Luke's side, and whenever Luke sat, Billy

Idol tracked him down.

They'd made honey-cinnamon ice cream again last night because it was Luke's favorite. He inhaled two bowls of it. He would have eaten a third bowl if there had been any left to eat. That boy was a bottomless pit.

Okay, she admitted it. She loved that Luke enjoyed her ice cream. Aunt B would caution her against feeding Luke ever again. Paul Glick would admonish her for her vanity. But for sure and certain, Luke would be allowed to eat at her table anytime he wanted.

Luke had eaten dinner at their house last night, and Aunt B hadn't made one complaint about him in her prayer, but only because Luke, Dan, and Josiah had been kind enough to paint their barn door on Friday night. Sort of. Poppy seriously questioned their color-matching skills. The first time they had painted the Honeybee Sisters' barn door, it had turned out a muted shade of pumpkin orange. This time the door was reddish pink, much the same color as Paul Glick's face when he got angry.

When the door had turned out orange, Aunt B suggested to Rose that maybe the paint had faded in the sun. Rose wouldn't have believed that excuse twice. So Dan told her he had painted the door in the middle of the night to surprise them, which was technically true. The color had definitely surprised them.

Poppy felt a little twinge of guilt for not telling Rose the truth. Poppy would have wanted the truth with no sugar coating. But was it bad to protect her sister from something sure to make her nightmares more vivid?

Poppy tended the hives that were close to the road in front of their farm. The mischief maker had tipped over one of the clover field hives in May and the one closest to the road nearly a month ago. She glanced past the two rows of trees that lined their property. She hadn't seen any suspicious cars down the road lately. But she was wary all the same. Had they driven a car last weekend when they spray-painted the barn? If they had, where had they parked it? Next time she should sneak into their car while they were sneaking onto her property and pull out some important engine part so they wouldn't be able to escape.

She'd catch the troublemakers and irritate Luke at the same time. What could be better than that?

Above the thick hum of the hives, Poppy heard what sounded like a high-pitched whine coming from the direction of the dirt road. She seemed to remember that the spray-painter's car had squeaky brakes.

She quickly stacked the honey supers back on top of the brood box and laid both her hive tool and smoker on the ground next to the hive. She clumsily took off her gloves and veil as she jogged toward their little bridge. Craning her neck to get a better view around the bend, she stuffed her gloves inside the veil, took off her sweat jacket, and laid them all on the bridge to retrieve later. She'd kick herself into next Sunday if she missed those boys again.

Once she stepped off the bridge and onto the dirt road, she paused long enough to listen for the car. She heard it, down the road to her right.

But it wasn't a car. Someone was crying for help.

Her heart flipped over like a pancake. Rose and Luke's little sisters were due home from the animal shelter soon. Were they in trouble? Was it Griff again? He was supposed to be at work. The three of them had left earlier this morning to avoid Griff altogether.

Poppy bolted in the direction of that sound. With her beekeeping jeans on, she could run much faster than when she wore a dress. When she turned the bend, her heart stopped and she couldn't get any air into her lungs. Right in the middle of the dirt road, Rose, Dorothy, and Joann were in some sort of struggle with a thick-necked boy a good head taller than Rose. He looked to weigh at least twice as much.

It took Poppy a moment to recognize Griff Simons. Rose had been right. He was a lot bigger than he used to be.

Griff had his burly arm wrapped around Rose's waist, and it looked as if he was trying to give her a kiss. Rose pushed against him with one hand while Joann screamed at the top of her lungs and tugged Rose's other arm in an attempt to pull her from Griff's grasp. Dorothy, who at thirteen years old couldn't have been more than four feet ten inches tall, pounded her fists on Griff's back while tears streamed down her face.

Poppy felt the anger burn in her throat. With nearly irrational rage and little forethought, she ran toward Rose. Plunging herself between Griff and her sister, she shoved Griff away with all her might. Griff didn't expect Poppy's attack, and she knocked him off balance just enough that he released his hold on Rose and stumbled a few steps backward. He didn't go far. Poppy had never shoved herself against someone so solid — except maybe Luke Bontrager.

Surprise popped like a pimple on Griff's face before he smiled a smug, hateful smile that stretched across his crooked teeth. Aunt B would have slapped braces on that boy before he could say another word. Griff didn't seem the least bit concerned or cowered by Poppy. "Go away, Poppy," he growled, showing those very bad teeth.

"How dare you pick on three helpless Amish girls!"

Griff looked her up and down. He'd probably never seen her in jeans and a T-shirt before. "You leaving the Amish?"

"Leave my sister alone."

"Poppy, it's okay," Rose said, taking Poppy's elbow and whimpering softly right against her ear. Rose had never told such a big lie.

Dorothy and Joann had pulled back and stood a few feet away, holding on tight to each other. Joann's *kapp* lay in the dirt, and her hair fell over her shoulders in unruly tufts. Dorothy's sleeve was torn at the seam and two trails of tears made their way down her face.

Poppy extended her arm and gently nudged Rose farther behind her. "Rose, take Dorothy and Joann and get home."

Rose took a step back and took Poppy's elbow with her. "Come with us, Poppy. Let's just go."

Poppy hesitated and glanced at her sister. Much as she would have liked to teach Griff Simons a lesson, he'd grown a lot bigger since the last time she'd given him a black eye. Judging by the condition of his teeth, he probably ate nails for breakfast and washed them down with a swig of kerosene. No matter how furious she was that he had scared sweet, guileless Rose and Luke's little sisters, it was best to get the girls safely away. Whatever she did might put the girls in more danger than they already were. Maybe she'd pay him a visit later when Rose and Luke's sisters were safely at home.

Keeping her eyes trained on Griff, she took two steps back and hooked arms with Rose. "Okay, come on."

Rose let out a shuddering breath. *"Denki."*

Griff scowled. "Don't look at me like that, like I'm nothing. You Amish girls are so stuck up."

"Just stay away from us," Poppy said. "Or you'll answer to me."

When she turned away from him, he shot out his hand and yanked Poppy hard by the wrist. She winced as the pain traveled all the way to her shoulder, her good shoulder.

340

Without thinking, she made a fist with her free hand — no longer hampered by a sling — whipped around, and brought it up hard against Griff's fleshy lips.

The impact moved from her hand up her arm like sharp lightning and made her dizzy with pain. She cried out involuntarily as the old injuries seemed to flare to life.

Griff released her arm, touched his fingers to his lips, and uttered several curse words. With something primal and brutal flashing in his eyes, he raised his hand and slapped Poppy hard upside the head before she could even think about moving out of the way.

Agony seared through her cheek as her head snapped back and stars danced at the back of her eyes. She tasted the salty blood in her mouth, and in her dazed condition the idea that she might lose a tooth floated in and out of her brain. Oh, *sis yuscht*! Please let her keep all her teeth.

She'd been slapped twice in two weeks. Jesus said to turn the other cheek. Was *Gotte* trying to tell her something?

She felt a tug at her elbow and realized Rose was pulling her away from Griff with a force and speed she hadn't thought Rose capable of. Joann grabbed her hand on the other side, and the two of them pulled

Poppy down the road with Dorothy leading the way.

They walked as fast as Poppy could manage, though Griff didn't follow them. Maybe she'd scared him off. If her face hadn't felt like it would crack into a million pieces, she might have grimaced. She wasn't so vain as to think she'd intimidated Griff Simons, no matter how tough she thought herself.

More likely, Griff was too lazy or too out of shape to chase after them.

Or, maybe, just maybe, his lips ached a little, and he wanted to put some ice on them before they swelled up like a pair of bloated fish in a chum bucket.

They probably wouldn't swell that big.

But she could always hope.

"Keep going, Poppy," Rose said. "We've got to get you home."

"Are you all right?" she said, wincing at the pain that traveled up her face when she moved her lips. "Did he hurt you?"

"Luke said Griff wouldn't be home," Dorothy sobbed.

"He tore my *kapp* off," Joann said. "And he tried to kiss Rose, but he didn't hit us or anything."

Rose nudged Poppy forward. "We're okay, Poppy, but we need to get home. Aunt Bitsy will know what to do."

Poppy's shoulder ached and her hand was on fire, and she couldn't even blink without making her face hurt, but Rose and Luke's sisters hadn't been injured. That was all that mattered.

An invisible hand squeezed her lungs until she couldn't breathe. Except for Luke. He mattered very much.

And he would be furious.

He'd yell at her until she went deaf.

CHAPTER TWENTY-ONE

The gas generator that powered Luke's air compressor and other tools hummed loudly outside the workshop window. It was a comforting sound, a sound that said Luke had furniture orders and work and a livelihood. He was glad for all three.

If he asked Poppy to marry him, he would be able to assure Bitsy that he could provide for a wife and family. He could even build them a house with his own two hands. He had a lot to offer a girl if she didn't mind being married to a grumpy, stubborn man who often opened his mouth without using his brain first.

Ach! A girl like Poppy could have any boy in the community. Why would she ever pick someone like Luke Bontrager?

Dinah Eicher might still be available.

His heart felt like a stone in his chest. Now that he knew Poppy, he could never bring himself to settle for Dinah Eicher.

The door to the wood shop swung open and slammed against the wall behind it. Startled, Luke jumped to his feet and almost smacked his head against the shelf above him. Joann, with no *kapp* and hair running wild around her head, shot into the room and threw herself into Luke's arms. "Oh, *mein bruder,*" she said, before disintegrating into sobs.

Luke tightened his arms around his hysterical sister as blood raced through his veins. "What happened? Are you injured? Was there a buggy accident? Where's Dat?"

"Griff Simons attacked us."

Luke lost the ability to breathe. "Attacked you? Where is Dorothy?" When Joann didn't answer immediately, he grabbed her shoulders and nudged her away from him. "Joann, look at me. What happened? Is anybody hurt?"

"We were coming home from the animal shelter, and he tried to kiss Rose Christner," Joann said, barely able to get the words out between sobs. "Poppy shoved him away, and he hit her. Hard. He was supposed to be at work."

Luke flinched. "He hit Poppy?"

"There's a big purple mark on her cheek, and Bitsy thinks she broke her hand." Joann took in great gulps of air as her body shook violently. "She saved us."

Luke pulled Joann close again. No doubt his heart pounded as violently as hers. "Where is she now? And what about Dorothy? Is Dorothy okay? And Rose?"

"We didn't know what to do, so we ran to Bitsy's house because Rose said she has a shotgun. Dorothy pounded on his back when he wouldn't let Rose go. Her sleeve tore, and she has a scratch on her leg and she can't stop crying. Rose's arm got scraped, and she's crying too, but not as bad as Dorothy. Poppy's cheek is swollen something wonderful."

Luke took a few deep breaths to calm his raw anger. It didn't help. A boy who would strike a girl would surely answer to *Gotte.* "You said she broke her hand."

"She wasn't even afraid. She only wanted to help us get away from him. He grabbed her, and then she punched him." Joann shuddered. "He hit her back. But then we ran away."

Rage and shock clamped around his throat like a noose, and Luke thought he might be sick. "Mamm and Dat went into town."

Joann sniffled into his shirt. "I know."

He smoothed his hand down her hair. "Can you run out to the cornfields and tell Matthew and Mark what happened? Tell them I've gone to the Christners'."

The sobbing started up all over again. "I can't go out there alone."

He pressed his lips against her forehead. "You made it all the way from the Christners' house by yourself."

"The cat came with me."

"The cat?"

Joann pointed to the open door. Billy Idol stood guard at the threshold looking as fierce and dangerous as a robber cloaked in black.

That stupid, *wunderbarr* cat.

"Take the cat with you to the fields. He'll protect you." He cupped her chin in his hand. "He got you this far, didn't he?"

A faint smile played at Joann's lips.

"And stay with Matthew and Mark until Mamm and Dat get home. Okay?"

She nodded.

Luke grabbed his hat from the hook and shoved it onto his head. He scooped Billy Idol from the floor and handed him to Joann, who cradled him in her arms like she would a nice, fluffy kitty. Luke narrowed his eyes and got face-to-face with the ugly cat. "Billy Idol, take care of my sister. If anyone frightens her, you have my permission to scratch."

Billy Idol hissed and bared his teeth, but

347

Luke figured it was only to prove to Joann what a good protector he was. Joann took a shaky breath and squared her shoulders. "I'll go find Matthew. We'll be okay till you come home."

"Okay. *Gute* girl."

He watched Joann until she disappeared behind the house with Billy Idol clutched tightly in her arms. If Luke didn't hate that cat so much, he'd give it a hug.

The anxiety and anger nearly suffocated him. Joann was scared to be by herself, Dorothy was certainly traumatized, and Poppy had been assaulted. The girl he loved had been assaulted. And he hadn't been there.

The despair crumpled him like a thin piece of tissue paper. First his *mamm* and now Poppy. How could he ever hope to win her love? He couldn't even protect her when she needed him the most.

CHAPTER TWENTY-TWO

Poppy could barely remember changing back into her dress. She could barely remember Aunt B helping her tie a scarf around her head. But here she sat in the kitchen in her dress and a head covering, obviously dazed beyond what she thought she was.

Her face hurt something wonderful, but it was nothing compared to the dread that filled her chest at the thought of what Luke's anger would be like. Joann had gone to fetch her brother, and any minute now he would crash through that door and yell at her for putting his sisters in danger. She was already poised to burst into tears. She didn't think she'd be able to hold it back once Luke got here.

Maybe she could go hide in her room.

Poppy pushed aside that cowardly thought. She had always stood up to Luke

Bontrager before, no matter how angry he was.

Sometimes it was very inconvenient to be so contrary.

Poppy sat at the table with the hand that wasn't broken wrapped around Rose's wrist. Rose clutched a tissue in one hand and stroked Dorothy's arm with the other. Dorothy sat next to Rose, sniffling softly, but she seemed calmer than when they had first come into the house. The sight of Aunt B's shotgun had eased her mind considerably.

Aunt B knelt on the floor next to Dorothy's chair. "*Gute* as new," she said as she peeled the paper backing off an extra-large Band-Aid and placed it over the scratch on Dorothy's leg.

"*Denki,*" Dorothy said. "I'm just a big *buplie.* It's a little scratch compared to Poppy's face."

Poppy tried to give Dorothy a reassuring smile. It didn't come out well. Her face hurt too much.

"You're not a baby, and we don't want it to get infected," Aunt B said. "How is your scrape, Rose? Do you need a Band-Aid?"

"I'm okay. There isn't any blood."

Aunt B put the Band-Aid box back in the drawer. "There doesn't have to be blood. Look at Poppy. She's not bleeding anywhere, and she looks terrible."

"*Denki,* Aunt B," Poppy said, smirking with half her face.

"It's temporary, little sister. Imagine having a face like Paul Glick's, that never got better."

"Aunt Bitsy," Rose scolded. "That's not nice to say. Lily used to be very happy with Paul Glick's face."

Aunt B looked toward the ceiling. "*Denki,* dear Lord, that Lily has seen the light. But what would You have us do about the Simons boy? Do you have time to give him a yeast infection?"

"Aunt Bitsy!" Rose said.

Rose never ceased to amaze Poppy. Griff Simons had given her quite a fright, and she was still willing to forgive him. Poppy would have liked another crack at his face.

Dorothy sniffed one last time for good measure. "Do you think Joann made it home okay?"

"Of course she did," Rose said. "Luke will be over in two shakes of a lamb's tail."

Poppy couldn't even swallow. She and Luke had been getting along so well, but she'd never speak to him again if he yelled at her.

When he yelled at her.

She nearly sobbed out loud.

Aunt B came back to the table and took Poppy's chin in her hand. "We should probably put some ice on that bruise. And your hand."

"Okay," Poppy said. Maybe ice would numb her to the pain. All the pain.

"When Luke comes to get Dorothy, we'll ask him if he can go to the phone shack and call a driver," Aunt B said, laying her hand softly against Poppy's cheek. "I hate to tell you this since you took off the sling only this morning, but I think you're going to be in a cast at Lily's wedding."

"I know," Poppy said, whispering past the lump in her throat. She really should go upstairs. Her throbbing cheek and Griff's horrible smile and the thought of what might have happened and what would happen once Luke came battered her fragile self-control. The tears were mere seconds away.

Dorothy squeaked when someone knocked on the door. Poppy stiffened her spine and held her breath. She refused to indulge in the tears now. Luke would see nothing but obstinance.

Aunt Bitsy picked up her shotgun, opened the door, and trained it at Luke's chest. He didn't even flinch. Poppy's stomach plummeted to the floor. Luke looked as angry and riled as a mother bear. He was definitely going to yell.

"I'm glad you have a shotgun," he said.

Bitsy nodded. "Only for emergencies. I don't believe in guns." She propped her gun against the wall next to the door. "I'm not usually happy to see you, Luke Bontrager, but Dorothy needs her big *bruder.*"

He quickly glanced around the room, letting his eyes linger on Poppy's face for a split second. "Is everybody okay?"

Dorothy jumped from her chair and ran into Luke's arms.

Luke's eyes got a little watery, and he cleared his throat three times. "Are you okay? Did he hurt you?" he said, lifting Dorothy off her feet and squeezing the air out of her.

She relaxed her grip around his neck, and he set her back on her feet. "I ripped my sleeve and fell down when he shoved me, but he didn't shove very hard."

"Joann says you hit him."

Her voice trembled, and Poppy thought Dorothy might start crying again. Heaven knew she had every reason to. "I'm sorry, Luke. I know I should have run away, but he hurt Rose. I had to help her, even though we shouldn't use violence."

Nonviolence. One of the eighteen articles

of the Confession of Faith — the one Poppy had always struggled with — especially when someone harmed the people she loved.

Luke tucked an errant lock of hair behind Dorothy's ear and attempted a smile even though Poppy could see the muscles of his jaw tense with anger. "You're a *gute,* brave girl for not running away. *Gotte* would not have wanted something bad to happen to Rose." A dark shadow passed across his already dark expression, and he gathered his sister into his arms again. At least he wasn't mad at Dorothy. She desperately needed his comfort, not his censure.

"I hit him as hard as I could in the back," Dorothy said. "But he didn't even notice."

"Oh, he noticed, all right," Luke said. "For sure and certain he'll have some big bruises tomorrow."

"I'll pray extra hard for it," Aunt B said.

Dorothy glanced at Aunt B. "You don't think hitting him was a sin?"

Aunt B shook her head. "I would have taken a chunk out of his arm with my teeth."

Dorothy bloomed into a smile. "I had to help Rose. I just had to."

Aunt B nodded. "You did a *gute* thing, Dorothy. I'll be grateful forever that you watched out for my girl."

Luke gave Aunt B a soft look and cleared his throat again. Poppy's muscles went taut as his gaze traveled in her direction. She turned her face from him and stared at the sofa. Lord willing, he wouldn't even notice the bruise.

What a silly notion. Of course he'd notice. It was why he had come.

His eyes flashed with unmistakable outrage as he came to her and knelt next to her chair. With more tenderness than she would have expected from someone so angry, he gently took his finger and nudged her chin so she would look at him. She winced as the heat of his touch traveled all the way up her jawline. "*Ach,* Poppy. You should put some ice on that."

"I don't need ice," she said.

His frown cut deeper into his face. "I don't blame you for being mad at me. You put yourself in danger for my sisters again, and I wasn't there."

Poppy lifted her chin to keep it from trembling. "Go ahead and yell at me." Might as well get it over with. Like as not, the anticipation would be worse than the actual yelling.

He furrowed his brow. "Yell at you? Poppy, I am not going to yell at you."

She wasn't sure what that meant. The

silent treatment? *Gute.* She never wanted to talk to him again.

"Oh, no," Dorothy cried out as she looked out the window. Whimpering, she ducked down on the window seat as if she were hiding. "He's coming. He's riding up the lane on a motorcycle."

Aunt B rushed to the window to have a look. "And his *dat.*"

Luke frowned. "Who is it?"

"Griff Simons," Dorothy said.

Luke shot to his feet. Poppy held her breath and tightened her grip around Rose's wrist. Aunt B grabbed her gun.

"Bitsy, don't," Luke said. "He could take it right out of your hand."

She scowled at him. "It's for show. I don't believe in guns, remember?"

Luke wrapped his hands around Dorothy's shoulders and pulled her away from the window. "Poppy," he said, his eyes flashing with fury, "can you take Dorothy and Rose upstairs?"

They all jumped at the three loud, unapologetic raps at the door. Poppy and Rose stood up, and Poppy gathered Dorothy into her embrace.

Luke snapped his head around. "Poppy, take them upstairs."

Poppy wasn't about to run away and let

356

Luke and Aunt B fend for themselves. "Rose, take Dorothy upstairs."

Rose eyed her doubtfully, too frightened to argue. Dorothy's safety was the most important thing to all of them.

Poppy gave Rose's hand a squeeze. "Everything is going to be okay."

Rose nodded and shepherded the terrified Dorothy out of the room.

Luke's glare could have set the house on fire. "Poppy, you go too."

Aunt B slowly opened the door and pointed the gun at the scowling middle-aged man standing there. Griff Simons stood behind him, and they both took up a lot of space on the porch. While Luke's glare merely annoyed Poppy, Griff's father was positively terrifying. Poppy momentarily thought twice about staying downstairs.

Griff's *dat* wore a leather vest and leather gloves that covered his knuckles but not his fingers. Aunt B's tattoo fetish paled in comparison to the tattoos covering Griff's *dat*'s arms. There was more blue ink than skin. His head was shaved bald, and he had two or three days' worth of scruff on his face.

Poppy took a deep breath to calm her racing heart. Not all people with tattoos were criminals or murderers. Surely Griff's *dat*

357

wasn't as mean as he looked. Of course Aunt B's tattoos were always nice, fluffy, lovable temporary tattoos of kitties and butterflies and daisies. Skulls and spiders were a little more intimidating.

Griff's father squinted in the bright sunlight and scowled at the gun as if he'd seen scarier things in his fridge. "You're Amish. You're not going to shoot me."

"Maybe I am, Kyle," she said. "What do you want?"

"I want to talk to whoever did this to my son." Kyle Simons motioned to Griff's face, and Poppy couldn't help but feel a perverse sense of satisfaction. Griff's bottom lip was three times the size of his top one. His mouth looked as if it was sculpted into a permanent pout. She'd hit him hard, and she had a broken hand to prove it.

"Dad," Griff mumbled, shuffling his feet and keeping his eyes trained on his shoes, "I already told you. I don't care. Let's just go home."

Kyle snapped like a tree branch laden with snow. "Shut up, Griff. When someone pushes my son around, they answer to me."

Luke immediately stepped forward and nudged Aunt B's gun aside. "You can talk to me. But outside. I won't allow you in the house."

Griff's dad frowned. "It's better that way."

With barely contained anger Luke glanced at Poppy. "Stay here."

Poppy shook her head. "I'm the one they want." Though she was shaking in her shoes, Griff and his *dat* would see nothing but contempt. Someone had to stand up for Dorothy and Rose. If the Simons were low enough to take satisfaction in bullying an Amish girl, then they would prove to be the weak ones.

Several emotions traveled across Luke's face before rage took over. "You stubborn, bullheaded girl. I don't care what you think. You will not put yourself in danger while I have the power to keep you from it."

Poppy stepped back as if she'd been shoved. It didn't matter how nice Luke had been in the last few days. It didn't matter that he'd built them a chicken coop or painted their barn twice. He hated her, plain and simple. The heartache made her dizzy. If she didn't lash out at him, she'd melt under his hot glare. "You don't have any power over me, Luke Bontrager, and don't you forget it."

Aunt B pinched her lips together as her eyes darted from Kyle Simons to Luke to Poppy and back again. "Wait there," she said to Kyle as she slammed the door shut with the barrel of her shotgun. She turned to Luke and Poppy and rolled her eyes. "Maybe you two should work this out before it turns into a wrestling match." She propped her gun on the floor and leaned her hand on the stock. "But make it quick. Kyle Simons is not a patient man."

Luke scrubbed his hand across his forehead. "Poppy, Griff Simons hit you. His *dat* is even worse. Who knows what he'll do? Please stay in the house."

"Why? Because you think I'm weak and helpless? Or because you think you know what's best for me?"

He shook his head. "If you did things my way, you'd be so much happier."

"I won't be bullied into doing what you want."

Luke erupted. "I wasn't there to protect you or my sisters," he roared, "and I can't bear it."

Poppy closed her mouth. There was real pain behind his words.

In an instant, he came to rest, folded his arms across his chest, and propped himself against the closed door, tilting his head back until it rested against the door and his gaze pointed toward the ceiling.

One of the men on the other side pounded as if they were trying to break it down. The force of the blows rattled the door against Luke's back.

Aunt B looked daggers out the window. "Hold your horses, Kyle," she yelled. With her gun draped over her elbow, Aunt B placed one foot on the window seat as if she were settling in. She watched Luke and Poppy with barely disguised impatience, but she didn't say a word.

Luke didn't seem to notice the tempest on the other side of the door. "I know how mad you are, Poppy," he said, his voice like a soft caress against her cheek. "I thought Griff would be gone this morning. I sent Rose and my sisters into danger."

Poppy's anger fizzled like a campfire in the rain. "You couldn't have known."

"I couldn't protect them, but you did, Poppy. You will never know how grateful I am that you are so brave."

She studied his face. "You're not mad at me?"

He groaned. "How could you think I was mad?"

She threw up her hands. "I wonder why."

He lifted his head, and his dark eyes were filled with so much sorrow, she wanted to cry for him. "*Ach,* Poppy. I don't even know how to begin to make it right with you." He pushed himself away from the door and grasped her arms with his strong hands. "I said some very *deerich* things because I was afraid."

"Afraid I would die?"

He nodded. "And afraid that I would be responsible. My mom lost her foot because of me." A shadow of pain passed across his features. "It's a shame I live with every day."

"You can't hide," Kyle yelled from outside.

"Be patient," Aunt B fired back.

Poppy had no idea why Luke felt ashamed. "Your *mamm* lost her foot in a farming accident. How could that be your fault?"

He seemed to lose his strength. Exhaling slowly, he pulled out the nearest chair from the table, sat down, and buried his face in his hands. "My *dat* was sick. Mamm and I had to care for the farm. She asked me to help her fix the flatbed. I was full of pride and told her I could hold up the wagon bed by myself, but I turned out to be too weak. It slipped out of my hands and crushed her foot." His voice cracked into a thousand pieces. "They had to amputate. My *dat* was furious that I was the cause of it. He taught me better than that, and I let him down. I promised myself I would never let something like that happen again."

She reached out her good hand and laid it on his shoulder. He flinched, but he didn't pull away. "That is *Gotte*'s burden, Luke. Not yours."

With his hands still covering his face, he shook his head. "It's my *mamm*'s burden. A woman should never have to do anything that a man is better suited to do."

She knelt at his feet so she could look him in the eye. "You are talking to the wrong person. I don't think a man is better suited for anything. And sometimes a woman doesn't have a choice about the situation she's in."

"Also my fault." He took her hands, stood up, and pulled her with him. "I don't so much like you kneeling at my feet."

She tried to ignore the pleasant sensation of his rough hands. Now was not the time to lose her wits. "You take too much responsibility for things that belong to *Gotte.*"

"I take care of what I can with *Gotte*'s help."

"That's why you were so nervous about me using the hammer." She curled her lips. "But I won the race."

His eyes flashed with a scolding. "That's why I am so nervous about you using anything."

Five loud knocks came at the door. "Elizabeth Kiem, let us in."

Aunt B puffed out her cheeks with air and

then slowly released it. "I was hoping he'd get tired of waiting and go home."

Before they opened that door, Poppy had to make Luke understand. "I forced you to let me use the hammer, Luke. If I am careless enough to hit my own thumb, that's my fault, not yours."

He slumped his shoulders. "It feels like my fault."

Aunt Bitsy peeked out the window. "I hate to interrupt, especially when you two are finally getting somewhere, but Kyle looks to be foaming at the mouth."

Luke pled with his eyes. "Poppy, I would never forgive myself if I let you go out there unprotected. I need to make everything right again. Won't you let me?"

Gone was the gruff, rough-around-the-edges boy who wouldn't let her play football and used a drill behind her back. In his place stood a vulnerable, aching young man, the heavy responsibility of the family farm thrust upon him, the guilt of his *mater*'s accident choking him like a rope around his neck.

Poppy's determination crumbled like dry leaves in late autumn, and for probably the first time in her life, she gave in. Sort of. Her lips curved into a conciliatory smile. "We won't be unprotected if we go out together."

He gave a low growl, but it was more of an I-surrender growl than an I'm-mad-at-you growl. "Will you at least stand behind me?"

She opened her mouth to protest, but the anxiety in his eyes made her change her mind. She would let Luke win this one time, but only because he might die of anxiety if she didn't. She took a deep breath and nodded.

"Promise?"

"I promise."

He looked as if she'd just given him ten loaves of nut brown bread. "*Denki.* And will you promise not to say anything? I need to do all the talking."

She rolled her eyes. That boy could not relinquish one iota of control. "Okay. No talking unless absolutely necessary."

"Not even then," he said, pinning her with a look that invited no argument.

"I'll do my best."

Luke looked as if he might start yelling again. Instead, he pressed his lips together and nodded. "Bitsy, will you stay inside so I don't have two people to fret about?"

A dozen worry lines appeared on Aunt B's forehead. "I've got your back." She opened the door. Griff and his dad were standing right where they'd left them. Aunt B tapped her hand on the barrel of her gun. "No trouble, Kyle, or I might have to load this thing."

"I don't start trouble," Kyle said. "But I finish it."

"I'll be standing right inside the door," she said. With the heart tattoo on her neck and her dangly black earrings, she looked more intimidating than the average Amish *fraa*. Poppy frowned. Kyle's tattoos could have eaten Aunt B's tattoos for supper.

Luke marched out onto the porch, and true to her word, Poppy followed him and stationed herself directly behind him. She couldn't see much but Griff's head around Luke's broad shoulders. Aunt B shut the door behind them. With her back to the house, Poppy couldn't know for sure, but she suspected that Aunt B had her nose stuck right up against the window. Would she have to load her gun? Did she even have ammunition?

Poppy felt ridiculous standing behind Luke, but he would be very upset if she broke her promise. She should at least attempt to make him happy.

Griff looked pale, as if he wanted to be in Canada or Milwaukee or anywhere else in the whole world. Poppy couldn't feel sorry for him. He'd brought the community nothing but trouble.

The muscles of Luke's neck and back looked so taut, Poppy could have bounced a penny off them, but his stance was casual and nonthreatening, with his hands at his sides and his feet spread apart. "I'm here," he said. "What do you want to say?"

Kyle's scowl got even deeper, as if it would never find the bottom of his face. "What gives you the right to punch my son?"

Indignation boiled inside Poppy like honey on an overheated stove. Griff, the coward, obviously hadn't told his father who had really hit him, but she wasn't about to let Luke take the blame. She braced one hand on Luke's shoulder and stood on her tiptoes so she had a clear view of Kyle. "It wasn't —"

Luke's warning glare could have shriveled her tongue. She had promised not to say anything — unless absolutely necessary. She thought it was time for absolutely necessary. He obviously didn't.

Luke nudged her hand off his shoulder like a piece of lint. She took a step back and growled softly. Why wouldn't Luke at least tell Kyle the real story?

Because Luke Bontrager was the bossiest boy she had ever met. Hadn't he just told her that the world would be a better place if everybody just did what he wanted?

Bossy and arrogant. There was no reasoning with him.

"No one should hit anybody else," Luke said.

Without warning, Griff's father made a fist and popped Luke in the nose. Poppy shouted as Luke's head snapped back, but he didn't fall over. He was as solid and immovable as a tree trunk.

Poppy staggered as if she were the one who'd been hit. As soon as she got her bearings, she darted between Kyle and Luke and pushed up against Luke's chest so he'd be forced to step back, farther away from Kyle. "Don't touch him," she yelled.

Stubborn, aggravating Luke would not be pushed. He took her good hand and tugged her behind him again. If she hadn't been so *ferhoodled* by his touch, she would have protested. As it was, she felt powerless to do anything but let him lead her wherever he wanted, even if he did have blood trickling from his nose.

Griff's face turned a sickly shade of green. *Jah,* he wanted to be in Canada.

Luke calmly pulled a handkerchief from his pocket and dabbed at his nose. Lots of blood. Too much blood. "If you want revenge, Kyle, you or Griff can punch me in the face as many times as you want, and I won't fight back. But you have to let Poppy go in the house first."

Poppy squeaked in protest. Luke squeezed her hand as a signal to keep quiet. She squeaked in protest again.

"Poppy," he growled, "stay behind me and stay quiet."

Ach. She hated Luke Bontrager.

Kyle flexed his hand as if hitting Luke's face might have been hard on his fingers. "Are you satisfied, Griff?"

Griff nodded mutely.

Kyle turned back to Luke. "Now we're even. But come near my son again, and you'll get worse."

Poppy was nearly beside herself. She wanted to shout at Kyle for hitting the wrong person and at Griff for scaring her sister and at both of them for being despicable people, but if Luke could keep his temper, then so could she.

Kyle jabbed a finger into Luke's chest. Luke didn't move, but Poppy flinched. "We haven't had no problem with the Amish before. We don't want no trouble again."

"We'd like nothing better than to be left alone," Luke said, sniffing back the blood dripping from his nose.

"Then we understand each other."

Luke folded his arms across his chest. Still confined to standing behind him, Poppy could only guess that the blood dripped down his shirt. "I want to talk to Griff alone," he said. "Would that be all right with you?"

Kyle's eyes were tiny slits. "Why?"

"Man to man," Luke said. "No fighting."

Kyle frowned. "I suppose you deserve that. You took it like a man."

Griff sneered, and Poppy could tell he tried to muster a little swagger. "I got nothing to say to him."

Kyle grabbed a handful of Griff's T-shirt and pulled Griff toward him. "You listen to what he has to say, like a man. You understand?"

Griff nodded, his eyes full of resentment.

Kyle motioned to the shiny black motorcycle parked in the lane. "I'm on my bike right over there." He took the porch steps in one jump, got on his motorcycle, and started the engine. Although he was near, he wouldn't be able to hear a thing.

Griff crossed his arms over his chest, giving Poppy a *gute* look at the tattoo on his forearm, which was a skull with a snake coming out of its mouth. She swallowed hard and thought of Aunt B's heart tattoo.

Poppy much preferred cute little hearts, but Griff Simons wasn't so tough.

For sure and certain, he didn't look tough. His arms were folded as if to protect himself from Luke, the Amish boy who hadn't fought back, but who looked like he could break Griff's arm with a flick of his wrist. Griff's eyes were downcast, his shoulders stooped. He looked scared and weak and even a little contrite. Had that been Luke's doing?

"What do you want?" he said, as if he hated the very thought of Amish people. He probably did.

"What would have happened if I'd told your *dat* you hit a girl?"

Griff pressed his lips together and lifted his chin. "Nothing."

She could see the muscles of Luke's jaw tighten. "Do you know why I didn't?"

Griff stared at the barn as if Luke hadn't just asked him a question.

"Because I didn't want him to hit you." Luke tilted his head to force Griff to meet his eyes. "He would have hit you, wouldn't he?"

Griff exhaled a puff of air and stared at his shoes again.

"Griff," Luke said. "I didn't want him to hit you."

Poppy could have growled. She could have stomped her feet and yelled at the top of her lungs. She could have thrown her arms around Luke's neck and kissed him silly. She felt so turned over every which way, she had no idea which urge was the strongest.

Luke had known all along what Griff's father would do, and he not only wanted to protect Poppy, but he had wanted to protect Griff Simons, who in many ways was a victim himself. Luke could have explained it to her instead of asking for a promise that only caused her aggravation.

Part of her hated to let Griff get away with anything. If his *dat* had struck Griff, he would have deserved it. Part of her wanted to hug Luke and make him a cherry pie for being a better person than she could ever hope to be. He had already forgiven Griff Simons, and now he was watching out for him — at the expense of his own nose.

Ach. She didn't hate Luke Bontrager. Not one little bit.

Luke turned and gave Poppy a cautious smile. His nose was red, but the blood wasn't dripping anymore, although there were several spots on his shirt. "Poppy," he said. How could that one word from his lips send her head whirling like a swarm of honeybees?

He wrapped his protective arm around her and pulled her forward. Poppy couldn't have been more surprised that Luke would let her come out from behind him, but her shock was soon overshadowed by the warm sensation of Luke's arm around her, as if she belonged tucked neatly next to his heart. It didn't help her pulse that he smelled of freshly cut cedar. She could breathe in that scent all day.

He ran his finger along her jawline and nudged her cheek so Griff could see the bruise. "Are you proud of what you did to Poppy, Griff?"

"She hit me first," Griff said, mumbling so that Poppy could barely understand him. Well, the enormously fat lip probably made it hard to talk.

Ach, she was such a wicked girl.

"Are you proud?" Luke said, his tone demanding an answer that Griff didn't want to give.

Griff hung his head. "No."

"Are you proud of scaring three Amish girls who have never done you any harm?"

"I was having a little fun, that's all."

Luke's glare would have scared Billy Idol. "Are you proud, Griff?"

"No."

How did he manage to make his voice soft and authoritative at the same time? "Next time you see my sisters or Poppy's sisters walking down the road, will you remember how I could have told your *dat* what really happened but didn't, and just let them be?"

Griff glanced toward his *dat*'s motorcycle. "I suppose."

Poppy didn't know if Griff was convinced, but at that moment, Luke could have persuaded *her* of anything. His goodness astounded her.

Maybe she should at least try to show some forgiveness, even if Griff didn't deserve it. "Wait here," she said before running into the house.

Aunt B stood on the window seat with her gun pointed at Griff's head through the glass.

"Did you load it?" Poppy said.

"*Nae.* I could see that Luke had it under control. And it never hurts a boy to get some sense knocked into him."

Poppy went to the cooling rack where four loaves of wheat bread sat. "May I?" she said, taking the wax paper from the drawer.

Aunt B swiped her hand through the air. "It's a waste of a good loaf of bread, but go ahead. Griff might be the worst thing that ever happened to the neighborhood, but he is still a motherless child."

Poppy tore off a piece of wax paper as best she could with one hand and wrapped it around the bread. She ran outside and handed it to Griff, who acted like he didn't quite know what to do with it. He probably suspected she'd poisoned it.

"That bread is like gold," Luke said. "Guard it with your life."

"Oh. Okay," Griff said.

She hadn't expected a thank-you. She didn't get one.

Griff clomped down the stairs, climbed on the back of his *dat*'s motorcycle, and they drove away.

Luke exhaled deeply and gave Poppy a smile that set her heart racing. "I thank the *gute* Lord that you are safe, and nobody got hurt."

"What do you mean nobody got hurt?" She took the handkerchief from his fist and dabbed at the blood under his nose.

He hissed and pulled back. "Careful. It stings something wonderful."

"Did he break it?"

"I don't wonder that he did."

"You should put some ice on it."

He cocked an eyebrow. "Only if you put ice on your hand."

She batted her eyes. "I was planning on

375

doing that all along."

He growled. "Poppy Christner, you delight in aggravating me, ain't not?"

"*Jah,*" she said. "Almost as much as you delight in aggravating me."

"I do not."

Dabbing at the blood on his shirt was futile, but she did it anyway. It kept her close to him and his wonderful-*gute* smell. "At first I thought you didn't tell Griff's *dat* what really happened just to spite me," Poppy said. "And then I thought maybe you wanted to take the credit for giving Griff a fat lip."

He laughed. "I'll bet you surprised him with how hard your fist is."

Poppy grinned. "He slapped me more out of shock than anything else."

Luke reached out and gently stroked his hand along her cheek. His cool fingers felt heavenly against her warm bruise. "*Oy, anyhow, Poppy,*" he said in his low, musical voice. "I wish I could have taken this one for you."

"Why didn't you tell me your plan instead of making me promise not to speak?" she said.

His hand found a wisp of hair from beneath her scarf, and he twisted it between his fingers. "Because, no matter how much you dislike me, I knew you wouldn't willingly agree to let Griff's *dat* punch me. Either that or you thought Griff deserved to be hit."

Poppy lowered her eyes. "*Ach.* I am wicked. I *do* think he deserved it."

"You're not wicked. It shows you have a tender heart for my sisters and Rose."

"So do you, but you thought of Griff too. I didn't."

"There was really no time to argue about it. Another minute and Kyle would have broken down the door," he said.

"Did you know he would hit you?"

"*Nae,* but I suspected if he didn't turn his anger on me, he'd take it out on Griff. I live close enough to know what goes on at that house."

Poppy had been wiping at the same spot of blood on his sleeve for a very long time. She smiled sheepishly and handed him back his handkerchief. "I shouldn't have been so difficult, but I didn't want you to boss me around."

He smirked as if he knew he was going to annoy her. "I told you, the world would be a much better place if everybody just did things my way."

"*Ach,*" Poppy said. "What an imagination you have."

Someone knocked on the window, and they turned to see Rose and Dorothy grinning and waving at them.

"They look like they're feeling better," Luke said.

"Cum reu," Poppy said. "I will get you some ice for that face and a slice of bread because you have done a very *gute* thing."

He pursed his lips and shook his head. *"Nae.* I will get *you* some ice. Your cheek is purple and your hand is swelling like a dead fish."

She glanced down and winced. Her right hand looked decidedly chubby. She'd be wearing a cast at the wedding and weeding the garden with one hand. But she could still make bread if Luke helped. Her heart did a double somersault twist at the thought of Luke Bontrager coming over every day to knead bread. It didn't even matter that she only made bread once a week. Surely she could find something for him to do the other six days.

"Cum," he said, cupping his hand over her elbow and leading her into the house as if she were a frail old woman. "It must be hurting something wonderful."

"At least there is nothing that needs to be glued," she said. "Remember all the time we spent gluing each other back together? I have such fond memories."

He gazed at her as if he were looking into her heart. "Me too. What would I do without you?"

Her pulse pounded like a charging bull. "Well, you wouldn't have that scar on your finger. You wouldn't have had to pull me out of a car window, fish me from the ditch, or buy me a drill. You'd be sitting at home in a rocking chair playing Scrabble with one of your *bruders*. You'd be enjoying a lot more peace."

He shrugged and gave her a dazzling smile. "Nah. I've kind of gotten used to the excitement."

CHAPTER TWENTY-THREE

Poppy, Rose, and Lily each pulled two bags of tomatoes from the buggy. Poppy hung both bags on her *gute* arm. It was a *gute* thing they had handles. She hated it when she couldn't do something to help.

One of their errands in town was delivering tomatoes to the Yutzys, who sold some of the Honeybee Schwesters' produce at their fruit, vegetable, and donut stand. The Yutzy girls, Hannah and Mary, were *gute*-natured and friendly and unapologetically loud, and they never seemed to let anything ruffle their feathers. Poppy liked them very much.

The Yutzys' vegetable stand stood on one of the busiest corners in town, where tourists liked to stop for Amish donuts and produce. Tables of cherries and beans, corn and peas lined the sidewalk for several feet. Even in the early morning, a few tourists and some Amish neighbors were looking at the produce.

Poppy's stomach lurched. Dinah Eicher and her *mamm* stood near the flowers looking at a flat of petunias. Poppy pretended she hadn't seen them and hoped Dinah would pretend too. There was no need for them to say anything to each other.

So what if Luke liked demure, pretty Dinah? That didn't hurt Poppy's feelings at all. Luke could like whomever he wanted. But that didn't mean Poppy had to be friendly. She slid her broken hand behind her back. Dinah was sure to gloat over it.

Hannah and Mary stood inside the little enclosure that housed the vegetable stand's cash register and the propane stove where they cooked donuts. Hannah looked up as she counted out change to a customer and squealed in delight. "Lily! Poppy and Rose! *Ach, du lieva,* it's the Honeybee Schwesters!"

The customer, an *Englisch* tourist, pinched her lips together in annoyance, as if Hannah had just broken her eardrum.

Hannah giggled and patted the woman's hand. "I'm sorry if I scared you. I'm just so happy to see my friends."

The *Englischer* softened and cracked a smile. "Good friends are the greatest treasure, I suppose."

Hannah's head bobbed up and down. "*Jah, jah.* Nothing better than friends. Have a wonderful-*gute* day." She came out from behind the counter and gave each of the sisters a hug. "*Ach, du lieva,* it's been ages, *ages* since I've seen any of you."

Poppy smiled. Maybe not ages. They brought some cherries here just last week.

Hannah furrowed her brow. "Poppy, what happened to your face?"

If only she could hide her cheek like she could her hand. "It's nothing."

Hannah was always a little flighty. She turned and called to her sister, who was sprinkling sugar on some donuts just out of the deep fryer. "Mary, look who's here."

Mary beamed like a lantern as a giggle tripped from her mouth. She came out from behind the counter and hugged Poppy and her sisters just as Hannah had done. Poppy never felt unloved around the Yutzy sisters. "*Ach,* Lily and the Honeybees. We sold all your cherries in about two days. People love them. I think the bees make them extra sweet."

Lily held up one of her bags. "We brought some tomatoes if you want them."

No one ever had a hard time hearing Hannah. "Do we want them? Poppy Christner tomatoes are famous. I mean, famous." She turned around again and called to her brother James, who stood behind the counter staring at Poppy and her sisters. James had a crush on Lily, and unlike Hannah and Mary, he fell silent whenever the Honeybee Sisters were around. "James, come and get these tomatoes and put them on the table."

Red in the face, James came out of the enclosure, took Lily's and Rose's bags, and laid them on the table with the other tomatoes.

Hannah leaned in and lowered her voice. She was still significantly louder than a whisper. "James used to have a crush on Lily, but now that Dan has come home, James has taken a shine to Poppy."

"Me?" Poppy said.

Hannah giggled. "Of course you. The Honeybee Sisters are all so pretty, James had no problem switching."

Lily smiled. "I don't wonder that he did. Poppy and Rose are a hundred times prettier than me."

Rose's cheeks glowed red. "That isn't true, Lily. No one is prettier than anyone else. *Gotte* looks on our hearts."

Hannah gasped. "Poppy, what happened to your arm? Did you break it?" She quickly took the bags hanging from Poppy's elbow. "James, come over here and get the rest of these. Can't you see Poppy is hurt?"

Silently and obediently, James took the bags from his sister, then went to the table and started arranging the tomatoes so they looked nice and neat. The Yutzys knew how to sell produce.

"Ach," Poppy said, fingering a thread sticking out from the cast that went halfway up her forearm. "I'm afraid I hit somebody."

Both Mary and Hannah widened their eyes.

"You hit somebody?" Mary said. "Not something?"

Bless their hearts, Lily and Rose stood ready to defend her from anyone who dared suggest that Poppy shouldn't have punched Griff Simons.

"Dorothy and Joann Bontrager and I were walking home from the bus stop," Rose said.

Lily leaned in. The rest of them did the same. "Griff Simons moved back in with his *dat.*"

Mary shook her head. "That's too bad."

"He tried to kiss Rose," Lily added.

Mary's gasp sounded like her dying breath. *"Nae!* Rose, what did you do? Did you cry? I would have cried."

"I would have screamed my lungs out," Hannah said.

Hannah was noisy and outgoing. Poppy

384

would have been very interested to hear how loud Hannah could scream.

Rose's expression darkened with a painful memory. "I screamed."

"Poppy was in our yard," Lily said. "She heard the screaming and punched Griff so he would let Rose go."

The Yutzy *schwesters* gazed at Poppy as if she could control the weather. "*Oy* anyhow, Poppy. You're so brave," Mary said.

Hannah slapped her hand over her mouth. "Look at her cheek, Mary. Did he hit you back?"

Poppy nodded. The thought still made her a little jumpy.

"She broke her vow of nonviolence. She should be shunned." Paul Glick, Lily's ex-boyfriend, stood on the sidewalk in front of the vegetable stand with his arms folded across his chest and a smug scowl on his lips. His puffy face held the petulant expression that Poppy had come to know and dislike. No doubt he was on his way to his family's market.

Mary's face looked as if she'd just sucked on a lemon. "Shunned? Paul Glick, you don't know anything."

James came from behind and tapped both sisters on the shoulder. "Mary, Hannah, there's customers."

Hannah gave Poppy a swift kiss on the cheek. "Griff Simons is the meanest boy in the world."

The Yutzy sisters went back behind the counter. Paul didn't seem to have anywhere he had to be. "You Christners have caused trouble in this community long enough."

"Paul," Lily said, with a fake and cheerful lilt to her voice, "how have you been?" Lily had broken things off with Paul. Maybe she felt a slight tinge of guilt about it. Poppy felt no guilt at all.

Paul didn't even look at Lily, didn't even acknowledge that she existed. Poppy shouldn't have expected anything better from him, but she still thought steam might come out of her ears. "We are a peaceful people, Priscilla," Paul said. "You hurt more than yourself when you use violence on our *Englisch* friends."

Eyes flashing with anger, Lily opened her mouth to say something. Poppy beat her to it. Lily shouldn't have to speak to Paul ever again, and Poppy was eager to defend herself. "What would you have done, Paul, if Griff had attacked your sister?"

"I would have let him kiss her."

"And hit her?"

"It would have been *Gotte*'s will to test my faithfulness. I would have let *Gotte* exact

His vengeance."

Rose hooked her elbow through Poppy's. "Maybe Poppy was *Gotte*'s vengeance."

"God is able to do His own work," Paul said. "Ours is not to question His commandments."

"I didn't want Griff to hurt my sister," Poppy said.

Paul narrowed his eyes and glared at Poppy as if she were preaching evil doctrine. "It was *Gotte*'s will."

"You pledged to follow the Confession of Faith." Poppy turned to see Dinah Eicher lurking just outside their little gathering. When had she sneaked into the conversation? "Do your baptism vows mean nothing to you?"

Paul glared at them the way Aunt Bitsy had looked at Kyle Simons yesterday. "Time and again I have cautioned the bishop and the ministers about your family's behavior. Your Aunt Elizabeth dyes her hair and wears earrings and tattoos. Someone has seen her with lipstick. Lily breaks her promises and deceives people. All of you wear pants and flirt with boys."

Flirt with boys? What he really meant was that Lily had chosen Dan Kanagy over him. Poppy clenched her teeth. Paul liked nothing better than to twist facts to justify himself. If she hadn't sworn off hitting any more boys, she would have seriously considered clobbering him over the head with her cast. How dare he talk about Lily and their family that way?

Dinah nodded so hard, Poppy thought her *kapp* might fly off her head. "You flirt with lots of boys."

A look of understanding passed between Dinah Eicher and Paul Glick. They must have realized they were allies in the imaginary battle against the Honeybee Sisters. But what did Dinah have against Poppy except that she thought Poppy had stolen her recipe for Nestlé Toll House cookies?

Since she had called things off with Paul, Lily had become almost as bold as Poppy. "Paul," Lily said, "don't insult my family as if you know them. You know nothing."

"You are the worst offender, Poppy," Paul said, still ignoring Lily as if he'd cut her completely out of his heart and therefore she didn't exist anymore. "You have never been able to fully accept the Confession of Faith. You use violence to solve your problems. It will only bring damnation to you and trouble to our community."

Dinah was so eager to share her opinion with someone who would agree with her. She stepped forward and stood next to Paul.

"She wants to be a boy. She is not content in the place *Gotte* has placed her."

Rose tugged at Poppy's sleeve. "Let's go. Paul is too angry to speak any sense."

Poppy nodded at Lily. Lily nodded back. Paul would not be allowed to bully either of them today.

"I'd like to hear what else Paul has to say," Poppy said, lifting her chin and daring Paul with her eyes. She took one of Rose's hands and Lily took the other. They stood together, a wall Paul would not be able to breach no matter how many cruel words he threw at them.

Paul pasted a look of fake concern on his face. "You can make this right, Poppy. The man is the head of the woman. Find someone to marry you and prove that you are willing to submit to him. You might just keep from getting shunned."

"It's why she's been throwing herself at Luke Bontrager. She needs a husband to make her respectable."

Poppy did her best to school her expression even though Dinah's words had hit their mark. Sweet, pretty, helpless Dinah Eicher had a nasty streak. Did Luke know about that particular quality?

Rose looked as deeply troubled as Poppy felt. Her skin turned pale, and her eyes pooled with tears. She practically yanked Poppy's shoulder out of its socket. "Let's go, Poppy. Please, let's just go."

Poppy wasn't about to be wounded or chased away by two people who would take great satisfaction in seeing her put down. "I don't need a husband," she said. Luke or Owen Zimmerman or Wallace Sensenig could just leave her alone. Why did she even think of Luke? He wouldn't ever consider marrying her, not when a lovely girl like Dinah Eicher was available. "I don't want a husband. I am enough of myself."

"Not in *Gotte*'s eyes," Paul said.

She'd never felt such a surge of outrage before. Not when Luke had yelled at her, not when vandals had painted her barn, not even when Griff Simons attacked Rose. "*Nae,* Paul. I am unworthy only in your eyes, and you are so small, your voice is like the buzzing of a mosquito in my ear."

Hannah Yutzy practically burst from around the counter with a box of donuts in her hand. "Here you go!" she said, her smile so painful, Poppy could tell she forced it as wide as it would go. "Donuts hot out of the fryer." Starting with Poppy, she went around the circle and handed a fresh, hot donut to everyone, including Paul and Dinah.

She shoved one in Paul's hand before he

could refuse it. He made a point never to buy anything from Yutzys' produce stand. His family's market stood just down the street. "I don't want this," he said. He tried to hand it back to Hannah, but she seemed awful busy handing out napkins.

"What do you mean, you don't want it?" Hannah said, giving him a look of wide-eyed innocence. "Didn't you order a glazed donut with sprinkles on top?"

Paul scowled. "*Nae.* I did not."

Dinah had already taken a bite out of hers. "I didn't order one either."

Hannah sighed a very deep, to-the-tips-of-her-toes sigh. "Well, I can't take it back now. You've put your fingers all over it. We'd have to throw it away and lose all that money."

Paul probably could have breathed fire out of his flaring nostrils. "Fine. I will pay you for it, but I'm not going to eat it. I'm saving room for my *mamm*'s rolls. How much?"

"Three dollars."

"Three dollars? For a donut?" Paul said.

Dinah frowned and handed Hannah two one-dollar bills and four quarters. She glared at Poppy, lifted her nose in the air, and flounced away with her mouth full of donut and powdered sugar clinging to her bottom lip.

Paul shoved his hand into his pocket and

391

pulled out some bills. "Three dollars? We charge a dollar a roll at the restaurant."

Hannah's cheeks had to be aching from all that fake smiling. "Prices are going up."

Paul handed her the money and turned his attention back to Poppy and her sisters. Shaking his donut in their direction, he said, "Let this be a warning. Don't be surprised if the deacon pays you a visit." He turned on his heels and marched away without another word.

Lily handed her donut to Rose and dug into the canvas bag where they kept their tomato money. "Have you got change for a twenty, Hannah?"

Hannah reached out and tapped Lily on the arm. "The Honeybee Sisters never pay at Yutzys. You are like family to us."

"I insist," Lily said, holding out the twenty-dollar bill. "We feel guilty taking your donuts for free."

"Don't feel guilty," Hannah said, glancing behind her and making an attempt to stifle a loud giggle. "Paul Glick paid for yours."

Chapter Twenty-Four

Poppy was so unhappy, Luke could have cut it with a knife. Two days ago she had gifted him with that irresistible smile. She had laughed at his jokes and seemed devastated when Kyle Simons had socked him. She had invited him to come over and make bread any time he wanted. Luke thought he was making real progress. Tonight she could barely stand to look at him.

The Honeybee Sisters had invited him to dinner, probably because he'd made a point to show up at their house right before dinnertime with Dan Kanagy. They couldn't very well invite Dan without inviting Luke. Mamm was starting to wonder if she should be offended that Luke seldom ate at home anymore. In truth, Lily had invited him to dinner while Poppy had stood in the background trying to slice tomatoes with her left hand. She didn't even say hello, didn't even acknowledge when Luke walked into their house. It was as if she didn't want him there.

Trying to make sense of Poppy's dark mood left Luke with little appetite. He wracked his brain, trying to remember if he'd said something that had offended her. Stupid things flew out of his mouth all the time, but he usually didn't realize they were stupid until hours or days afterward. It made it kind of hard to pinpoint just what he'd said that had made Poppy act as cold as a frosty night in January.

The bruises on her cheek looked worse than they had two days ago. Had they X-rayed her face when they X-rayed her hand? He should have suggested that. She could very well have a fractured cheekbone or something.

Her cast went almost to her elbow, and her fingers were swollen and a light purplish color. She had paid a steep price for hitting Griff so hard. Luke shuddered at the thought of what could have happened. Poppy really had no choice but to hit Griff with all her might. A softer blow might have saved her hand, but might not have stopped Griffin his tracks.

When the pork chops were ready, Bitsy called for everyone to sit. Poppy set a bowl of buttered corn on the table and sat next to Luke, but he might as well have been invisible. She didn't look, didn't smile, didn't send so much as a glance in his direction.

His heart sank. What was wrong, and how could he fix it? He cleared his throat. "How does your cheek feel, Poppy?"

She instinctively touched her hand to her face. "Still a little swollen."

Luke swallowed hard. "Did they X-ray your cheekbone at the hospital? There might be a fracture."

She didn't even bristle at the idea that he might be trying to boss her around. Her green eyes showed him nothing except defeat and sorrow, and his heart ached for her without even knowing what was wrong.

Billy Idol stationed himself at Luke's feet and hissed to get Luke's attention. "Not now, cat," Luke said, more harshly than he meant. Billy Idol was a nuisance, for sure and certain, but in his own way, he had tried to protect Joann. Luke would be very ungrateful if he didn't at least acknowledge Billy Idol's kindness. He reached down and scratched behind Billy Idol's half ear. "I'll pick you up later," he said. "But not while I'm eating."

Billy Idol meowed and twitched his ears, which was probably as good a reply as Luke would get. He looked up to see Poppy staring at him. He smiled sheepishly. "He likes me."

"I've never been able to figure out why," Poppy said, as if she truly meant it. Why didn't she just go ahead and take a hammer to his face?

Dan was blissfully unaware of anything going on between Luke and Poppy. Usually Dan was blissfully unaware of anyone but Lily. "You don't even have a black eye, Luke. I'm disappointed."

Luke pretended to be cheerful. "Dat says my nose isn't broken. I got off easy."

"I can't believe you let him hit you," Rose said. "It was very brave."

Luke bowed his head. "*Nae.* Poppy was the brave one."

Rose choked on her words. "*Jah.* She saved us."

"Let's talk after the prayer," Bitsy said. "The pork chops are getting cold."

At least he would be able to have some sort of connection with Poppy during the prayer. He reached out his hand to her, and she hesitated only briefly before placing her hand in his. It was the hand without the cast. The hand with the black thumbnail. *Ach,* Poppy was beat up something wonderful. The thought made him feel even lower.

But he loved the feel of her skin.

"Dear Heavenly Father," Bitsy said, without waiting to see if everyone was ready. "We are grateful that Rose got some new paints today and that Lily is engaged to Dan — not that I'm all that thrilled with Dan, but at least he's not Paul Glick. We ask You to heal Poppy's hand and face and Luke Bontrager's nose, and give him the wisdom to see past it."

Past what? His nose? Luke nearly opened his eyes. What was Bitsy talking about?

Bitsy pitched her voice a little louder. "Keep evil, Griff Simons, and Dinah Eicher from our door. Amen."

Dinah Eicher? How had she made it into Bitsy's prayer?

Bitsy looked up, scowled, and bowed her head again. "And, dear Lord, bless the food."

Reluctantly, Luke let go of Poppy's hand as he bowed his head for the silent prayer. *Dear Father in heaven, will You show me the way with Poppy?*

Was it selfish to pray for himself? If *Gotte* didn't help him, no one would.

Luke opened his eyes. Dan's smile could have illuminated the road all the way to Luke's house. "Aunt Bitsy," he said, "you've never thanked *Gotte* for me before."

Bitsy smirked. "Don't get cocky. It's only

because Paul Glick is such a chucklehead."

Chucklehead? Luke couldn't begin to guess what that meant.

Lily frowned. "I can't believe I nearly married him."

Dan took a shuddering breath. "Don't even mention it, Lily. I still have nightmares." He leaned over and gave Lily a kiss on the forehead. "I am the happiest man on earth."

"No kissing," Bitsy said as she scooped a helping of cheesy potatoes onto her plate.

Dan merely grinned. He could get away with just about anything with Bitsy. He'd saved her niece from making a terrible mistake.

Dan passed the potatoes to Luke, who took more than he wanted to eat — not because they didn't look delicious, but because his insides were tied up in knots about Poppy and he could barely bring himself to eat anything.

"Why all this talk about Paul Glick, anyway?" Dan said. "It will give me indigestion."

The look Lily gave Poppy didn't escape Luke. Was Poppy worried about Paul's threat to have them shunned? Maybe her unhappiness had nothing to do with Luke. He didn't like the thought of Paul upsetting

Poppy, but he'd feel a whole lot better if he knew Poppy's distress hadn't been his fault.

Luke passed Poppy the potatoes but held on to the serving spoon until she made eye contact with him. "Poppy, did something happen with Paul?"

She pressed her lips together and took the spoon from his hand. "We can take care of ourselves."

That short answer said more than a whole day's worth of talking. The thought of Paul Glick was like fingernails on a chalkboard. Did Luke need to pay a friendly visit to Glick's Market? Nobody would be allowed to upset his Poppy while he had something to say about it.

Luke clenched his teeth. Poppy didn't need him to defend her against anybody, least of all Paul Glick. Judging by the look on her face, she didn't even want him to. Poppy fought her own battles, no matter how much Luke would have liked to fight them for her.

A familiar longing grew in his chest until it threatened to suffocate him. Poppy didn't need him, but he would be worthless without her.

He couldn't speak. He couldn't even eat. He just sat there mutely staring at his pork chops and cheesy potatoes. He had never felt like more of an outsider. Poppy wouldn't let him in.

A line appeared between Dan's brows. "What happened with Paul Glick? Did something happen?"

Lily poured Dan a glass of milk. "Poppy's muffins are delicious with raspberry jam. You should try one."

The line between Dan's eyebrows got longer. "Lily, did something happen today when you went to town?"

Rose, the quiet one, seemed eager to talk where her sisters weren't. "Paul Glick said he is going to talk to the elders about having Poppy shunned."

"Poppy?" Luke said. "Why Poppy?"

As soon as it came out of his mouth, he realized what a dumb question it was. Poppy had broken her vow of nonviolence when she socked Griff Simons — at least Paul Glick thought so.

"Paul Glick is blowing hot air, like he always does," Dan said, flashing Poppy a half smile. Luke knew Dan well enough to recognize the anger behind the casual expression. Dan would probably volunteer to do all the dishes. He cleaned like an Amish *fraa* when he got angry. "They won't shun Poppy for protecting Rose and Luke's sisters. They didn't even put Jethro Schwartz under the ban when he bought a car."

"Only because he sold it," Poppy said as if she'd rather not talk about it.

"We should tell them that Luke took a punch from Griff's father," Dan said.

A shadow traveled across Poppy's already sad face as she pushed a kernel of corn around her plate with her fork. "*Jah*. Luke fixed it."

What had he done? She acted as if he'd thrown a kitten into the ditch.

Rose gazed pointedly at Luke. "Dinah Eicher accused Poppy of trying to be like the boys. She said Poppy needs a husband to be respectable."

Poppy smiled a painful, flippant smile. "Apparently, I'm nobody without a husband."

Time stood still as every person at the table, including Poppy, turned to Luke and stared at him as if they expected him to say something. Was it a subtle hint for Luke to ask Poppy to marry him? His heart beat double time as hope flooded through his veins. They didn't even have to make the suggestion. He'd jump at the chance to marry Poppy.

Wait. What about Dinah Eicher?

His heart plummeted to the floor. Dinah Eicher had told Poppy what? Luke had

401

heard the word *husband* and disregarded everything else — he was stupid like that sometimes. Dinah Eicher told Poppy she needed a husband to be respectable? Poppy didn't need anyone to make her respectable. She was brave and strong and *wunderbarr* all on her own. Dinah Eicher knew nothing.

One look at Poppy's stricken face and it became obvious that Dinah's words had stung worse than a whole nest of angry wasps. But how? How could Poppy ever believe such things about herself?

Maybe because at one time, he had told her the very same things.

The pain of guilt was so raw, he couldn't draw a breath.

Poppy folded her arms, which wasn't easy with a bulky cast. "I don't care what Dinah Eicher says," she lied.

They were all still staring at Luke as if they weren't quite sure they liked him. "Luke," Rose said. "What has Dinah told you? Does she think Poppy should be shunned?"

"How should I know what Dinah thinks?"

Poor Rose widened her eyes and pursed her lips together as if she would never speak again. Oh, *sis yuscht,* he had never spoken to Rose that way before. There was no excuse for it, except that he was feeling as low as a cockroach in a cellar.

"I'm sorry, Rose," he said. "I guess I just don't understand."

Lily nodded her head and held his gaze as if willing him to say the right thing. "Dinah said some very cruel things about Poppy. You don't agree with her, do you?"

Realization hit him upside the head, and he couldn't even see straight. They thought he and Dinah were still seeing each other. But how could they? Hadn't he spent every spare minute on the Honeybee Farm?

He slapped his palm against his forehead. "Didn't you tell them, Dan?"

Dan frowned. "Tell them what?"

Bitsy stood up so fast her chair toppled over behind her. "Do you smell that?"

Luke sniffed the air and caught the unmistakable smell of smoke. He sprang to his feet, being careful not to step on Billy Idol. Soon everybody was on their feet. They'd all smelled the smoke.

It seemed like a race to the door. Dan opened it while Bitsy grabbed her shotgun. Luke was the first out on the porch. A plume of smoke rose above the honey house. With his heart already halfway down the lane, Luke leapt from the porch and ran for the honey house. Dan and the Honeybee

Schwesters were close behind. "Dan, get the hose," Luke yelled.

"There are buckets in the barn," Poppy called, already headed there with her sisters.

Luke nearly yelled for her to stay in the house. She had one good arm, an injured face, and a freshly healed shoulder. She shouldn't be fighting a fire. He thought better of calling her back and growled in frustration. He'd put the fire out himself before Poppy lifted a bucket.

A hose and attachment abutted the barn near the chicken coop, but there was also one behind the honey house near the windmill. Luke raced to the back to turn on the hose.

Black smoke billowed from a smoldering pile of boxes and garbage that had been pushed up against the honey house. Flames were already lapping against the back window. The honey house was constructed completely of wood. It was only a matter of seconds before the wall would catch fire.

Rose and Lily ran toward him with buckets, and he turned the water on full blast to fill them. Dan raced around the side of the building with a bucket and a rake. He handed his bucket to Lily and took a rake to the fire, doing his best to pull the debris away from the building without setting the surrounding weeds or himself on fire.

Luke's heart did a flip. "Where's Poppy?"

Lily looked toward the barn. "She was right behind me. I don't know."

Luke dropped the hose and bolted for the barn. He couldn't hope that she had decided it would be dangerous to try to put out the fire with a cast on her arm. She would never run for safety, especially if her sisters needed her.

Ach! He loved that about her.

Ach! He hated that about her.

Luke didn't see Poppy anywhere between the barn and the back of the honey house. He opened the barn door and called her name. No answer.

He worked himself into a panic without much effort. Where could she have gone in a matter of seconds? Hearing a faint meow and a loud hiss, he looked down the lane to see Billy Idol standing sentinel in front of the honey house door. He liked that cat more and more all the time.

Of course Poppy would be doing something *deerich,* foolish. He kicked up the gravel under his feet, sprinted to the front of the honey house, and went inside. He almost passed out with relief. There was Poppy trying to drag a large metal tub across the floor with one hand. Wisps of smoke seeped through the cracks in the wood on the backside of the building. Once the wood caught fire, it wouldn't take long for the whole building to go up yet.

"Poppy," he yelled, not even attempting to be nice. "Get out of here now."

"We can't support ourselves without this honey," she screamed. "I've got to save the extractor."

He grabbed her by the arm. "It's not worth your life."

She pushed him away with all the force of her broken hand. "Don't tell me what to do. Just leave me alone, Luke Bontrager."

He considered throwing her over his shoulder and carrying her out, but she'd put up a fight and probably hate him for saving her life. She wanted the extractor. If he took the extractor out, she'd come with it, wouldn't she?

Sometimes, only sometimes, he kept his head well enough to be smart.

"Come on then," he said, grabbing one of the handles of the extractor.

Poppy met his eye and grabbed the other handle. It wasn't light, not even for Luke. Together they carried it out of the honey house and set it down before a fit of coughing overtook both of them.

"We've got to get the tools and the empty

supers," she said.

"No more, Poppy."

"We can't support ourselves without the honey."

Bitsy came stumbling down the lane dragging two of the biggest fire extinguishers Luke had ever seen. They must have been heavy. She wasn't making much progress.

Luke rushed to her side and took both of them from her hands. "Get them to the fire," Bitsy said, completely out of breath. "Hurry."

Luke glanced at Poppy. "Do not go back in there."

She looked as if she were just waiting for him to go away. He growled but couldn't spare the time to make her promise to stay out of trouble. All he could do was pray she'd decide she'd rather not die in a fire.

Bitsy followed him as Luke lugged both extinguishers around to the back. Lily and Rose were filling buckets and throwing them on the fire, but their efforts were futile. The flames were over six feet high, blistering hot, and getting hotter. Luke handed one of the fire extinguishers to Dan. He showed him how to pull the pin and squeeze the trigger. "Aim for the base of the fire," he yelled.

Dan nodded. The fire extinguishers popped and hissed as Luke and Dan swept the stream of white, powdery liquid across the base of the honey house.

The fire was no match for two heavy-duty fire extinguishers. It sputtered and seemed to disappear almost instantly. Luke sprayed every possible hot spot even when the fire seemed to be completely out. Dan picked up his rake and spread the garbage out so Luke could spray all of it for *gute* measure.

They studied the damage and breathed a collective sigh of relief. Nobody needed to ask how the fire had started or who started it. The troublemaker had been momentarily forgotten in their happiness of putting it out. Dan threw down his rake and hugged Lily. Bitsy surprised Luke by smiling and slapping him on the back in a rare show of approval. "It is a *gute* thing you are so strong, Luke Bontrager. I would still be dragging those fire extinguishers down the lane."

"I'm glad I could help. I'm glad you had those fire extinguishers."

She shrugged. "The handicapped workers were having a sale."

One corner of the honey house was singed, but there didn't look to be any major damage. Luke would make sure the walls were sturdy before he let anyone back inside.

Inside.

Luke gazed around for Poppy and frowned when she didn't appear from around the front of the honey house. His heart sank. For sure and certain, she'd gone back in to save the hive tools. *Ach!* He would give her the biggest scolding of her life.

The door was halfway open, and he shoved it so hard it slammed against the wall behind it. He didn't mean to be quite so forceful, but his muscles were taut and his nerves were frayed and he didn't temper his own strength. Poppy sat on the floor of the honey house surrounded by a half dozen upended supers. No doubt she'd been trying to carry a whole stack out with one hand and dropped all of them. Blood dripped from a wound in her shin that didn't look too serious, and she tried to scoot her way backward out of the room on her bottom. She didn't make much progress with her injured leg and her one good hand.

Billy Idol, bless his heart, kept vigil over Poppy as if he were guarding her from harm. He wouldn't have been able to drag Poppy from a burning building like a dog might have, but he was a comfort to Luke all the same.

That stupid, adorable cat.

Luke's first impulse was to yell at Poppy for being so stubborn, but he remembered it was one of her best qualities and bit his tongue. She only made him so mad because he loved her so much. He squatted next to her and laid a gentle hand on her shin just above the bleeding cut.

"You should go help with the fire," she said. Tears pooled in her eyes. She blinked, and they slid down her cheeks.

He pretended not to notice. "The fire's out," he said, swiping supers aside like blocks. Without asking permission, he slid one hand under her knees and another around her back and lifted her into his arms. Her sigh sounded like a surrender as she snaked both arms, cast and all, around his neck and relaxed into his embrace.

His heart swelled bigger than the sky. He never wanted Poppy to leave the safety of his arms.

She buried her face in the crook of his neck, and he could feel her warm tears against his skin as he carried her out of the smoky honey house with Billy Idol following close behind. "Don't cry, Poppy." He curled his lips upward. "I'm not so bad. Most girls would love it if I carried them out of a burning building."

She stiffened and pushed herself away from him. "Most girls? Put me down."

Stunned, he let her slip from his arms and

onto her feet without even asking if she could stand on that leg. As it turned out, she could stand just fine. She swiped the tears from her eyes, threw back her head, and growled in frustration. He'd said something stupid, though he couldn't for the life of him guess what it was. "I didn't mean to upset you," he said, because he could think of nothing else.

"Most girls might throw themselves at you, Luke Bontrager, but I never would."

He furrowed his brow. "I never said you would."

"I didn't throw myself at you. You're the one who picked me up and carried me out of there even though I didn't need your help."

Luke curled his fingers around the back of his neck. "*Nae.* You never need my help."

"Dinah Eicher says I throw myself at you because I want a husband." She glared at him with all the force of a bolt of lightning. "Let me tell you something. No matter what you and Dinah think, I don't need a husband. I don't want a husband, and I certainly don't want you," she said, as if the very thought stabbed her in the heart. "Just go marry Dinah Eicher and leave me alone."

Her tortured expression stole his breath. As usual, he had messed up somewhere down the line, and he wasn't sure how to fix it. She turned away from him and limped up the lane. "Poppy, wait," he said, catching up with her in three giant steps.

She kept walking. He felt as if he'd been forever chasing her. "I challenge you to a race," he said.

That made her pull up short. She squinted with her entire face. "What?"

"I'll race you to the bridge, and if I win, you will stop glaring at me and listen to what I have to say."

"I don't want to race."

He tried to give her a teasing smile even though it was a pretty *gute* bet that he was just as miserable as she was. "Can I just claim victory?" She started to walk away. "It would make it so much easier if I didn't have to chase you into the bathroom. You know how persistent I am."

Poppy stopped walking, huffed out a shaking breath, and folded her arms. He could see the tears collecting in her eyes, threatening to spill out at one cruel word from him. She didn't understand that he never wanted to make her cry again.

He reached out to take her shoulders and thought better of it. Poppy was in no mood. "First of all, you have never thrown yourself at me, and I have never told Dinah that you have."

"Then why did she say . . . ?"

He held up a finger to stop her from talking. "I won the race, remember? You promised to listen."

She looked away. "You didn't win anything."

"I can't help it if you decided to forfeit." He couldn't resist. She looked so sad, so weary, as if she were holding the entire farm on her shoulders. He placed a hand on her arm. "I am the one who throws myself at you. I've been doing everything I can to show you how I feel, but you won't take the hint. You are very thick, Poppy Christner."

Her eyes glinted with surprise, and she looked completely and utterly offended. He obviously wasn't getting through.

"I called things off with Dinah the night at the park, and if you think I want to marry her, you're as crazy as a Betsy bug."

She opened her mouth to argue before it even registered what he had said. "Why . . . what? What are you talking about?"

Her expression was a puzzling mixture of strength and vulnerability, as if one word from him had the power to crush her or make her walk away forever. Her eyes, awash with tears, were a brilliant, nearly

413

blinding, color of green, and her lips, full and perfect, pulled him to her like a magnet. In an unbridled moment of utter insanity, he clamped his arms around her waist, pressed his mouth to hers, and stopped the argument that was surely on her lips.

She stiffened and pulled back slightly, but she knew how persistent he was. He felt it the second she decided he was serious. Her posture softened, and she tentatively snaked one arm around his neck, then stood on her tiptoes to bring herself closer to his heart.

Fireworks exploded inside his head. It seemed she had finally grasped what he'd been trying to tell her for days. He loved Poppy Christner so much he thought he might float away to heaven before his time.

With his arms still around her, he pulled away slightly, his lips a mere two inches from hers. "I've been wanting to do that since I cornered you in the bathroom at the park."

"I probably would have punched you," she said, softly, breathlessly.

"You are a stubborn, feisty, unconventional girl, Poppy Christner, and I love you so much I can't sleep at night."

It was a *gute* sign that she seemed more surprised than upset. "Are you teasing me, Luke Bontrager? I don't —"

"You don't need me. Of course you don't need me, but I need you so bad my bones ache. I'm stupid and arrogant, and I've been cruel just because I wanted to be right. I've hurt your feelings a thousand different ways and lectured you up one side and down the other. There is no reason in the world that you would ever love me, but I'm asking it anyway."

A slow, tentative smile formed on her lips. "Really?"

"For sure and certain."

She sighed, whether in resignation or contentment, Luke couldn't tell. "Don't gloat, but I believe I love you too."

He tightened his arms around her. "Then will you marry me?"

She closed her eyes as relief and jubilation flooded her expression. "I never thought I'd hear those words from you." She giggled. "I never thought I wanted to hear those words from you."

"I hope you've changed your mind."

Tiny worry lines appeared around her eyes. "Are you sure you want to marry me? I won't be submissive or demure. You'll hear my opinions whether you want them or not, and I'll insist on using a drill without your permission."

"How boring to have a wife who never

gives me several heart attacks a week. Why would I want someone who wouldn't dream of jumping in the ditch or punching *Englischers* twice her size?"

She drew her brows together. "I just can't believe you would want to marry me. You could have any girl in the community, even Dinah Eicher."

"Why would I want Dinah Eicher? I've just kissed the prettiest, most exciting, bravest girl in the community. There's no going back. The real question is: Can you stand being married to an arrogant, stubborn man who loses his temper too often and makes clumsy apologies and sometimes can't see past the end of his own nose?" His heart would shrink to nothing if she didn't say yes this minute.

She placed her good hand on the side of his face. He thought he might dissolve into the gravel at his feet. "I'll tell you what," she said. "I'll race you to the bridge. If you win, I'll marry you."

"And if you win?"

She grinned. "Then you'll marry me."

He'd never felt so gloriously happy, like he could run and never get tired. He pretended to calculate the odds in his head. "I can live with that." He took her hand in his. "May I escort you to the finish line?"

They strolled to the bridge, which wasn't much of a walk from the honey house but still slow going for Poppy since she limped all the way. Luke made a point to take a decisive step on the bridge before Poppy did. "I win," he said. "Does that mean you marry me or I marry you?"

"Jah," she said, her smile lighting up the dimming sky.

He gave her another kiss. Every cell in his body seemed to come alive. Had he ever known real happiness before this moment?

Something pricked his ankle, and he looked down to see Billy Idol trying to claw his way up Luke's trousers. The stupid cat.

Poppy giggled. "Why he likes you, I'll never know."

Luke growled in mock indignation. "Oh, really? What do you know? You never did like me all that much."

She tilted her face to his, inviting him in for another kiss. "I still don't like you, Luke Bontrager, but somebody's got to make the sacrifice and marry you. I'd hate for you to end up a bachelor."

He chuckled before kissing her again. His legs got wobbly.

"Kissing is not allowed on this farm. You'll scare the bees." Bitsy stood in the lane, grasping her two fire extinguishers and eyeing them with raised brows.

Ignoring Billy Idol, who was still climbing up his trousers, Luke braced his arm firmly around Poppy's shoulders and grinned. Poppy grinned right back.

"Bitsy, I touched Poppy's leg a few minutes ago. I think I need to marry her."

Bitsy smirked. "It's up to Poppy. Ever since you've started coming around, you've been nothing but trouble. Poppy is missing a thumbnail. She has a new scar, a nasty bruise on her face, and a broken hand. And she had to get a tetanus shot. At the rate she's going, she'll end up in a wheelchair at her own wedding."

Poppy nudged closer to Luke and smiled up at him as if he was the whole world. He thought he might burst. "I love him, B. I'll take my chances."

"Well, don't say I didn't warn you," Bitsy said as she turned and walked toward the house. "And, Luke, you have a cat crawling up your leg." Luke thought he might have seen the faintest of smiles on her lips — either a smile or a painful grimace. He couldn't be sure.

Maybe he didn't want to know.

CHAPTER TWENTY-FIVE

Poppy kept glancing out the kitchen window as she helped Lily and Rose roll out cookie dough. Luke would be here any minute, and she thought she might go crazy with anticipation.

"Poppy, that will never do," Lily said.

Poppy tore her gaze from the window. Her dough ball was the size of a lemon, sitting like a giant on the cookie sheet, overseeing all the normal-sized cookies. *"Ach,"* she said. "It's hard with only one hand." It was a *gute* thing she hadn't been the one to read the recipe or measure the ingredients. She couldn't concentrate on anything but the heavenly thought of seeing Luke.

"I think she's a little distracted today," Rose said, smiling and picking up Poppy's mammoth ball of dough. "I'll fix it."

Lily's grin matched Rose's. "He's so handsome, Poppy."

"And so nice," Rose added.

"And too big for his britches," Aunt B chimed in. She sat at the table with a cotton ball and some fingernail polish remover, trying to take off the stubborn black nail polish she'd worn for two weeks. It wasn't going well. Even after she removed the polish, her fingernails looked dirty, as if she hadn't washed her hands for days. "I'll have Luke whipped into shape before the wedding."

The wedding.

The thought stole Poppy's breath. She was going to marry Luke Bontrager, the most *wunderbarr* boy in the whole world. Was there ever a girl so blessed? Surely not even Lily could be as happy as Poppy. Dan was a fine young man, but Luke was everything a girl could want. He was handsome and kind and stubborn, and she could barely keep herself from laughing at the pure joy of being the one he'd chosen. No wonder Dinah Eicher hated her so much.

Lily rolled another ball of cookie dough in the cinnamon and sugar. "Luke will be happy about a double wedding, won't he?"

"Of course. Dan is his best friend. He'll love the idea."

Lily curled her lips and eyed Rose. "Now we just need to find a husband for Rose. Wouldn't a triple wedding be wonderful-*gute*?"

"There's no hurry," Aunt B said, concentrating very hard on her fingernails. "I don't think I can bear having another boy loitering around the house. They're a lot more trouble than they're worth." She pointed a finger at Rose. "Don't feed anybody."

Rose turned a bright shade of pink to match their barn door. "I don't dare talk to a boy."

"You have no trouble talking to Luke and Dan," Lily said. "And Luke is about the most frightening boy you'll ever meet."

Poppy raised an eyebrow at Lily. "That's my fiancé you're talking about."

Rose placed another ball of cookie dough on the sheet. "I knew Luke had a *gute* heart and that he was the perfect match for you. I was never afraid of him."

"The perfect match? He hated me."

"Nae," Rose said. "He just needed to get to know you. I knew he'd fall in love."

Lily opened the oven and slid the full cookie sheet inside. "We just need to find the perfect match for you."

Rose frowned. "I wouldn't know the first thing about getting a husband. It terrifies me."

Aunt B was on her seventh cotton ball. "You won't have to *get* a husband. Unfortunately, the boys who are interested will come to you. And eat all our food."

"I hate to put anyone to so much work," Rose said, looking increasingly troubled.

Lily put both her arms around Rose. "Don't spend a single minute worrying about it. Falling in love should not be scary. If it happens, it will happen naturally."

"Gute," Rose said. "I don't have to have a husband at all."

"Jah," Aunt B said. "Being an old maid has its advantages. I don't have to share the covers when I sleep."

Three strong raps came at the door. Poppy's heart galloped as if no one had ever come to the door before in her life. She dropped her cookie dough back in the bowl, wiped her hand, and ran to the door. Luke stood on the other side holding a kitten and a drill and smiling as if he couldn't stop himself.

She stepped outside, closed the door behind her, and since his arms were full, threw one arm around his neck and kissed him. He didn't object. *Ach.* She felt like a sliver of light floating across the sky. She loved him to the bottom of her toes.

"If you do that every day," he said, "I think I will die of happiness before my next birthday."

"Me too."

He held up the drill. "I thought you and I could do a little drilling together today."

She loved that he trusted her to use a drill safely. "Sounds like a fun activity. Did you bring the kitten to keep us company?" Poppy stroked her finger along the orange ball of fur.

Luke smiled sheepishly. "The kitten is a present for Bitsy."

Poppy shook her head. "She won't accept it."

"I know. I'm hoping Rose will butter her up." He opened the front door and motioned for Poppy to go in first.

"Luke," Lily and Rose said at the same time.

Aunt B groaned. "I suppose you'll want to stay for dinner."

Billy Idol started hissing at Luke the moment they entered the house. Luke laid his drill on the table and scooped Billy Idol into his free hand. Billy Idol immediately stopped hissing, but he still wore the scowl on his face. Luke showed Billy Idol the new kitten. "This is Fluffy. Poppy saved her from the ditch, and now she needs a new home. Honeybee Farm needs another cat, don't you agree?"

Aunt B tightened the lid on her polish remover and grunted derisively. "Luke Bontrager, if you think I'm going to let another cat into my house, then you breathed in a little too much smoke yesterday. Farrah Fawcett and Billy Idol are trouble enough."

From her comfortable pillow on the window seat, Farrah Fawcett eyed Aunt B, Luke, and the new kitten with haughty indifference. She'd borne the indignity of Billy Idol in the house. She probably wasn't eager for a pesky kitten to invade her space.

"My *mamm* says we can't keep all four cats, and Dorothy and Joann would be devastated if we took it to the pound." The kitten, obviously sensing some resistance, mewed pathetically and looked at Aunt B with those big, blue, captivating eyes.

Aunt B folded her arms. "Absolutely not."

"Male or female," Rose said.

Luke nodded. "Female."

Rose cleaned off her fingers and took the kitten from Luke's hand. "*Ach,* what a beautiful kitty," she said, nuzzling the kitten against her cheek and cooing softly. "Aunt B, we have to keep this cat. Poppy saved it from the ditch. Do you want her dislocated shoulder to be in vain?"

"We've got lots of room, Aunt B," Poppy said. "And lots of mice to go around."

Aunt B seemed to dig in her heels as she sat there. "We don't need another cat."

"*Jah,* we do," Lily said. "Billy Idol could use some help keeping the mice out of the beehives when winter hits, and there are ever so many grasshoppers in the garden."

Aunt B pushed her lips to one side of her face. "Cats don't eat grasshoppers."

"She's pretty too, and she needs us. How sad to be an orphan with no one in the whole world to care for you," Rose said.

Aunt B twitched at the mention of orphans. Lily, Poppy, and Rose were orphans. Aunt B had taken them in out of the goodness of her heart. Poppy thanked the *gute* Lord every day that Dawdi Sol, with his harsh version of life, hadn't raised her.

"Please, Aunt Bitsy," Rose said. She put the kitten on the table so Aunt B could get a closer look. "Please let us keep this sweet little orphan cat."

Aunt B slumped her shoulders, grunted, and huffed a breath so forcefully that she stirred up a breeze in the kitchen. "I'm turning into a cat lady."

Rose clapped her hands, snatched the cat from the table, and hugged it to her breast. Poppy and Lily cheered. Luke gave Aunt B one of his best smiles. "*Denki,* Bitsy. I know she'll have a *gute* home."

Aunt B waved her hand in his direction. "You don't care about a *gute* home. You just want to get rid of those cats."

Luke merely grinned and took his drill from the table. "I hate to leave you just as we're getting to know the new cat, but Poppy and I are going to fix the fire damage on the honey house. It shouldn't take too long." A shadow crossed his face. "I wish we could find who did it and make them stop. I don't like how close Poppy came to getting hurt."

"I invited the sheriff by this morning," Aunt B said. "He poked around in the ashes but didn't find anything important."

"I'm going to tell you plainly," Luke said, glancing at Rose. "I'm worried about it. You all need to be more careful. Never go out of the house alone."

"Unless we have the shotgun," Lily said.

"As frightening as it was, I don't think they meant to burn the honey house down," Aunt B said.

"Why do you say that?"

"They piled that fire with things that would burn slow and make a lot of smoke. They wanted to scare us but not necessarily burn anything down. Maybe whoever it is has a conscience after all."

Luke took Poppy's hand right there in plain sight of Aunt B. "You give them too much credit, Bitsy. Someone who scares four women living alone doesn't have a conscience."

"We still need to do our best to forgive them," Rose said. "And pray they will leave us alone from now on."

Aunt B looked up at the ceiling. "Lord, I'm still waiting for that yeast infection for Paul Glick and the troublemakers, and I don't much like Luke holding hands with my niece."

Nothing Aunt B said ruffled Luke. He didn't let go of Poppy's hand. *Ach,* he didn't even have to look at her to make her heart race.

"Do you really think Paul Glick is mad enough to try to have Poppy shunned? His *dat* is one of the ministers," Rose said.

Aunt B nodded. "He's already tried. I had a visit from the deacon this morning."

Luke squeezed Poppy's hand, and his eyes flashed with concern. "What did he say?"

"I wasn't expecting him, and I still had my black fingernail polish on, so I slipped on two oven mitts and wore them the whole time he was here. My hands got really hot, but at least he couldn't chastise me for wearing nail polish."

"Is Poppy going to be shunned?" Luke asked. "Because if she is, they will have to shun me too."

Aunt B pushed air out between her lips. "Stuff and nonsense. I explained to him all about Griff Simons. He was very understanding and said if it had been his daughters, he might have been tempted to do the same thing. He was more concerned about the honey. Paul says we cheated him."

"Jah," Lily said, her expression in shadows. "He's been spreading that all over the community."

Aunt B swatted away Lily's concern. "I explained as best I could without saying any bad words about Paul. The deacon understood. Shunning is done out of love and a need for correction. You girls have done nothing wrong. The deacon agreed that none of you needed correction, and he didn't get a glimpse of my nail polish. We'll be fine."

"Did the polish help you think of a *gute* idea for your book?" Luke asked.

"I've given up on writing a Mennonite vampire romance. The Mennonites are very nice people, and I wouldn't want to offend them. We'll have to come up with another way to pay for two weddings."

Poppy pulled closer to Luke, who was still holding her hand. "We want to have a double wedding. Me and Lily. Is that all right with you?"

"Don't ask what he wants," Aunt B said. "The groom should keep any opinions to himself. The wedding is for the bride."

Luke looked at Aunt B, then Poppy. "She's right. I should keep my mouth shut."

"I'm liking you better and better," Aunt B said.

Poppy tugged at his hand. "But I want it to be okay with you." Especially since Aunt B was planning fireworks for the wedding. Luke needed to be prepared.

He gave her a heavenly smile. "I wouldn't want anything else."

She thought she might faint. Or fly. Or float. Her happiness overflowed to fill the entire house. She would be Luke Bontrager's wife. *Oy,* anyhow!

Aunt B breathed deep. "It's going to be a big event. We've got to come up with a way to make some money. Maybe we could start by selling the cats."

Lily gasped in mock horror. "I'd be desolate without Farrah Fawcett."

Luke held Billy Idol up so they were face-to-face. "I won't let that mean lady sell you," he said, talking to Billy Idol as if he were a baby. That cat had wheedled his way into Luke's heart.

Rose hugged the kitten against her neck. "You can't sell Fluffy either."

Aunt B threw up her hands. "All right. I won't sell the cats, but if that kitten is going to be living with us, she'll have to be renamed. Fluffy is no name for a cat."

Luke placed Billy Idol on the floor and winked at Poppy. "We should get to work. There's no telling how much time we'll need to repair the honey house."

Aunt B shot darts at Luke with her eyes. "You're too cheerful for your own good, Luke Bontrager. No kissing behind the honey house."

Luke gave her a look of wide-eyed innocence. "Would you prefer we kiss in front of the honey house?"

"No shenanigans in front of or behind the honey house."

Luke fingered the stubble on his chin. "I'll think real hard on that, cat lady."

Poppy giggled at the look on Aunt B's face. Luke refused to be intimidated.

Billy Idol followed them to the porch, where Luke shut the door behind them and paused to put his arms around Poppy. "I love you with everything I've got, Poppy Christner."

"I love you back."

"And I promise to always keep you safe."

Poppy laid a swift kiss on his lips. "We'll keep each other safe."

"All the better," he said as he tugged her in for another kiss. Her heart did a cartwheel across her ribs. The fireworks had already begun.

Billy Idol sat on the mat and watched the shenanigans with that permanent sneer on his lips. He adored Luke. He wouldn't think of tattling to Aunt B.

Poppy always forgot that Aunt B had a sense about these things. The door swung open and startled Luke and Poppy apart. Luke cleared his throat and tried to act as if he hadn't been caught doing anything wrong.

It was too late. Aunt B had seen everything. She stood just inside the door with a scowl on her lips and the cat formerly known as Fluffy in her arms. "Luke Bontrager, you have been warned. Stay away from Poppy's lips, or I'll throw you off our property."

Luke did his best to stifle a grin. "You're right, Bitsy. Poppy is always safe with me. I promise to behave myself."

"You'd better," Aunt B said, holding the kitten up as if she were Aunt B's eyes and ears. "Leonard Nimoy and I will be watching."

RECIPES

HONEY APPLE PIE

Note from Poppy: If you love honey, you will love this pie! If you like your apple pie more tart, you can decrease the honey to 1/2 cup. Luke loves it with the full amount of honey and of course, the cinnamon.

Pastry for 2-crust pie
2 lbs. tart apples (7 to 10 depending on the size)
1 1/2 tablespoons lime juice
3 tablespoons flour
3/4 cup honey
Dash of salt
1 teaspoon cinnamon
3 tablespoons butter
Canned milk
1 tablespoon sugar
1 tablespoon cinnamon

Prepare the pastry and refrigerate 30 to 40

minutes. Return to room temperature before rolling it out. Roll out and line pie plate with the pastry.

Peel apples; slice. Place in the pie shell. Sprinkle with lime juice, flour, honey, salt, and 1 teaspoon cinnamon. Dot with butter.

Cover with top crust, brushing edges of lower crust with cold water before pressing together. Flute. Cut slits in top of pie to allow steam to escape, or decorate with pastry cutouts.

Mix 1 tablespoon of sugar and 1 tablespoon of cinnamon together. Brush top crust with canned milk. Sprinkle with sugar-cinnamon mixture.

Bake at 375 degrees about 1 hour, until nicely browned. Put a cookie sheet under pie pan while baking in case the pie drips. Aunt B won't stand for a dirty oven.

MAMMI SARAH'S
NUT BROWN BREAD

Note from Poppy: This hearty bread goes well with soup or salad, or you can serve it for breakfast. It doesn't burn easily, so make sure it's cooked all the way through.

2/3 cup molasses
2 teaspoons baking soda
2 2/3 cups buttermilk
1/2 cup sugar
1/4 teaspoon salt
1 1/2 cups chopped walnuts
2 cups raisins (softened in hot water and drained)
2 1/2 cups whole wheat flour
2 1/2 cups white flour

Mix together molasses and baking soda. Mix in all the rest of the ingredients. Divide the dough into three bread loaf pans sprayed with nonstick cooking spray. Bake at 350 degrees for 40 to 45 minutes.

NOT DINAH EICHER'S
COFFEE CAKE

Note from Lily: This is the best coffee cake I've ever tasted. And *nae,* I have not tried Dinah Eicher's recipe.

Ingredients for the Cake
3/4 cup butter, softened
2 cups (scant) sugar
3 cups sifted flour
4 teaspoons baking powder
1 teaspoon salt
1 1/4 cups whole milk

3 egg whites, beaten until stiff

Ingredients for the Topping
3/4 cup butter, softened
3/4 cup flour
1 1/2 cups brown sugar
2 tablespoons cinnamon
1 1/2 cups chopped pecans

Preheat oven to 350 degrees. Sift together flour, baking powder, and salt. Beat egg whites and set aside. Cream butter and sugar. Add flour mixture and milk alternately until combined. Don't overbeat. Fold in beaten egg whites with a rubber spatula. Spread in a well-greased 9"-×-13" baking pan. A cake pan with higher sides is best.

In a separate bowl, combine topping ingredients with a pastry cutter until crumbly. Sprinkle over the top of the batter.

Bake for 40 to 45 minutes, or until no longer jiggly. Serve warm.

HONEY CUSTARD WITH SWEET CHERRIES
Note from Bitsy: This recipe might have singlehandedly made Luke fall in love with Poppy. Do not make this if you do not want the boys hanging around.

Ingredients
6 eggs
1/2 cup honey
1 teaspoon vanilla
1/4 teaspoon salt
1 quart (4 cups) skim milk

Topping
2 cups sweet cherries
4 teaspoons honey for drizzling

Break eggs into large bowl and beat well. Add honey, vanilla, and salt; beat again. Heat milk to just below the boiling point (when fine skin forms on top).

Add milk to egg mixture, stirring to blend well. Pour into small cups or large casserole dish.

Place cups or casserole dish in pan of hot water to a depth of at least 1 inch. Bake at 300 degrees for 1 hour or until a wet knife comes out clean when inserted in custard. Chill in the fridge for at least an hour before serving. Serve topped with fresh cherries and a drizzle of fresh honey.

ABOUT THE AUTHOR

Jennifer Beckstrand is the bestselling author of *The Matchmakers of Huckleberry Hill* series and the *Forever After in Apple Lake* series, set in two Amish communities in beautiful Wisconsin. She has always been drawn to the strong faith and the enduring family ties of the Plain people and loves writing about the antics of Anna and Felty Helmuth. Jennifer has a degree in mathematics and a background in editing. She and her husband have been married for thirty years, and she has four daughters, two sons, and two adorable grandsons, whom she spoils rotten. Readers can visit her website at www.jenniferbeckstrand.com.